Chapter 1

"Well Tom, that must have been one of our busiest days since we have moved into this place. We must have done well over what the hub expects of us and I think they will have a shock when we phone through the order."

"Do you want me to go round the rooms and see what we need or have you already done it?"

"If we both go round then you can lift up all the floor boards and I'll put the list together. Then as soon as we have phoned it through I think that is us just about done for this week with it being Sunday tomorrow."

As they went round the various rooms what Tom didn't realise was that Clive was watching him closely. Tom was a good looking guy in his early twenties and as he bent over lifting the various boards Clive was scheming.

"Have you got anything planned or is it just going to be a lazy day at home Clive?"

"I will be playing squash in the afternoon as usual but other than that not a lot else, what about you? I guess that within five minutes of me going you will be going home, getting all spruced up and then out on the town for the rest of the night."

"Not tonight I won't. With it being nearly half ten now by the time I get home, washed, and changed it will hardly be worth it by the time I get into the city centre. I might pop out just for a couple of pints tomorrow lunchtime if I can be bothered."

"Well you look sporty enough why don't you come over to the squash club and give it a go. I will be there for a couple of hours and so far I have only got one twenty minute court booked other than that I am free." Clive was eager to see exactly what Tom looked like without being fully clothed and had just thought of a way of achieving just that.

"I've never even picked up a squash racket and as for the rules I wouldn't know where to start."

"Well I take it that you have got a pair of shorts and trainers, I've got a spare racket and it could turn out to be just your cup of tea."

"Yes but I know that you have been playing for years so you'll probably get me running all round the court while you just stand there in the middle."

"So you obviously know something about the game then for you to say that. I bet on the quiet you have played the sport loads of times."

"Well I'm twenty two now and I'll be honest with you when I was about fifteen we did have a squash court at school and I did give it a try a few times."

"There you go then, so what do you think? Get to mine for about half one and we can go from there in my car."

"Go on then, I know that you won't give me a minute's peace all next week if I say no. What do I need to bring other than shorts and a t-shirt?"

"Well unless you intend coming back smelling then I would suggest a towel and shower gel for when we've finished."

"Right then. Let's get on with putting this order together and phone it through. Then I'll have to go home and start digging through all my boxes in order to hunt out a pair of shorts. I know I have got some but to be honest I have still got about eight or nine boxes in my flat that I haven't got round to unpacking."

It was half an hour later by the time that Clive left the Coventry house and headed for his home in Warwick. Tom on the other hand locked the house up and after double checking all the doors then went along the road to his flat and started looking through the various boxes. All he was hoping was that not only could he find the shorts but that when he did they would still fit him, he'd put on a few pounds since they were last worn.

Eventually he did locate them and to his surprise they did still fit although they were a little tighter than they used to be. He stood looking in the full-length mirror wearing nothing but a pair of socks and his shorts and thought to himself that he had got a pretty good body on him, considering that it had been four or five years since he had last done any sort of regular exercise. After admiring himself for a good few minutes he then decided that it was time for him to get some food, as he hadn't eaten since breakfast. The question was should he cook something healthy or shall he just pop along the road and grab a pizza from the takeaway as usual. The pizza won and he was soon getting dressed again and heading back downstairs and out of the front door.

Having waited for the pizza to be cooked he headed home only to find Gavin, his older brother, waiting on his doorstep.

"Hello you, don't tell me you are on the scrounge for either money or food, well I've got bad news for you I've just spent my last tenner on this pizza and now I am going in to eat it. I told you the last time you came round that brother or no brother I won't stand for anyone who nicks off me, so you know what you can do."

"Bloody hell Thomas, you had a bad day or something and I wasn't nicking from you anyway, they were my CD's that were in the bag."

"We both know that you haven't even got a home to go to let alone any means of playing CD's. You were nicking them to sell so you could get more drugs. I spoke to your supplier when he came round to the house earlier and he was telling me that he won't supply you any more on tick until you've cleared your debt with him. That is why you are here, you haven't got any money to buy your next fix, well you have come to the wrong place mate you're getting sweet nothing out of me from now on. For the last three years I have been mug enough to fall for your tricks, always saying that you will come round with some money for me when you get your benefits through. What happens? as soon as you get your money you get totally out of your head and that is it until you can't afford anymore, then it's round here again. Well you can forget where I live as far as I am concerned."

"Come on bro, I'm getting some money next Thursday and I promise you that I will come straight round to the house and give you twenty quid."

"For starters you know that we don't want you anywhere near the house, my boss would give me severe grief if you were to turn up there. Besides which we both know that you don't get your money through for another week and a half. I've fallen for your lies before and I'm not going down that road ever again. Now if you don't mind my supper is getting cold so I'm going in to eat it. Bye."

"So is that the way it's going to be then Tom, you won't even help your own brother out?"

"Well you won't help yourself so why do you expect me to. Why don't you get off the drugs and go out and get yourself a job like I have. Perhaps then it won't be a case of you turning up here after anything but in order to start paying back some of the hundreds of pounds that I must have given you over the past couple of years. Now sod off and don't bother coming round here again unless it's to bring some money for me."

With that Tom let himself through his front door and immediately shut it behind him before giving his brother a chance to continue with his begging.

While eating his pizza Tom was deep in thought, he knew that his brother was an addict and that one way or another he would find a way to get hold of his next fix. If it was earlier in the day then Gavin would probably head for the high streets and do some nicking from shops, if there were any left that he was still allowed to go into that is. The last Tom had heard was that his brother was barred from at least fifty percent of all the ones in the precinct, and there wasn't a pub in the city that he was welcome in. Good old pub watch, when it came down to people like his brother then he was all for barred from one and you are barred from them all. Gavin was a pain in the backside at the best of times but when he had got a drink inside him he was an absolute nightmare.

Tom had just gone to take a bite out of the last slice when his phone alarm sounded and he straight away grabbed his phone in order to check what was going on. The alarm system from the house was linked into both his and Clive's mobile and if there was anything happening then they could check out the CCTV within the house from wherever they were. He could not believe what he was seeing. Without wasting a second he was out of the chair and while slipping into his shoes was reaching for his gun and coat. The house was his responsibility with Clive living so far away and he knew that he had to deal with this matter himself without phoning any of the firm's heavies.

As he made his way down the stairs and out through his front door he was keeping an eye on the screen of his phone watching his own brother rummaging through the house. Unfortunately, Gavin went out of shot and Tom guessed that he had made his way upstairs in order to get his hands on the heroine. He knew exactly which floorboards in which room to head as he had been there with his old supplier when they had picked up stock before. With Tom only living just a few doors along the road it took but minutes before he was quietly opening the front door. He noticed that the front room window had been forced and was still half open and knew that as soon as his brother had got what he wanted then he would be heading for that same window as his method of getting back out. Tom was pleased that he had never told Gavin about there being hidden security cameras in the place, but there again if he had perhaps the idiot wouldn't have broken in. If Tom allowed his brother to leave with a stock of drugs then not only would he be losing his job but he quite possibly could end up losing his life as well. If Clive, his boss, had received the alarm as well and was watching his brother going through the place like he was there would be big trouble. Tom waited by the light switch in the front room in the dark for his brother to come back down the stairs hoping that he would be able to stop him. He heard Gavin coming back down and readied himself, the gun in his right hand and his left on the switch ready to bring light into the situation. He was hoping that the surprise element would stop Gavin in his tracks.

Light on. "What the fuck do you think you are doing?" Tom shouted at his brother who was nine years his senior and currently had his arms full of various products.

As Tom looked at what his brother had got in his arms he couldn't believe what he was seeing. Gavin hadn't just grabbed enough to keep him going for a few days but with what he'd got in his hands it would have lasted him weeks and must have been worth tens of thousands of pounds.

"Point a gun at your fucking brother would you?"

"Yes and if you go one step closer to that window I won't only be pointing it, you are not worth me losing my life over and if I let you go through that window with what you've got in your arms then that is what would happen. Now I strongly suggest you put all that stuff down on the floor and get back through that window and if I ever see you anywhere near here or my flat again then I promise you that it will be the last thing you ever do."

"As if you are man enough to use that thing little brother, you were always scared even when you were at school and I always had to fight your battles for you. You hadn't got any bottle then and you haven't got enough now for you to ever pull that trigger. Now I'm going. Bye."

As he crossed the room Tom had only got chance to quickly warn him again by which time he was at the window.

"Sorry Gavin but it's your life or mine and mine is worth one hell of a lot more than yours has ever been."

With that Tom pulled the trigger, the bullet hitting Gavin in the right leg just above the knee thinking that it would stop him in his tracks. Unfortunately, the drugs that he was on were clearly making Gavin oblivious to pain and as he went to climb out of the window Tom fired a second round. This time however, it wasn't aimed at just wounding his brother but rather it was straight to the back of his head. Gavin fell back into the room, the drugs that had been in his clutches going everywhere. Tom just stood motionless for what felt like ages but in real terms was but a few seconds. He knew that there was no way that his brother would be alive and that he now had got one huge problem on his hands. He stood there looking at his brother lay face up on the floorboards, the pool of blood slowly growing under his head.

"Why the fuck did you have to try and leave Gavin, why did you have to try and leave?"

Tom was at this point not really that bothered about having killed his brother, there was no real love lost in that department. What was filling Tom's mind now was how the hell was he going to get everything sorted before Monday morning. If he had a car then there would have been a chance because he could have dragged the body out into it in the dead of night and gone and ditched it somewhere. As for the blood that could have been dealt with, it would only need a real good mopping and then nobody would be any the wiser. His mind was in overdrive as he tried to come up with a solution. Yes, he'd got a full clean driving licence and enough money in the bank for him to be able to hire a car first thing in the morning for twenty-four hours, but he couldn't risk moving the body until well into the night. He thought things through. If he hired a small van then tomorrow night or in the early hours of Monday morning he could load the corpse into it, and then what? Where could he take it where it wouldn't be discovered, or would it matter even if the body were to be found? He'd also somehow got to then get back here and get every trace of the blood cleaned up before Clive turned up which would be about eight o'clock Monday morning, with them expecting a delivery. Tom looked down at the gun still in his right hand and for just a split second he did think of turning it on himself, if he couldn't get everything sorted in time then he was as good as dead anyway. There was no way that the firm would just ignore the fact that he had killed someone in one of their houses, that was not done. Kill people who deserved it yes, but not right on your own doorstep, you take them somewhere before you do the deed.

He looked back at the body and the pool of blood that was rapidly spreading and was now covering quite an area of the wooden floorboards. If he left Gavin's body there until the early hours of Monday morning then the blood would not only have dried on but there was a good chance that it would stain the boards which then wouldn't be easy to disguise.

He went over and closed the window and put the catch back on it although it had been bent where Gavin had forced his way in. it will do for now, he thought. Then he closed the curtains tightly making sure that there was no gap that anyone would be able to look through and see what was within. It was now that he had a thought of what to do about the pool of blood. If he dived home and grabbed a couple of bin bags and some old towels then he could put the bin bags down on the boards then with the towels on top of it. He'd then lift the body onto the towels. That way any further leakage would be soaked up and keep the floor clean. He could then mop the boards that were already covered by his brother's blood and that should sort it. Yes, he thought, that should do it. He made his way to the front door but turned back. Firstly he would take all the drugs back and replace them under the floorboards where they had come from. As he started picking up the many small packages strewn across the room he still could not believe that his brother was dumb enough to have grabbed so much. If Tom hadn't killed him being in possession of this lot Gavin would probably have ended up overdosing on the stuff anyway. Tom's only concern was for himself, which although they had never been close he was having difficulty believing that although he had just killed his own brother he was not feeling bad about having done so.

There was one real good thing though, if Clive had received an alarm on his phone then without any doubt he would have called Tom before now in order to see if there was a problem. The alarm system had only been installed about four weeks ago and had proved nothing but trouble since day one, but now Tom was really glad that it wasn't as reliable as the installers reckoned it was.

He ended up making two trips upstairs with packages and it had taken him some time to get everything back in its rightful place so when Clive lifted the floorboards on Monday when the delivery turned up then he would not suspect anything.

As soon as the drugs were all safely stashed back in their rightful place Tom left the house in order to dive home to get the old towels and some bin bags only to return five minutes later to start cleaning the mess up. Although Gavin, from appearance, looked as though he was just skin and bones Tom found him a lot heavier to move than he had imagined he would. He did however get the job achieved although in doing so and looking at his own clothing he then realised that he was absolutely covered in claret himself. He checked his watch, where was the time going? It was already gone half two in the morning and he envisaged that he would still have well over an hour's work here mopping the floor to such a level that there would be no trace of the blood remaining.

He went to the kitchen and started filling the mop bucket with the hottest water available and then returned to the front room and started the clean-up. To his horror although the blood hadn't had a chance to dry it seemed that it had already achieved one thing, as he mopped the area for a third time he was convinced that there was already staining. However he couldn't be certain until the boards had a chance to dry, he'd have to wait till then before knowing for sure.

It was gone four in the morning before Tom eventually turned the key in the front door and headed back to his flat. All that remained for him to do now was to get a van hired in the morning and then wait until late tomorrow night at which time he would go along to the house, load up the body and go and ditch it somewhere. Then he needed to go back to the house just to do the finishing touches. The only one issue that he could see was that somehow he would have to return the van to the hire company on Monday morning and with a delivery due that would prove difficult. He then decided that he'd have to hire it for two days. That way first thing on Tuesday morning he would take it back as there wouldn't be a delivery and as such he wouldn't be starting work until half nine.

It wasn't until he got into bed at just after five in the morning that Tom remembered that later he was going to have to go over to Warwick and to Clive's place, and then go and play squash. He

tried to create a timetable in his head. Up at eight, go to hire
centre and get a van which will probably take about an hour by
the time he got back home. Between nine and ten he would spend
by going to the house in order to check to see how the boards are
drying and to make certain that there was no further blood
escaping onto them from where he had moved the body. Then he
would have to go and purchase some sort of covering in which to
wrap the body ready for when he drags it out to the van in the
early hours of the morning, which would take him the best part of
another hour. That would have taken him up till eleven which by
that time he would only have a couple of hours maximum before
having to go and catch a bus over to Warwick. He could always
drive over there in the van that he hires but there again that would
cause Clive to start asking questions as to why he had it. Before
allowing himself to go to sleep Tom got back out of bed and put
all his blood stained clothes in the washing machine so they were
all washed before giving the blood a chance to really dry and
therefore stain them. He got back into bed and having set his
alarm for eight o'clock he knew that he would be getting very
little sleep between now and Tuesday evening. What a night he
thought as he drifted off.
He was up and with a hot drink before the alarm actually
sounded, having had a restless two and a bit hours under the quilt.
As Tom drank his coffee he then realised that he also needed to
come up with somewhere to take the body to as well that
wouldn't be covered by cameras and as a result lead the police
back to him. He thought things through and pondered for a while
on purchasing some concrete blocks and then with the aid of rope
attaching them to the body and dumping it in a lake somewhere.
He then thought better of it because that would mean him
spending too much time with the body. No he needed to be able to
just push it out of the back of the van and drive straight off.
Where though that was the question?
By half ten he had achieved a lot more than he thought that he
would have. He'd got the van and on the way back from the car
hire company had popped into a builder's merchants where he'd

bought more than enough sheeting to not only wrap the body in but also to line the floor of the van with as well. He had even popped into the house to check that all was okay there. Luckily now the floor had dried a little there didn't appear to be any staining, in addition there was no further blood from where he had moved the body. The only one down side of this morning was when he had removed the washing from the machine, he'd discovered that both his jeans and shirt were still badly stained. Oh well, they will have to end up in the bin and be replaced.

He set his alarm clock for midday and got under his quilt in the hope of getting an hour's sleep in before he had to make his way to the bus stop.

He didn't achieve a wink and it was not long before he was on his way over to Clive's place. He'd remembered that he had got a good twenty minute walk from where the bus dropped him to Clive's so ended up having to catch an earlier bus than he was expecting to.

"Afternoon Tom, I had this funny feeling that you wouldn't turn up. I thought something would have cropped up to prevent you from coming."

"No not at all. I said that I would come and I don't normally let you down do I?" Tom replied as if nothing had happened the previous evening.

"I will say that for you Tom, you are very dependable. So was it a quiet night in then last night or did you end up going out for a few beers after all?"

"Now if I had gone out for a few beers then I might well have ended up phoning you to say that I wasn't coming. From what I can remember the game is not something you want to attempt playing if you have any sort of hang over."

"Right then I guess that we might as well get on over there and see what the bookings are like for the courts. Recently there hasn't been any problem getting a court without having to pre-book one which is what you always used to have to do. Saying

that you watch today the place will probably be as busy as hell
and we'll have to hang around for ages before getting one."
"So when you said yesterday that you had already got a twenty
minute session booked are you meeting up with someone there?"
"No, I normally book just the one and when I get there you can
normally find someone hanging around that wants a game. So at
least we will have twenty minutes even if we can't get any more
time."
"It has been that long since I have done any exercise I will
probably be knackered by the end of twenty minutes anyway,
especially if you get me running all over the place."
"I'll be gentle with you don't you get too worried about that.
Besides although I play often it does not mean that I am any good.
I can tell you here and now that I am no star player by any stretch
of the imagination."
"I've heard stuff like that before and then been absolutely
hammered, it happened at snooker just the other week. The guy
had two breaks both over fifty and then he turned round and said
that he was just lucky with how the balls were placed."
With that they jumped in Clive's car and travelled the couple of
miles from his to the squash club. On arriving Tom was very
impressed with the place and hadn't thought the sport that popular
to warrant a club having eleven courts, but soon realised that it
was very well attended. Having signed in his guest Clive was then
showing Tom through to the changing rooms.
As Tom got changed out of his jeans and pulled on his shorts he
was oblivious to the fact that he was being watched. As he
removed his shirt to replace it with a t-shirt Clive was very
pleased with what he saw, there was no doubting that Tom had
got a pretty good physic. Having both readied themselves they
then made their way out to the courts and it was not long after
getting onto court four that Clive had got Tom sweating. Clive
was a much better player than he had told Tom and was in total
control of the court.
"Bloody hell Clive will you at least give me a bit of a chance to
return a ball? I don't think that I have got one back to the wall

between the lines yet and we've been playing for a good fifteen minutes."

"Sorry Tom, I thought that you were hiding your true ability from me and I didn't want to allow you a chance to get settled back into the game, otherwise it would have been me running all round the place. I'll take things a bit easier on this last five minutes for you. Do you think that after a bit of a break that you will be able to handle another twenty minute session?"

"If I do I know one thing for certain, I'll be as stiff as anything tomorrow."

With what Clive had got in mind it wasn't as much tomorrow but the following Sunday he certainly would be, but not in the way that Tom was referring to.

"We'll have a bit of a break for half an hour or so during which time we can get an orange juice in the bar and then just the one more go before we call it a day if that is okay with you?"

"I guess that it would hardly have been worth me coming all the way over from Coventry if we didn't, but can you go a bit easier on me on the next session though please otherwise although I'm only in my early twenties I'll end up having a heart attack."

"No problem, we'll just have a bit of fun the next time and not even bother scoring if you want."

Having finished the first period they went through to the bar, stopping off in the dressing room on their way in order to get some cash to pay for their drinks. While they were in there Tom went to use the urinals in order to relieve himself, and Clive took the opportunity and went to have one as well. He wanted to see just what Tom was hiding in his shorts, although he knew that he would be getting a real good look when they both showered later. After finishing the second spell on court both the men headed back to the changing room where they undressed totally before going into the wet room area in order to get showered. It was now that Clive was able to see Tom completely naked and he liked what he saw. Yes Tom had got just the right sort of body for what he had got in mind and in addition had also got quite a presentable manhood. Although totally flaccid at this point in time Clive imagined that when Tom was aroused that it would then be of a decent size and good enough for what he had got planned for the following weekend, he then thought, why wait till next weekend?

"So Tom, have you got anything else lined up to be doing this afternoon?" Clive asked once they had got back into his car in order to head back home.

"I've got one or two things that I need to attend to, besides, I didn't get much sleep last night so was thinking of getting another couple of hours this afternoon if I can."

"That's right, I almost forgot that you had quite a busy night despite the fact that you didn't go out for a drink. How is Gavin by the way? Is he sleeping well?"

It was only now that the truth hit home to Tom that Clive must have been watching on his phone everything that took place at the Coventry house the previous evening. The question was exactly how much did Clive know and what had the cameras captured.

"So you clearly got the alarm call then although you hadn't given me a shout to see what was going on."

"I did Tom and the main reason why I didn't bother calling you at the time was when I saw you enter through the front door carrying your gun I just knew that you would make sure that I wouldn't end up having to explain to the hub where all our stock had gone."

"So can I ask what exactly you saw because once I got into the house I was concentrating on the job that I knew I had to do and was not watching the footage."

"Well put it this way Tom, I know for a fact that Gavin broke in and was upstairs when you got there. You then waited for him in the lounge until he came back down and it was then that you challenged him. I must admit that when you turned the lights on it certainly made much better viewing. I also know that you took two shots, the first just wounding him in the right leg but the second one certainly did the trick. That was why I was surprised when you turned up today, I thought you would still have been busy tidying up."

"What can I say Clive, I am really sorry about what happened. My brother had turned up at mine earlier on the scrounge as normal and I guess it was because of the fact that I sent him packing that he resulted to breaking into the place. He is an addict and we both know well enough that they will go to any lengths to get their next fix."

"Don't you mean that he was an addict, I have a feeling that he will not be taking any more drugs ever. So I saw your efforts moving his body across the room and putting it onto bin bags and then watched as you mopped the floor but haven't really had a chance to watch anything from there on."

"So you were up till five o'clock this morning watching everything that I was doing."

"No Tom, I have got it all recorded and was in fact still watching when you turned up at my door this afternoon. As yet I don't know if you have managed to get rid of Gavin's corpse but I guess when I get back indoors I will have plenty of time to see. That is unless you want to bring me up to date with what the current state of play is."

Tom now hadn't got a clue as to what Clive was likely to do and who he was going to tell about what had gone on the previous night and was beginning to get very worried.

"So what happens now then Clive? Are you going to get in touch with top man to tell him what I have been up to, because if you do I have a funny feeling that you will end up having a new face helping you in the house from tomorrow. I think that my days working for the firm will come to a sudden end, and what's more I don't think I will be around long enough to apply for any other job."

"Well I do believe that if Marcos were to find out that you shot someone dead in one of his houses then you might be right there Tom. I think that if I were to call him right now then I would say that within just a couple of hours you would be in the same state of not breathing as your brother is."

"I take it that you haven't contacted him then?"

"Not yet I haven't, as yet I am trying to come up with a real good reason for me not doing so, if I don't inform him and he finds out then my neck will be on the block as well."

"If you tell him Clive I am a dead man we both know that."

"I know you would be and as I say my problem is coming up with a good enough reason to keep myself from going down that road. After all I have got every second of what took place recorded, it isn't a case of it just being my word against yours is it?"

"Please Clive, whatever you do please don't tell Marcos about what I did."

"So how desperate are you for me to keep my mouth shut then Tom?"

"I'll do anything Clive, just anything but please don't let on about what took place."

Tom was now really grovelling, as he knew he had to if he was going to stay alive. What he didn't know was that he was playing straight into Clive's hands. Clive had waited for an opening to get Tom involved in his other little businesses and the way he was viewing things he now had just that opening.

"Just a quick question then Tom, have you got rid of the body yet or is it still in the flat?"

"It's still in the front room but I hired a small van this morning in which I can get shut of it somewhere. I haven't got a clue at the moment as to where I am going to take it though."

"Would I be right in thinking that you could really do with a hand getting the body out of the way? You know what they say about a dead weight being a lot heavier than when someone is alive. I bet you had a job moving it just the short distance across the room didn't you?"

"If you were watching you would have seen that I did. Having said that it isn't exactly a job that I could really ask anyone to give be a hand with, it isn't like moving a washing machine or something like that is it."

"No Tom, but I think that I might know someone that will give you a hand later on this evening as long as you play your cards right. When we get back to mine you can stay for a couple of hours and then I'll drive you back over and give you a hand if you want."

"If you would that would be absolutely fantastic as I'd been wondering how I was going to manage it on my own. Can I ask though what you meant by if I play my cards right?"

"Well it is quite clear that if you don't keep in my good books then you are as good as dead already, so I guess that at the moment I have got hold of all the cards and we'll just have to see which ones I deal you."

"So what you are saying is that I am now going to be your puppet and that I will have to do just about anything that you ask of me, am I right?"

"I suppose you could put it like that. Let's face it Tom just how much do you value your life?"

"So can I ask what it is that you have got lined up for me then Clive, from the way you are talking it sounds to me as though you have got things already planned out in your head."

"Well we will be back at mine in just a couple of minutes and before I let you know what I am thinking I'll let you have a viewing of the recording that I have got from last night and early this morning. As I said earlier I haven't seen it all yet so it could be interesting for both of us to watch. I take it that you will not be in a hurry to get off will you Tom?"

The way Clive had said it Tom knew that leaving Clive's place straight away was not going to be an option if he was going to keep Clive's mouth shut, as well as have a hand later getting rid of Gavin's body.

"Well I haven't got anything to do until well into the night so I guess that I might as well stick around. Come on then are you going to let me in on what it is that you have got lined up for me to be doing."

"I'll give you a bit of a clue Tom but at the moment I will not go into details as they are best left until after we have watched the recording that I have got of you. I know it's changing the subject quite a bit but I haven't seen you with that girl you were going out with for quite a while. Have the two of you split up?"

"Yes, we finished a couple of months ago, she was getting far too demanding and serious and I just couldn't be doing with it all."

"So would I be right in thinking that you are still young and not ready to start putting your roots down just yet. Still playing the field as they say."

"I guess so although I haven't had much of an opportunity to enjoy my freedom with having moved into the new flat, and with the hours that we are now working."

"So are you trying to tell me that super stud hasn't had sex since he finished with his ex a couple of months ago. That must be murder for a guy like you. We'll have to see if we can do something about that then won't we young Tom, mind you if it has been that long I bet it will be all over in no time if you were to get a girl's mouth down round your cock."

"I would like to think that I would be able to give a girl a good time even with it having been so long."

By this time Clive was parking the car up on his drive and as soon as he had killed the engine he got out and headed for the front door, Tom following.

Chapter 2

Once inside Clive got a couple of cans of lager from the fridge and the two of them took a seat in the lounge where Clive wasted no time in getting the recording from last night showing on his television.

As he sat there watching Tom couldn't believe how clear the picture was, up until now he had only caught images on his mobile phone but when displayed on a big screen TV the clarity was perfect. He remained speechless as he watched events unfold. It was immediately clear that with what Clive had got here it was either enough to get him killed by those that he worked for or if the police ever got their hands on it then he could say goodbye to his freedom for quite some years. Even in the dark the picture was good, but when it got to the point when Tom switched the front room light on then everything was crystal clear. There was no disputing the fact that he had shot his brother twice, the second time being in the back of the head. There was no way that if it ever went to court that he could possibly say that it had been in self-defence.

"So what do you think of the CCTV system then Tom, I reckon that it is pretty good. I bet you are really glad that there are only the two of us that can get access to the images from it. Just think, if Marcos had insisted on having it wired through to his mobile then you wouldn't have been playing squash with me this afternoon."

"It's frightening to see it. So what are you going to do with it now?"

"Well that does depend chiefly on you, and how much you want it to be kept just between the two of us. Our little secret, well not so little actually, but it could remain our secret forever as long as you play your cards right."

"I guess you could say that you have got me by the bollocks in a really big way. If this ever got to Marcos or the police then I would be in deep shit. So what do I have to do in order to keep it just our secret then Clive?"

"I could ask you what you are prepared to do?"

"If I want to stay breathing then I guess the answer to that one has got to be just about anything."

"Really? So you would do anything I asked of you, is that right?"

"I haven't got much choice have I when you think about it, as you said earlier you are definitely holding all the cards."

By this time, the film had got to the point where Tom had picked up all the drugs from off the floor in order to take them back upstairs.

"Well I think you have seen enough for now haven't you Tom, how about me putting on a bit of a different film for us to have a look at now."

With that he got up from his seat and slipped a different disc into the player.

"I take it you are not opposed to watching the occasional porn film are you Tom?"

"Not at all, mind you I haven't seen one for years. I think the last time that I watched porn must have been when I was about fifteen or sixteen, but I can remember that it was really good."

"I guess with it being when you were that young I can imagine what happened, I bet you ended up getting quite a bulge in your trousers. Would I be right?"

"I think I did at the time, but back then I was still a virgin and I don't suppose that it would have the same effect these days with me being that much more knowledgeable and experienced."

With that the film started and Clive sat back down in his chair, one eye on the television and the other keeping a watch on Tom to see what effect it was having on him if any. They sat there for a good few minutes watching this guy being given head by this very attractive young blond haired female.

"I bet you'd just love to be in his shoes right now with you having gone without any for the last couple of months, wouldn't you Tom?"

"Too right, it certainly looks as if she knows exactly what she is doing and she wouldn't have to ask me a second time."

"So go on then Tom, you said that when you watched one when you were sixteen you ended up getting a stiff cock, tell me has it had the same result this afternoon?"

" Not completely but it certainly isn't totally soft. I guess that's down to the fact that I have been without any for the past few weeks."

"So if you are getting hard down below then I guess with those jeans being quite tight that it must be getting a little bit uncomfortable for you."

"Put it this way if I carry on watching this and I keep going the way that I am it will become unbearable. It's only half way there and it is already getting rather tight."

"In that case Tom why don't you stand up for me and prove you are telling the truth. I reckon that if you are getting rather stiff down there then there should be quite a bulge to be seen. Come on Tom, stand up and show me just how tight those trousers are getting."

Tom was feeling rather uncomfortable in two ways now, there was not only his stiffening cock pressing against the material but Clive now was asking him to stand up so he could see just how tight the jeans had become. Although really wanting to tell Clive that he had to be having a laugh he knew that at present he was in no position to deny Clive any request that he made. Reluctantly he stood up and turned to face Clive about four or five feet away from where he was sat.

"It does give the impression that it is a little on the hard side, but I think you had better undo your jeans and lower them a little in order for me to see just how hard it is."

Now Tom was in a really awkward position, he knew that Clive used to be married until his wife had died in a car accident a couple of years ago, otherwise he would have thought from Clive's request that he was in fact gay. He'd got a daughter so couldn't possibly be so Tom thought that Clive was just telling him to do it in order to see just what sort of hold he'd actually got over Tom. If Tom was to reveal his manhood then that showed that he hadn't been lying when he'd told Clive that he would do just about anything for him.

"Come on Tom, surely you can't be shy. Go on drop those jeans." He did as instructed, lowering his jeans till they were just clearing the bottom of his boxer shorts.

"Well with your boxers where they are I am still unable to see just how hard that cock of yours is, you'll have to do a bit better than that if you know what I mean."

Tom knew exactly what Clive was asking him to do and very slowly he lowered his boxers enabling Clive to see everything that he had got. Although Tom couldn't quite work out why, but his dick was by this time much harder than it had been before he had stood up.

"Well that is quite a bit of kit you have got there, and I thought you said that it was only partially hard, from where I am sat it looks as if it is about as firm as it can get. I am right aren't I?"

"I guess it does get a bit harder but not that much. Can I pull my shorts back up now you've seen it?"

"Not just yet Tom. I bet with it being as it is that you would just love to have a girl's mouth go down on it right now wouldn't you. In addition if you got that aroused just watching a porn film I bet you'd be shooting your load in next to no time, would I be right on that one as well?"

"If she did as good a job as that bird on the film I guess that it wouldn't take me too long before I filled her mouth."

"So Tom what do you know about sperm banks?"

"Not a great deal other than birds use them when their old man is incapable of getting her pregnant. And I believe some lesbians use them if they want kids but don't fancy the idea of having sex with a fella. Other than that I can't say I know that much. Why do you ask, and can I pull my shorts up now?"

"Not yet Tom. What you possibly don't know about sperm banks is that sometimes it can take months before you eventually get the offer of any, and even then there is no saying who it has come from, or how fresh it is going to be. As a result there is getting to

be quite a black market for sperm that comes from good stock. Now although you are in no way appealing to me, to a lot of girls they would think that you were quite a good looking guy, as a result they would love to get hold of any sperm that you can produce. Are you understanding what I am trying to say?”
“If I am getting you right you want me to donate my sperm to a sperm bank, I wouldn’t know the first thing of how you go about doing it but I guess that if that is what you want to happen then I will have to do it.”
“So you would have no problem in shooting your load into a beaker then for someone that you will never meet to use.”
“Although it is something that I have never thought about I guess there isn’t really that much to get concerned over, especially when they will never meet you.”
“Okay then Tom, now I have already told you that the sperm banks don’t seem to be that efficient I’ll let you in on a little secret that I’ve got, seeing as though I have got a very big one of yours. I donate to this private place on a regular basis, and for each load that they get from me as long as it is a decent amount I get paid five hundred quid and all that they want is a photo of me to show their client. Of course it is just from the neck down so they will never know exactly who it was donating it. Are you with me so far?”
“I think so, what you are saying is instead of going to an official bank to donate you bypass them and deal almost direct and, get a decent pay-out for doing so. So what happens then do you have to go to some sort of clinic and do it there and then?”
“Oh it’s a hell of a lot easier than that Tom, you can do it in the luxury of your own home. That is why I have got a few of these films. If I sit here and watch one for a while I have no problem in producing more than enough to ensure I will get paid for it. Then all I do is make a phone call and keep it in a fridge until it is collected which is normally a few hours or so later.”
“So if I am reading things right what you are saying then is you are wanting me to do is to start donating my sperm and then you will earn all the money from it.”

"Not quite right, I was thinking more along the lines of a fifty fifty split, so you get two hundred and fifty quid each time, and I am sure you could put that sort of money to good use couldn't you?"

"So you are saying that you will hand me two and a half hundred for every time that I hand you a tumbler with my sperm in it. Well that is going to be easy."

"There are two small issues though, just red tape if you like. The first is, as I have already said they need a photo of you neck downwards. The other thing is that they insist on it being witnessed, for me I have got one of the neighbours that comes round and after we've watched a film or two we witness each other. So the first thing that you will need to do is to strip off to have the photo taken. Then I guess that I could be the witness, unless you want to do it in front of a total stranger, in which case I can phone my neighbour to come round."

"Am I right in thinking that you are on about me doing it right now?"

"Well from what I can see from here Tom you are pretty much well on the way already. Now if you go ahead and get those clothes off I'll go and get a camera to take the photo and one of their beakers for you to shoot into. See who can be first, me getting the stuff or you getting naked."

Without giving Tom an opportunity to give him any sort of reply Clive got up and headed out of the room. For Tom, he had no problem donating his sperm but he did have a problem in producing it while Clive was just sat there watching him doing so. He started removing his clothes hoping that he would be able to achieve the objective with having a bloke watching him. He knew that if it was a bird then he would be shooting in no time, especially if she were to offer to give him a bit of a hand, but in front of another man was something completely different.

By the time Clive came back into the room, camera in one hand and carrying two beakers in the other Tom was completely naked.

"I see you have brought two beakers in, does that mean that I have got to try and put half of it in the one and then finish off putting the rest in the other?"

"No not at all. You just shoot the whole lot in the one, but I thought that while you are at it and with the film being on I might as well earn myself five hundred at the same time. At least then it isn't just you doing it while I just sit here watching you. I thought that would probably make things easier. It almost reminds me of when I was really young and back then it was almost the fashion to have wanking races with your mates. There was a game that used to be played although I have never taken part myself. It was called soggy biscuit and what happened was that there were a group of you all having a race and when you were about to shoot your load you did so onto a biscuit. Well the idea of the game was that the lad who shot last ended up having to eat the soggy biscuit."

"I must admit I have heard of it but I have always thought that it was just a load of rubbish, I never thought for one moment that lads ever got up to that sort of stuff."

"How things change over the years, I bet you have never had a race with another lad because with you being that much younger I think it had gone out of fashion by the time you would have reached the age where you could take part."

"I did go to a boarding school don't forget, so in answer to your question yes when I was thirteen or perhaps fourteen I have done it along with other lads. But you do crazy things when you are that age."

"Can you remember back then if when you had a race if you shot more than if it had just been yourself giving it a hand in private."

"Strictly between the two of us there was this one occasion that there were about four of us all doing it together and there was this bent lad who shared the same dorm as we had and we always used to bully him. Well to cut a long story short between us we decided that it would be quite a laugh to teach him a lesson for being gay, and we each took it in turn shooting our loads into his mouth. We thought that it would turn the lad straight but instead he fucking loved it, for weeks after he kept asking when we were going to have our next race."

"So you shot your load into another lads mouth. I guess at the end of the day a mouth is the same whether it belongs to a bloke or a female as long as you are not looking, I suppose that the sensation is very much the same. Having said that I have never had it done to me. Was it good can you remember?"

"We are talking of nine years or so ago but I can remember really laughing at the time because I knew that I had delivered one hell of a lot into his mouth. Don't forget that would have been the first time that any mouth had got anywhere near it so it was a completely new sensation for me."

"Well with you not having had sex for the last two months it will almost be the same now because you will have forgotten what it's like having a girl go down on it. Anyway by the looks of things with all this talking your tool has lost its stiffness. What do you think to us both sitting back down and watching some more of this film and then once you are stiff again I'll take a photo and then we can get down to business."

"Well I'll have to put my boxers and jeans back on if I am going to sit down on your furniture."

"No you'll be alright as you are without bothering to put any of your clothes back on. It isn't as if you are dirty with only having a shower a couple of hours ago."

"So are you going to do the same then? Are you going to drop your trousers and pants?"

"Well I can't think of a way for me to collect my deposit in this beaker while my trousers and pants are still up, so yes I'll be doing the same."

At this point Clive unbuttoned his trousers and lowered them along with his boxers and Tom couldn't stop himself from taking a look to see if Clive was hard down below or not.

"I saw you having a look then Tom, I am at exactly the same stage as you are, while I was watching the film I too was rather hard down below but with all this talking mine has gone just as soft as yours."

Tom was quite surprised that he didn't feel in the least bit uncomfortable now with the situation. He was actually beginning to think that it could be quite a laugh seeing which one of them produced the most, and who out of them reached the point first.
"So Tom, there are loads of rumours about different things that happen in all boys boarding schools. You have already told me about the gay lad, tell me were there other times that you were, how shall I put it, a little bit more personal with another pupil than you should have been."
"You know what you're like when you're kids, there were times that we helped each other reach the goal as it were, but that was then and there was nothing gay about it but rather done as just a bit of fun."
"So you had other boys wank you off and you have done the same to them, is that what you are telling me, or was it more than just the hand that you all used?"
"It was always just the hand other than the time that I said with the gay lad. I'll tell you one thing though he could have taught some of the girls that I have been out with how it should be done because from what I can remember he did do a pretty good job."
"I guess he must have, I have just noticed your cock and it's getting stiff with you just thinking about the job that he did on your tool. I think that seeing as you have got all the experience with how to help other lads shoot their loads that we had better just put it to the test. Why don't you come over here and show me what you used to do with them."
"You are kidding, you're asking me to come there and give yours a helping hand?"
"Well just think of it as revisiting your youth, don't forget that you have experienced something that I never have and I am just curious as to if another bloke can even get mine hard let alone getting me to shoot my load."
"Yes but back then it was a case where we helped each other out, and it was done as just a bit of a laugh."
"Just because we are both in our twenties doesn't mean that we can't have a laugh now does it. Besides, it isn't like either of us

are going to go down the pub tomorrow night and start telling all
our friends what we did. It will be strictly between the two of us
and nobody else will ever know. It's a bit like you and your
brother's little secret."
Tom had worked under Clive for the last two years and knew him
well enough to know that, this, if he were to go ahead with
Clive's wishes, would without doubt always remain a secret.
Whereas with what he had done to his brother that was for Clive
to decide on. He was in control of that.
He didn't want to, but he moved to where Clive was sat. He then
started fumbling with his flaccid dick, hoping that he would not
get any response from it and then would be allowed to stop.
Unfortunately within just seconds he could sense that it was
beginning to get stiffer with his handling of it.
"Well this reminds me of an old saying that I haven't heard for a
number of years. They used to say that any hand is better than
your own hand and I guess that there is some truth in it even
though it happens to be the hand of another bloke."
"I've heard the saying, I think in full it is 'any hand is better than
your own hand, any mouth is better than no mouth and any hole is
a goal." Having said it Tom immediately wandered on his
wisdom for having done so.
"I have just remembered what I haven't done which I need to
before we go any further, I haven't taken a photo of you yet. Also
I haven't noticed if you have got hard again yet"
With that Tom turned round so as to enable Clive to see that yes
he was now fully erect.
"So on looking at that it's clear it wasn't only me that enjoyed
what you were just doing to my dick."
"Don't get me wrong in any way, I am by no means gay but I
guess with touching yours I was thinking back to some of the fun
times I used to have back at school. It must be about eight years
since I have last touched any cock other than my own."
"It's quite clear looking at yours that you must have enjoyed
having mine in your hand, otherwise there would be no way that
yours would be anywhere near as upright as it is at present."

"I could say the same about you Clive, you must have enjoyed having another man playing with yours for that to have responded so well. I know that yours isn't quite at the same stage as mine is but if you hadn't stopped me when you remembered about the photo I think it would only have been a matter of a few more seconds."

"I'll admit that's a fair comment, now the quicker I get these photos done then the quicker you can get back to what you were doing and you can see if you can get mine as hard as yours is."

Tom thought from what Clive had said that he would just be having the one photo taken from a distance so Clive could get the whole of his body from neck to knee in it. Five minutes later Clive considered the task now completed, he must have taken at least twenty shots in total, including some rather close pictures of both his erect cock as well as having taken a couple of his backside for some unknown reason. With the camera now put to one side Clive went and sat down on the one end of the settee instructing Tom to sit next to him and carry on from where he had left off.

After a minute Tom turned round to Clive and pointed out the fact that it was a bit one-sided, he was having to handle Clive's tool while at the same time his own was getting no attention at all. With Clive having taken a very quick feel of Tom's penis he pointed out that Tom must be enjoying having another man's cock in his hand that much because without it having any attention it was as hard as it could get. Clive continued by saying that he wouldn't be surprised if Tom actually shot his load without having to touch it as he was clearly enjoying what was taking place.

"There's no way that I will shoot with just handling your cock, that I am sure of."

"Just a quick question Tom, do you normally go down on a girl?"

"Yes why?"

"And do you enjoy it, or is it just a case that it is the done thing?"

"I enjoy it, I always get quite a kick in getting them really aroused with having my mouth and tongue down on them."

"In that case Tom I think you had better get your mouth down on mine to see if it ends up arousing you as much as when you go down on a girl."

Tom was in total disbelief on hearing Clive suggest that he get his head down in order to give a blow job. He'd had it done to him once by a lad but he had never thought the occasion would ever arise where he was expected to do it himself.

"Am I right in thinking that what you have just suggested that I do is not optional, because if it is then I would say thanks for the invite but no thanks."

"You are right with your thinking, if I stand up and you kneel down in front of me then when I am about to shoot my load I will be able to deliver it into the glass. You never know you might just enjoy it as much as you do when you go down on a girl."

With that, and against his wishes Tom ended up on his knees and started carrying out Clive's latest demand. Although he would always maintain that he was totally straight as he worked his mouth on the now fully erect member he was finding he was actually quite enjoying doing so.

"I'll tell you what Tom, what you are doing down there is very nice I must say. I think if you start taking it further down into your mouth you might well end up getting me to shoot my load."

As Tom moved his mouth further onto the member and having taken more of it in his own pleasure heightened, although not believing it he was really enjoying having Clive's member in his mouth, so much so that he really started to work his mouth on it.

"Fuck me Tom. I said that what you were doing just now was quite nice but now you are really giving me enjoyment. What's more I can assure you that if you carry on doing exactly what you are then I will be shooting my load in next to no time, and it will be a better than average load as well. That is really nice."

Hearing that what he was doing was giving Clive real pleasure only fuelled his own enjoyment and he could tell that he was not too far from shooting himself although he hadn't even got his own hand anywhere near it. Both of his hands were now firmly attached to Clive's buttocks in order to pull Clive as deep into his mouth as he could.

"Now I am going to leave this totally up to you Tom. I am very close to shooting and I have got the beaker in my hand ready to catch it but if you want to keep your mouth down on it when I get there then you can. As far as I am concerned you have earned the right to choose to stay down on it. Carry on and I will tell you just before I shoot."

Tom was getting that much enjoyment that although on the one hand even the thought of taking another man's sperm into his mouth was not nice to even consider. But, on the other hand before he had got his mouth working on Clive's member he had thought the same about carrying out that action. Just seconds later Clive announced that he was about to shoot his load and to Tom's own surprise he stayed exactly where he was and kept the member deep inside his mouth. As Tom started receiving Clive's deposit inside his mouth he reached up and having taken the beaker from out of Clive's hand then made a deposit himself into it, such was the enjoyment that he had got from doing what he had to his immediate boss.

"Well I don't know quite if I should be saying thank you for that or not, on the one hand I did enjoy it, but on the other side of the coin you have just prevented me from earning five hundred pounds from what I produced."

"Sorry about that Clive but I guess that I just got a bit carried away, which I have to say came as a total shock to me as well as it probably did to you."

"Initially I had told you to do it just so I had more of a hold over you, but when you started going to work on it I thought that I might as well just see quite how far you were prepared to go."

Tom could not believe two things, no three. Firstly he could not believe for one moment that he would have got enjoyment from having another man's penis in his mouth. Secondly that he had not only chosen to keep the member in his mouth knowing that it was about to shoot, but had taken the sperm in his mouth and had not considered for one moment not swallowing it. The third was that the amount that he had delivered into the beaker was a much greater deposit then he would normally produce if he had just given himself a hand job, and by quite some margin.

"I can't believe what I have just done." Was the only thing that Tom was able to say, still tasting Clive's spent enjoyment in his mouth.

"Well I guess that opens up one huge question for you now then Tom."

"What's that?"

"Well from the way you so clearly enjoyed having done that, which is definitely a gay act, you now need to answer the question as to if you are really bi-sexual. Let's face it if you were totally straight then I can't see you having ever got so much of a kick out of having my tool in your mouth in the first place, not mentioning what you went on to do."

"Can we change the subject now please Clive because I really don't want to think too much about what has just taken place, and if it is alright with you can I now get dressed again?"

Chapter 3

Tom knew that he was now even more under Clive's control than he had been prior to the last few minutes and, was now concerned that if this did ever get out then his whole social life would be turned upside down. He knew that if all his friends were to find out what he had just done then there would be no way that he could remain living in the area, he just wouldn't be able to handle things.

"Before you get dressed I do have one question for you, I know with me it is normally no more than fifteen to twenty minutes before I am ready to go again, how long does it normally take you to be up for it a second time?"

"I guess that depends largely on the circumstances, if I'm with a really hot bird then it doesn't take me any time at all if the need arises. Having said that if I am just at home pleasuring myself then it can take quite a while. Why do you ask?"

"Well thanks to you I am now five hundred quid light on my possible earnings, so I was thinking that between us we can make up the shortfall just as soon as we have had enough of a breather. Besides which I want to help you to discover if you have got underlying gay tendencies or not."

"So am I right in thinking once we have had a rest then you will be wanting me to do the same to you again to see if I get the same amount of enjoyment a second time."

"No Tom, I think we both know that the answer to that would be a resounding yes, you enjoyed it that much. No I think we will have to try something slightly different in order to ascertain just how deep your gay tendencies really are."

Tom was now wondering just what Clive had got instore for him to do next. His mind was working overtime at this point trying to think of the different acts that gay guys get up to. He had got a pretty good idea that Clive would not be referring to the previous occurrence taking place the other way round as there was no way that he could ever see Clive taking Tom's member into his mouth. What else was there, only anal, the thought of that was something that set alarm bells ringing in his head. Yes in the past there had been occasions where he had taken a girl up the back passage. He'd got a feeling that with Clive if that was what he had in mind then it was almost definitely going to be Tom to be the one who was going to be the person that got penetrated. Was Clive gay after all, despite him having been married and having fathered a child?

"Well Tom if I am going to give you a hand getting shut of your brother's body we can't do that till about two in the morning at the earliest. So you'll have more than enough time between now and when we'll need to get going from here for you to have discovered without doubt just how gay you actually are. With the time now being just turned six then we'll have a good seven or eight hours in which time you can discover exactly what you are."

What had Clive got in store for Tom, that was the question and just how far was Clive going to take things before they left to go to Coventry? In seven hours depending on what Clive was thinking Tom thought that there was more than enough time for all sorts of things to take place, and how many times was Clive thinking that Tom would be making a deposit into beakers. He decided that there was one way of him getting some idea as to what was ahead for him.

"So Clive, just how many beakers do they give you at any one time, I guess with them collecting near enough straight away that you are only given two or three at any one time."

"Well normally they allow a bloke to have two always available, however with my neighbour coming round here to make his deposits as well it generally means that I have four here ready to be used."

"So if you have got four here and with me already having used the one then I guess that after another three deposits between the two of us then that will be it until you get fresh beakers delivered."

"I did say generally I only have four here but as it happens I have got five, which means that there are still four remaining available to use."

"So are you intending to get them all used today then?"

"Well with us having so much free time on our hands then it would be a waste of the evening if we were not to get them all used."

"So that means that with there being four left that we will both need to shoot another twice to get the job finished to your expectations. I shouldn't think that will be a problem at all, I know that I would be able to deliver my next load well within the next half hour, so by that reckoning then give it two hours max and we should have finished."

"Well if we use two beakers each then that will be right, I guess we will just have to wait and see how things progress."

The way things were going, in addition to how Clive was talking Tom got the feeling that it would be him that was going to be the only person to be using the beakers. This meant that he would have to shoot his load a further four times within the next few hours. The question that was now pressing heavily on his mind was where would Clive's deposits be going if he were to shoot the same number of times as it was clear that Tom was expected to?

"I'll just go and put your first beaker in the fridge, and then I guess we might as well take our seats again and carry on watching porn until one of us starts getting aroused again."

He took the beaker from Tom's hand and on looking at the amount that was in it he decided that he would have to pass comment before he left the room.

"Well Tom, looking at the amount that you've delivered into this then I can only assume that you really did enjoy having my cock in your mouth."

"And Clive from the amount that you delivered into my mouth I guess that I could say the same, that you must have really enjoyed having that thing of yours there."

"As you quite rightly said earlier any mouth is better than no mouth, now what was the next part of the saying?"
Without giving Tom an opportunity to answer Clive went through to put the beaker in the fridge and returned without a fresh beaker in his hand. To Tom this just seemed to re-enforce his thinking that it would only be himself that would be filling the beakers. In addition he'd recalled the next part of the saying and chose to take Clive up on what was being implied.
"We both know that the following line of the saying was that any hole is a goal, are you thinking of getting that thing of yours inside my backside by any chance?"
"And if that was what I had got in mind then just what would you have to say on the matter? I hope you are not thinking of saying that no way is that going to happen, because I really would like to give you a hand getting rid of Gavin's body. I guess if you were to insist on me not going there then that is your choice, just as me making a certain phone call is my option."
"I really don't want it to, but by the sounds of things I have got no say in the matter and I'll just have to let you do it no matter how unpleasant and painful it is for me."
"I did say that I wanted to help you work out if you are really gay or not. But there is no need for you to start getting concerned about it being painful I have done it to females a number of times and I've even got some lube especially for those occasions."
With that Clive went to the bookcase to the right of the lounge and having opened the top draw pulled out a tub of lube.
In one way Tom was relieved to hear that with the use of lube then it shouldn't be quite as painful, but he still thought that it would be the most unpleasant of experiences he'd ever encountered.
It was at this point that Clive suggested that they once again focussed their attention on the porn film that was showing, but after just a minute Clive voiced a suggestion that Tom had difficulty in believing.
"Well I think it might be a good idea if I changed film to one that you just may or may not end up enjoy watching."

With that Clive fished out a different disc from within his collection and was soon inserting it into the machine. Within just seconds of it having started it was clear to Tom that it was one that had been designed purely with the gay market in mind, it was all just men on men.

"Now I really do insist that you watch this Tom as it will really help you to find the real you to my thinking. I'll be keeping an eye on that tool of yours and if it starts getting in the slightest bit stiff then I think that we will both be able to say that you must be bi if not gay. What do you think?"

"I think that there is as much chance of me getting any enjoyment out of watching this as there will be when you do what you have got planned for me."

"Well you say that though Tom, but I dare say you would have said a very similar thing to that before you got my dick in your mouth, and just look at how much you enjoyed that once you had started."

"So please don't take this as an insult but are you that way inclined? The only reason why I ask is that for you to have this sort of film in your collection it would imply that you might be. Also from how much you put inside my mouth it was quite clear that having a blokes mouth down on you it didn't hold you back in any way."

"For me Tom I can assure you that it is just sexual gratification, remember any mouth, any hole. Now how about you being quiet and concentrate on watching the film."

Knowing that Clive was keeping a close watch on him Tom started watching the film and within just a few minutes he could sense that there was an awakening down below. He was watching a bloke being given head from another guy at the time and it did cause him to get somewhat aroused.

"There you go Tom, I can see something is definitely happening below your waistline. I think that I had best fast forward the film to a different part as we have already established the fact that you love having a cock in your mouth."

With that Clive moved the film on until instead of oral sex taking place it was now anal. Again he ordered Tom to keep watching, while he carried on taking more than just the occasional glance to see what affect it was having on Tom's manhood. Just a short time later there was a further comment heading in Tom's direction.

"Well from how your cock is responding I think it must be about time we got back down to action as I have also got a rather stiff cock again, oh and by the way it just so happens that I have got the lube right here ready. I think if you kneel down on the floor and bend forward facing the telly then you will be able to continue watching while I get to work."

Tom was aroused but he had been thinking of when he had done a similar thing to girls. He was not viewing it from the aspect of the guy who was receiving the member up his anal passage. That for him was something that he was sure that he would not enjoy being subjected to. With a bit of a push from behind by Clive he got onto his knees and bent forward, he was dreading what was about to happen.

"Well I have put some lube on my dick but if you think that you might need some round your back end then you had better dip your fingers in the tub and apply some for yourself because I am not about to do it for you."

Knowing that with the more lube the less it was likely to hurt him he begrudgingly dipped a couple of fingers into the pot and applied it to the required area. He was oblivious to the fact that he was being watched doing so.

"Right then if you are ready then Tom let's see just how much enjoyment either of us get out of this shall we. I'd better put one of the beakers on the floor in front of you just in case you get a little more excited by what is happening than either of us expect."

With that and having placed a beaker on the floor just in front of where Tom was knelt Clive then went round to the back of Tom. As he started feeling Clive's erect member touching his backside Tom braced himself for what was to come. He hoped that Clive didn't get any satisfaction from what he was about to do because although he had taken his last load into his mouth he did not want

Clive to shoot his next load inside his backside. As he started feeling it entering his passage he was relieved that at least the lube seemed to be doing its job and that there wasn't any real pain as he felt it going further inside him. To Tom's amazement he was aware that the full length was now inside his passage with feeling Clive's body firmly pressed against his buttocks. It was now that Clive started working his member in and out, initially very slowly and gently and then increasing both speed and force. "So what do you think then Tom, I certainly haven't heard you crying out for me to stop so does that mean that you are enjoying having my tool deep inside your arse?"

It was when Tom replied that he was not getting any enjoyment out of what was taking place in the slightest that he felt Clive putting a hand round and having taken a hold of Tom's member Clive then said that in his opinion Tom had just lied to him.

"Tom, if you are not getting any enjoyment from what I am doing then why is this as hard as it is? Can you answer that for me?"

Although not wanting to admit it Tom knew that Clive had caught him out. Yes his dick was now very firm and he was not about to admit it but yes he was beginning to get a little bit of enjoyment from what he was experiencing. Had Clive been right all along? Was Tom gay although until today he had never realised it. Tom's mind was in turmoil, he just could not deal with what was happening to him, yes he had enjoyed taking Clive's member in his mouth and now despite his earlier thoughts he was actually enjoying having it now inside another of his cavities.

With Tom not having replied to what Clive had said it was now that Clive really started to work hard at what he was doing. It was quite clear from where Tom was knelt that he wasn't the only one who was enjoying what was happening, it was plain that Clive was getting a fair bit of enjoyment out of it too.

"So Tom, when you first got mine in that mouth of yours had you got any intention of swallowing what I was to produce?"

"No, not at all. Why?"

"I was only asking because I was wondering quite what you were likely to do when I inform you that I am about to shoot my load again. Will you keep your arse round it like you did your mouth or will you move forward so I can deliver it into one of the beakers?"

Although Tom didn't want to admit it there was this thought wondering through his mind as to if you were able to feel it as it enters your back passage. He was enjoying having Clive's member working in and out of his backside and there was just a part of him that wanted to know what it felt like when a load was delivered inside. However he thought that as soon as Clive told him that he was about to shoot he would pull himself forward. It did not happen though.

"Well do I need to get a beaker ready then Tom because I am just about to shoot my load?"

With Tom staying where he was it was instantly clear to Clive that Tom wanted the deposit to be made up his backside, and with the realisation he put in just a few more really deep thrusts before he felt himself erupting into Tom's arse. For Tom as soon as he felt Clive's delivery entering him he immediately grabbed for the beaker and brought it to his own member just in time for the jets of sperm that exited his tool to be caught.

As Clive pulled out and looked round Tom's body in order to see what had been delivered into the beaker he just could not prevent himself from making a comment that Tom did not want to hear.

"Well there you go then Tom, I think we can safely say that you are gayer than either of us thought you were. If you deliver that much when you have a dick either in your mouth or one up your arse then to me that shows very clearly that you are either gay or at the very least bi."

For Tom this was a total head fuck. He had always considered himself to be one hundred percent straight and as such how on earth could he have got this much enjoyment out of what had taken place over the last couple of hours. He just didn't want to admit it but there must be more than just a bit of truth in what Clive had just said. Surely if he was, as he had always thought, totally straight then he would never have enjoyed for one moment what had taken place.

"Come on then Tom, what have you got to say for yourself? Is that honestly the first time you have ever had another man's cock in either your mouth or up your arse?"

"I can honestly say that yes it has been the first ever time for it to have happened to me on both counts, what's more it's doing my head in because you know full well without me having to admit it that I have enjoyed both experiences. I am not about to try and fool you into thinking different because it was that clear from what I chose to happen."

"Well fair play to you for your honesty, and I guess that it is only right that I am equally as honest to you as you just have been. For me both things were one hell of a lot better than if I had just given myself a wank. By the way have you noticed what the time is?"

 On looking at the clock Tom saw that it was still only just turned eight o'clock, and instantly began to wonder what else Clive had got in mind. As far as he was concerned he had already done the two main things, he'd taken Clive's member in both his mouth as well as up his rear end. What else was there to do.

"I think that I had better put this second beaker in the fridge and while I am there I'll try and work out which one has got the greater load in it. That way we should be able to get some idea as to which you enjoyed the most, my cock in your mouth or having it up your arse."

While Clive was in the kitchen Tom wondered just what was in store for him yet this evening. Although Clive was still saying that he was straight and was just using Tom in order to have a bit of fun Tom thought otherwise, Clive seemed to be enjoying things just a little too much.

"Well you might be interested to know that there really isn't much between the two loads that you have delivered so far. I must admit that I am quite impressed with the amount that you deliver each time."

"I think that you don't do too bad from what I have felt of you shooting, but you do have an advantage as you have seen my load each time but I haven't had the opportunity to see yours, I have only felt them."

"Well I have a bit of news for you Tom, I think that you'll be pleased to know that you will have more chances to feel me shoot my load yet before we call it a night. You know I told you about my neighbour who comes round, I am going to give him a quick call to see what he is up to. If he is free I think that he might like to pop round in order to see if you can bring him a bit of excitement as well."

Chapter 4

With that Tom listened as Clive phoned his friend and on hearing the name George he thought that with it being an old fashioned name that he was now going to have to do a similar thing for an old man. He sat there while hearing that this George would be round in just a few minutes.

"Am I right that you still want me to stay naked?"

"Well I think that it would be pointless you putting your clothes back on because they will be coming back off in a very short time. You see Tom George and I were talking just the other day about going two up on a girl and we kind of liked the idea of us teaming up. Well we haven't got a girl here but you seem to be that accommodating that I think that we both might get fun out of using you if you have no objections."

Tom heard the back door opening and assumed that it must be this George arriving and waited to just how old this other guy was going to turn out to be. He was feeling uncomfortable being totally naked with not only Clive now having pulled his trousers back up but with a total stranger just about to arrive. As the visitor entered the room Tom could not believe his eyes. Although he had visualised the neighbour as being an elderly gent it was just a lad that walked in.

"Hello George, I didn't mention the fact that I had got someone else here on the phone but I'd like you to meet Tom. Now Tom here has very kindly agreed to assist us both in relieving ourselves of certain substances, and before I gave you a call I must admit that I have tested him out and he is as willing as he said he was."

"I know when we were watching that one porno of yours the other evening I said that I wouldn't mind giving a few things a try, but I really didn't think that you would have organised for me to do so. So you are Tom then, I'm George and I must say that from where I am standing it appears as though you have got quite a good body on you. Can you do me a favour and stand up and turn round so I can have a good look please."

The lad must have been no more than eighteen nineteen and Tom just couldn't work out what the situation was. Why was a guy his age donating to a sperm bank and more to the point if Clive was as straight as he professed to be then why the hell did George come round here to relieve himself. Within just a few seconds of him having stood up and turned round in order for George to take a good look at him at least one of his questions was soon answered.

George walked across the lounge to where Tom was standing and soon started touching various parts of Tom's body. Initially just feeling what muscle he'd got to his upper arms then soon working his way down the body until his hands were feeling his backside before moving round to the front. Clive may well say that he was straight but from what George was doing Tom had got the distinct impression that George was far from being so, and decided that it only fair to try and even things up a little.

"So George, you obviously like seeing me like this, how about you let me see you in the same state of undress? How about you getting your clothes off so that I can see what you look like as you can see me?"

"Well George I think Tom has got a point there besides, you'll have to get your trousers down before long if you are going to do any of the things that we talked about the other night."

"Clive is right, but I really can't be bothered to undress myself so Tom if you want to see me naked then I guess you had better undress me."

With that although Tom was in one way regretting having voiced his previous comment as there was no way that he wanted to actually be the one who stripped off another guy. He knew though that Clive would not allow him not to carry out George's wishes. After he had removed the stranger's shirt he then started undoing the jeans. It was blatantly obvious from the bulge that not only had George got an erection, but from the bulge showing through the material he was quite a big lad down below. As he lowered the jeans, leaving the pants where they were he now had a much clearer impression as to just how large the guys penis really was, and although he had thought that it was very big it now looked not much larger than his own. He was conscious at this stage that his own member was getting increasingly hard.

"So Tom by the looks of things you are getting quite a kick out of undressing George. Now without you using your hands why don't you get those pants of George's down round his ankles. And while you have got your head down there I'm sure that he wouldn't mind too much if you accidently ended up getting his cock in your mouth. But Tom, I don't want you to be kneeling down while you do it, I think it will be better if you just bend over."

With that Tom did exactly as he had been instructed and was soon taking the erect member inside his mouth. He was aware that Clive had stood up and was now behind where he was bent over but was not able to see what was happening. It was just a short while before he realised what Clive had been up to as he started feeling a stiff cock entering his backside for a second time during the evening.

For Tom this was just absolute madness, he had got both a cock in his mouth and another up his arse and he was just really enjoying where both of them were. The more Clive worked his member inside Tom's backside the more he in turn worked his mouth on George's member that was in his mouth. Now George put his hand on the back of Tom's head and pulled it forward forcing more of its length into the mouth.

"Well I know that you won't be able to answer me Tom, but I really hope that you are enjoying what you are doing to my cock as much as I am. Clive have you got the beakers handy because I do believe that with the job that Tom is doing with his mouth it won't be too long before I will be emptying my sack."

"Well if you really want to put the contents into a beaker then there is one down the side of the settee. But I think you'll find that Tom here might end up getting a little upset if you deprive his mouth of it after he has done all the work to get you there."

"Are you meaning to tell me that Tom will be happy if I empty myself into his mouth, because if so that will be a first for me. I have never had anyone take it in their mouth before but I reckon that seeing as he is doing such a good job it's only right for him to get the fruits of his labour."

Hearing that George was not that far from shooting his load it only spurred Tom into working his mouth harder on the tool that was now deep inside his mouth. He was really loving the whole experience and was trying to work out when he had enjoyed sex so much when he had been with any of the girls that he'd had over the years. He now needed to pull his mouth free as he had to say something.

"Clive I think that I need to have that beaker close by because between the two of you I know for a fact that I won't be able to stop myself from shooting very soon."

"You're alright Tom, if you can hold on to it for just a few more seconds then as soon as I have emptied myself in your mouth I'll return the compliment if you are happy for me to do so."

"In that case George you had better hurry up filling my mouth because I just know that I'll be doing so very shortly."

With that George introduced his hand onto his own cock in order to get the job completed just that little bit faster although with the job that Tom's mouth was doing the goal would have been achieved without the use of his hand in the not too distant future. As Tom started receiving George's sperm into his mouth he had to grab his own dick in order to prevent himself from shooting. When Clive had shot in his mouth earlier he'd thought that it had been quite an amount, now he was receiving one hell of a lot more from George. He felt jet after jet hitting the back of his throat and carried on sucking on it until sure that there was no more to come. As soon as the task was completed George pulled out and straightening Tom up then dropped straight to his knees and Tom's member was soon taken into the mouth. It was now that Clive was reaching his climax and as Tom felt the sperm entering his anal passage once more he in the same instant offloaded his own produce into the waiting mouth.

"Well that was quite a surprise George, I was really not expecting you to have gone down on Tom's dick like you did. If you had told me that you liked that sort of thing then you could have done that to me for the last few weeks."

"Clive, I didn't say anything because I thought that with you knowing that I was gay then if you wanted anything like that to take place then you would have asked."

"So am I right then Clive, George has been coming round here for some time donating his sperm for the bank or wherever it goes to and that you have never done anything like this between the two of you?"

"That's right Tom, yours is the first males' mouth that I have ever had my cock in and that arse of yours is the first one that I have ever been in as well the belonged to a bloke."

"So if you don't mind me asking if George has been coming round here and with you knowing that he is gay then why have you waited till today and with me?"

"When you first took my dick in your mouth I was just doing it to teach you a lesson for lying to me about having a quiet night last night. It wasn't until you got to work on it that I found that I was enjoying it almost as much as you were. From then I decided to take things one step further and I soon realised that having it up your arse was giving me even more enjoyment."

"So George admits that he is gay. I guess that I will have to accept the fact that I am bi, then Clive if you've enjoyed both having your dick sucked by another guy and then got even more satisfaction out of shagging another blokes arse then I guess that you must be bi too."

"I don't do labels Tom, as far as I am concerned I am having good fun and that is all that matters."

"So Tom, until you came round here to Clive's today you were straight then were you?"

"Yes George, I had not had another guys dick in my hand since I was in my teens at school let alone in either my mouth or up my back passage. Why do you ask George?"

"Well the way you were working your mouth on my dick I
thought that you must have had loads of experience doing it
because I was having to hold myself back from shooting much
earlier than I did as you were doing such a good job."
"Am I supposed to take that as a compliment then George?"
Without asking if he minded George drew right up to stand
directly in front of Tom and having put his right hand on the back
of Tom's head pulled it forward until their mouths met. With that
George started kissing Tom on the lips and was very soon trying
to force his tongue inside. For Tom at this point it was something
that he was not about to allow happen, a kiss on the lips was
shock enough for him but to start exchanging tongues was
something that he was not yet ready to go through with. As they
parted Tom felt the need to speak.
"Sorry about that George but it's all been a bit of a shock to the
system, and I'm afraid that is one step too far for me to take at
this stage."
"Tom, don't disappoint George like that, he's a friend of mine
and I really don't want to hear you doing anything to upset him.
Now go on, I think you had better apologise to George, and you
know what I mean don't you?"
With that Tom knew that he was going to have to carry through
with the instruction and having pulled George closer to him again
he then started kissing him, this time they both had open mouths
and tongues searched out the others mouths. It was after the initial
couple of seconds that Tom found himself giving his all into the
kiss. Again things were just fuelling the mental turmoil that he
was going through. Was there anything that was going to take
place this evening that he was not going to enjoy?
Having finished the kiss George turning to Clive said that Tom
was not just good at giving a bloody good blowjob but that he
was also a fantastic kisser when he put his mind to it.
"So Tom, from what I have seen so far from you today it appears
as though you have clearly wasted years bothering going out with
girls, you are certainly giving me the impression that you really
are enjoying what is taking place. Now be honest with me, how

does what is happening today compare with your usual sex with females?"

"Well you have told me to be honest with you and although I don't believe that I am going to say it. So far what I have experienced here today has got to be up there with the best ever sex session that I have ever had in my life."

"Well I noticed that you just said so far, does that mean that you are still wanting more?"

"Well it was you that pointed out that we didn't need to leave here till the early hours of the morning to go and do the other thing so I guess that seeing as we all seem to be enjoying things then we might as well carry on. That is assuming that you both would like to."

"Well Clive I am certainly up for having some more action if it is okay with you for us to continue."

"Tom, seeing that George here is keen to carry on then I think it would only be right for you to accommodate him further. Now before we start again and just to give ourselves a little breather I think that if I put on a slightly different film them you might get some idea as to what will be coming next. If the three of us all sit down on the settee then we will be able to watch it together."

With that Clive once again changed the DVD and as soon as the initial stuff had finished the four guys featuring in the film were getting up to some extreme sexual activities. They were using various sex toys and as Tom watched he thought that surely Clive would not be in possession of similar playthings. There again he had never thought that he would have films like this either so he could be wrong.

He was engrossed in what he was seeing taking place and for a time was ignorant to what was taking place at his side. He then found his left hand being moved over by George, the younger guy wanted Tom to become aware of the fact that he was once again quite firm.

"Well I don't need to ask if you are enjoying what you are seeing George because this thing that you have just put my hand round is speaking for you. And now I look I see that Clive is fully erect again also.”

“I knew he would be without even bothering to look, I know that this is one of his favourite films and he really gets off on watching it. When we have been here filling beakers when he has been watching stuff like this he shoots one hell of a lot I can tell you.”

Without saying a word Clive got up and left the room, only to reappear a minute or two later holding a carrier bag in his right hand.

“He’s got his toys out Tom, I knew that was where he had gone and what he was up to.” George commented with a smile on both his face as well as being heard in his voice.

“So what toys have you got then Clive, or is it a case that I will have to wait and find out?”

With the question having been asked Clive started taking out the various objects from within the bag. As each item was revealed Tom was taking a good look, again not believing it but getting more excited as each item came into sight. That was until the last two things were removed and brought out into the open, the first being a very large dildo. The final being a black rubber item that although at first he wasn’t able to see what it was he then asked Clive if he could have a better look. It wasn’t until he had picked the thing up and opened it out that he then realised what the item was, although could not quite work out what it was used for or exactly how. As he looked at it closer there was a mask and then running from the mouth of it was a tube that then led into a pair of rubber pants. He examined it further and soon realised that the pipe was attached to the pants in such a way that anything that passed from the penis of the wearer would then travel along the tube and into the mouth of the person wearing the face mask.

“So have you worked out what it is yet then Tom and how things work with it?”

“I think I have, but if the guy who is wearing the pants part shoots his load in them then how does it pass all the length of the tube?”

"You have almost got it right but not quite. If I tell you that it's called a pissing gimp mask does that make it a bit clearer as to what it is used for?"

As Tom heard the title given to the item there was a sudden realisation that he was going to be forced to be the one who would be wearing the mask part, and that he very shortly would be receiving into his mouth the urine from whoever was wearing the pants. Now this was definitely something that he would not be looking forward to happening although he just knew that he had got no say in the matter whatsoever. He was going to have to go through with whatever Clive told him to do.

"So George you said the other day that you wouldn't mind having a go using this, I hope you haven't had a piss just before you came round here and that you have got something in your bladder ready for Tom here."

"I think I'll be able to come up with something for him to drink Clive but before I get those on I had better get this dick of mine offloaded first otherwise I won't be able to have a piss with it being so hard."

"In that case George why don't you ask Tom if he wants to take it back in his mouth, or you could ask him if he would prefer you to put that thing of yours up his arse."

"So you heard Clive then Tom, which would you prefer? Me shooting my next load in your mouth again or would you prefer me to shag you?"

"To be really truthful with the amount that you seemed to deliver into my mouth earlier I would just love to see just how much you shoot. I'd love to watch you but I will be more than happy using my mouth in order to get you there."

"In that case Clive do you mind if I do that other thing that we watched the other night so Tom can have the best of both worlds?"

"Well I know for a fact that he will do a good job of cleaning it up so I will just be watching, you never know I might even add a bit to your donation if you know what I mean."

"Right then Tom, so you want to see me shoot my load. What I'll do is lie down on the floor and you can kneel between my legs and take it in your mouth until I am about to shoot. I'll tell you when and then I'll shoot over my belly so you can watch. After that I know you love the taste of it so once I have finished shooting you can then lick by stomach clean. Does that sound good to you?"

Tom answered him with actions and got up from off the settee and made it clear that he was just waiting for George to get in place on the carpet. Clive was now opening the tub of lube again and Tom thought that he would very soon be feeling Clive entering him again while he sucked on George's member. As soon as George was lay down Tom got straight to work and was soon taking the erect member deep into his mouth. He was aware that Clive was applying more lube to the entrance of his anal passage and unlike the previous time where once applied Clive's hand was immediately replaced by his penis this time things were different. He sucked while feeling Clive's fingers entering his backside, trying to work out just how many he had got inside him. Tom felt his entrance being stretched as more of the hand entered him and despite it being uncomfortable he certainly wasn't finding it unpleasant.

"So how is he doing on that dick of yours then George, do you think he is enjoying what I am doing back here?"

"I reckon so Clive because he isn't biting into it but he is going at it even better than he was earlier, why don't you try using the other thing. I am itching to know if a bloke can actually take something that size up him without having had years of experience taking things inside their arse."

Tom knew that the big dildo was now going to be coming into action and was dreading it. There was one thing taking a cock or even part of a hand up there but he was sure that if the big dildo was to be inserted then that was bound to hurt and in a really big way.

"Don't get worried Tom, I am not about to use the big one while you have got your mouth round George's tool because I have got a funny feeling that if I were to then you would end up biting it off. I'm going to use the smaller one for now and it will help to prepare your arse for things to come."

With that Tom felt the dildo entering him. He had seen it when being removed from the carrier bag and although not as big as the other one it was still some way bigger than Clive's member which up till now was the only thing ever to have entered him. As he felt it going deeper and deeper inside his arse he worked harder on the tool that was in his mouth.

"Tom, when I say you had better get your mouth clear because I can tell you that it will not be long before you are getting your wish and watching me shoot my load. And if you are almost there yourself then why don't you shoot in the same place as I do."

With hearing that it was okay for him to shoot all over the stomach of George he started working his right hand on his own cock, meanwhile continuing to feel the dildo being worked in and out of his arse as well as the dick doing the same in his mouth.

"Get that mouth off Tom."

As soon as Tom had raised his head clear George started despatching his latest load onto his own belly, and just seeing it was enough to send Tom over the edge, he too delivered a sizeable amount onto the same stomach.

Having raised his head from off the carpet in order to take a good look at the amount that was now on his belly George started laughing.

"Well by the look of that load I would say that we both really enjoyed that. The only problem I have got though is that I can't get my tongue down there to clean up your deposit so I guess that I will have to leave it all down to you."

"I am sure that Tom hasn't got any objection, but Tom don't waste too much time licking George clean because now he has shot his load I bet he is just itching to take that piss he was talking about."

Tom had taken both Clive's and George's sperm into his mouth and swallowed every drop but he was now going to have to take his own if he were going to clean up the mess on the stomach beneath him. He lowered his head knowing that he had no option, and as he did so and with him bending further down it allowed Clive to move the dildo further inside his anal passage. He raised his head momentarily, just long enough to ask a question.

"Clive, can I ask just how much of it is inside me because by the feel of it there can't be many more inches of it left?"

"I am glad to hear you say that Tom because I am beginning to think that you will be able to take the bigger one up there. The one I am using is as far up you as I can get it, and from what you have just said it is clear that you are still wanting more. By the way as soon as you have finished licking that lot up you had better get your mouth on mine and take some more off me while George puts on the pants, then I'll help you on with the mask."

As Clive had said would happen did. As soon as Tom had cleaned up both George's and his own discharges he then ended up getting another mouthful from Clive. By the time he had finished on that George was now comfortable with how the pants were on him.

"Right then Tom, we'll get that mask on you then if you lie down on your back then George will either stand over you or sit gently on your chest. But if you can have your legs bent right up and open wide for me at the same time that would be very helpful."

As soon as Clive was happy that the mask was on Tom correctly and that the tube wasn't kinked he then got Tom lying down. George sat gently on his chest as Clive had suggested.

"So I hope you are thirsty Tom because when it starts coming down that tube I think you will be quite surprised with the force that it comes through at. If you tell him when you are about to start pissing George then that will give him a chance to get a good breath beforehand."

As George started relieving himself of any urine that he'd got in his bowels Clive took hold of the large dildo and having parted Tom's legs wider started teasing the backside with it. He knew that with having the gimp mask on and with urine flowing down the tube into his mouth there was no way that Tom would be able to do anything to prevent Clive from inserting the dildo inside his anal passage. With the way the mask was designed there was no option open to Tom other than to take every drop that passed through the tube into his mouth, although he was having difficulty swallowing it all fast enough. He was having to concentrate that much on what he was doing with his mouth that he was almost oblivious of the dildo entering his rear hole. That was until Clive started feeding it in. Tom knew from looking at it that it must be a good four inches across and getting on for fifteen inches in length. He realised though that the full length couldn't be inserted because Clive would have to retain a hold of it in order to do what he intended. As George finished he lifted up to allow the tube to straighten out, he didn't want to deprive Tom of a drop that he had passed. Once happy that Tom must now have swallowed the entirety he then turned round in order to see just how Clive was getting on with the dildo. He was amazed to see that at least half of its length was now out of sight and yet Tom was not making any sound.

"Have you noticed something George, I think that Tom must either have liked the taste of your piss or is loving having this thing in him because there is definitely growth going on with that dick of his."

"I reckon that if I get my mouth down on it I can have a real close up of that dildo moving in and out of his arse, you don't mind me sucking Tom's do you Clive?"

"Not at all as long as you don't end up getting in the way of me doing this. I guess if you get those pants off and then help Tom to remove the mask he can be sucking on yours at the same time as you have his in your mouth."

As soon as the gimp mask had been removed from both parties they then took each other's members into their mouths. Tom wasn't able to see from where he was lay but was sure that nearly the full length of the dildo must be inside him from the feel of things. When he had looked at it earlier he had thought that no way would he have been able to have taken it, but having had his arse well lubed up as well as taking Clive's dick inside him the dildo was not too uncomfortable.

"Fuck me Tom, you ought to be seeing this, Clive has got nearly every inch of it in you and yet you are not even groaning in pain. And by the way you are working on my dick I think you are actually enjoying having it in there." George took the member back into his mouth.

Tom pushed George's hips up to allow his mouth to become empty of cock so he could reply to George's comment.

"You don't have to tell me that it is almost fully in me, believe me I can feel every inch of it. You want to try it sometime, it isn't that painful." He allowed the hips to lower so again was able to take the stiff cock back into his mouth.

Having heard what Tom had just said Clive now started working the dildo in an out, slowly. Tom was now groaning but neither Clive or George could work out if it was a groan of pain or shear ecstasy.

As soon as Tom's hand reached down onto the back of George's head pushing it further onto his cock so he was taking its full length inside his mouth it was then that Tom started shooting his load. He could not believe the sensation, it felt as though there was that much leaving his body that he was certain that it must have been by far the most he had ever shot in his life, it just seemed to keep pumping and pumping up his shaft. George was almost choking trying to retain it all in his mouth. Eventually Tom was totally spent, he breathed heavily trying to get his breath back such was the force of the orgasm that he had just had.

"Bloody hell Tom, I have taken a few guys loads in my mouth over the time I have been gay but never ever have I had to deal with that amount. I know that you won't be able to perform again for some time but the next time that dildo goes in you I want to watch to see just how much comes out of that cock of yours. Now can you get your mouth back onto mine because after tasting that load off you I think that I will have a decent load for you to taste." With that Tom finished George off, the dildo still being worked inside his rear end although now it was not having quite the same sensation with him having already shot his load.

"I have got a feeling that if I keep this in here for a few minutes that I'll be seeing Tom's cock getting stiff again in not too long. Do you fancy having a go with it George?"

"Are you meaning do I want to take over from you in feeding it in and out of Tom's arse, or are you meaning do I want to try taking it up my backside?"

"Well now you mention it if you want to then I am sure that Tom won't mind it being shared between the two of you, but I was meaning do you want to do what I am doing so I can have a chance to do something else."

"I can do Clive, what have you got planned next then?"

"As soon as you have shot your load Tom can then relieve me. I don't mean that I am going to shoot my load again just yet but I really could do with a piss and rather than bothering with the mask if he lies where he is I can piss into the open mouth if you fancy watching."

"In that case I'll give mine a bit of a hand so as soon as he has finished tasting my spunk then I'll watch as he starts drinking your piss."

George took his member in his hand allowing Tom to keep his mouth round just the tip of it until George could feel himself about to shoot at which time he removed his hand and pushed the rock solid member deep into Tom's mouth. He too was aware that he was shooting more than he normally did but was confident that it wasn't anywhere near the volumes that Tom had put into his mouth a few minutes ago. As soon as he was finished, and after allowing Tom time to lick off any residue he then pulled away in order to allow Clive to get into position.

"You are alright Tom I will control the flow so you are able to take it all down your throat, the last thing I want to happen is for any of it to end up on the carpet."

Tom was aware that the dildo had been just abandoned most of the way inside him. Although George was supposed to be taking over from Clive it was clear that he was eager to see Clive pissing into the awaiting mouth.

"Open your mouth then Tom, and if you need time to catch your breath if you tap me on the leg then I will stop the flow until you are ready to continue drinking it."

With that Clive started passing urine and George knelt at the side watching as it passed from the tip of Clive's cock and disappeared into Tom's mouth.

Twice Tom had tapped Clive on the leg before Clive deemed that he had finished and then lowering himself down he asked Tom to make sure that it was clean. Tom licked the end of the flaccid dick.

"Fuck me Clive, I have just noticed that he has got a stiffy on again."

With that Clive turned round in order to see for himself that George wasn't lying, he wasn't, Tom's cock was again standing to attention.

"So what do you think we ought to do with his next load then George? I know that you said that you wanted to watch him shoot the next time but with him only having done so five minutes ago I have a feeling that there won't be that much next time round."

"While that dildo is still up my arse I wouldn't be too sure of that Clive, I think if one of you starts working it in and out again then I will produce a good enough load for it to be worth George watching."

"In that case Tom, seeing as how you are that confident that it will be a good amount if you swap places with George then you can shoot onto his belly again before you lick it back off."

"Can't he just stay where he is please Clive, if he shoots all over his own belly then I can lick it up for him. It's only fair as he did clean my load up for me."

"Okay then George have it your way, I guess you will be asking me next if you can get Tom's in your mouth again to help it on its way."

"Tom, if I suck your cock while Clive works the dildo in and out do you think that would make you shoot the most?"

"I think if you get your mouth up this end and kiss me like you did earlier then that would have an even greater effect than if you were to be sucking me off."

No more needed to be said and they very soon had their lips glued together and both tongues at work in the others mouth. While they kissed it was George's hand that was working on Tom's penis in the hope that he could get him to peak. As they kissed Tom just couldn't stop looking right into George's blue eyes. This is all just magnificent he thought, the kiss, the dildo deep inside him, George's hand working on his dick, it was all brilliant.

He pushed George's head off signifying that he was just about to shoot his load for the sixth time since they had started, and as he watched George realised why he had such a job keeping all the last load within his mouth. George was wishing in a way that he hadn't just shot his own load because he was sure with having watched this just before he shot himself it would have caused him to produce more. As soon as Tom had finished George bent over and after having licked the tip of Tom's cock clean then got to the task of licking the rest of the body. Clive thought that the time had come for the dildo to be removed and finished with for this session.

"Well I don't know about either of you but I think that I am just about finished for today, I don't think I could get it stiff again if I tried. What do you guys think?"

"I reckon that Tom and I will both be able to manage once more if we spend some time giving each other a bit of encouragement if that is alright with you Clive?"

"What about you Tom, do you fancy having a time with it just being you and George while I go upstairs and dig out some suitable clothes to wear later and get myself a shower."

Tom lifted his head up from off the carpet and answered Clive's question while at the same time asking George one.

"Well I am up for another go especially if George would allow me to get my dick up his arse."

"I'll hurry up and get this cleaned up then get my mouth back up there and carry on kissing you while I think if I will allow you to shag me or not."

"I'll leave you two alone for a while, I think that Tom is now clear in his own mind and knows that he is bi."

"You haven't got that right Clive, before today I was totally straight, since things got underway I then changed it to me being bi. Now though there isn't a girl out there that could satisfy me anywhere near as much as I have been pleasured today. Sorry but girls for me are now a thing of the past as long as I can keep getting more of what I have experienced today."

"I think that Tom is trying to chat you up George, and in his own way is asking you if he can do this more often with you."

"Is that what you are trying to say is it Tom, do you fancy me and want this to become a regular thing and if so do you want Clive to be present every time we get it together?"

Tom was unsure how he was best answering the question, he didn't want to say anything that might cause Clive to get annoyed with him. He didn't voice a reply but instead waited until Clive had left the room before saying anything else.

"So Tom, now it is just the two of us will you answer me a question, and I won't let on to Clive what you have said. Is today the first time that you have had sex with another man?"

"I told Clive earlier that when I was at boarding school there was this one gay lad in our dorm that the one night we all took it in turns shooting our loads into his mouth. Other than that besides the occasional wanking competition then yes this is the very first time. I'll tell you one thing for sure though, I hope it isn't going to be the last."

"So how old are you then, at a guess I would say that you're twenty, twenty one?"

"Twenty two actually, what about yourself, you can't be anymore than eighteen?"

"You are nearly right, I'll be eighteen next week, and I expect you to be giving me a real nice present on my birthday if what Clive

was saying about you wanting to have me as your boyfriend is
right."

"I think I need to hold back on that for the moment, not that I
haven't enjoyed things with you but more because I need to get
my head sorted out first. It has come as a hell of a shock to find
out that I prefer sex with guys more than I do with girls if you can
understand where I am coming from."

"I think you need to stop talking and give me an opportunity to
convince you that you were meaning that you want me as your
fella. Why don't you get that mouth back here so I can get my
tongue back in it before I start working at getting that cock of
yours hard enough for it to enter me."

It was an invitation that Tom did not need to be repeated and
within seconds their tongues were exploring the other's mouth
again. George's hand down on Tom's flaccid dick trying to bring
it back to life, while in turn Tom was having a good feel of the
other lad's arse cheeks.

As soon as George had got Tom's cock hard enough he broke off
from the kiss and asked Tom how he was intending getting some
moisture round his point of entry. Following it up by casually
dropping the hint that once he had a tongue down there and found
it very nice. Again Tom didn't believe what he was doing. After
getting George to apply spit onto his now erect dick he then
turned George round and after bending him over dropped down
onto his knees. He then got his mouth working on George's rear
and, he made sure that it was wet in just the right place before
standing back up and getting his tool entering the now prepared
anal entrance.

"So I take it you want me to go all the way and shoot inside you?"

"Well seeing as I filled your mouth with mine earlier I think it
would be an insult if I were not to say yes please in reply to that
one. If you shoot as much as you did earlier I know for a fact that
I will feel it entering me. It will probably come out with such
force that I'll probably end up tasting it in my mouth."

With that Tom went to work and very soon was feeling himself
about to shoot his load. He reached round to the front of George

in order to get a good handful of the stiff cock. He then started working it in the hope that he would be able to bring George to his climax at exactly the same time as Tom emptied himself inside that arse of his.

"If you carry on doing that I will be shooting all over the place and I know that Clive will get really pissed off if he comes in here and sees that we have made a mess."

"In that case George when you are shooting I suggest that you catch it all in your hand and then just like I did with your belly earlier I will make sure that the hand is cleaned."

"You just can't get enough of my sperm in your mouth can you? If you stop working your hand on it then as soon as you have shot your load in me then you can get round here and take it directly into your mouth from out of my cock. I just know that with your mouth being round it again that there will be more for you to taste."

Just with George talking dirty in conjunction with the thought of taking more of George's juice into his mouth it was enough to bring Tom to his peak. He felt himself giving jet after jet inside the lovely arse that he had been working and decided then that he needed to tell George that he had just come to a decision.

"George, you know what we were talking about, well I have just decided that I want to get to know you a hell of a lot better if you know what I am saying?"

"Well hearing that I just know that there will be even more going into that mouth of yours just as soon as you get down on mine. By the way thanks for that, I enjoyed what you have just done and hopefully that will be just the first of many times that I take you up me."

"You are more than welcome George. Now let's see just how much you want me as your regular shag then shall we, I'll warn you though if you don't produce your personal best then I might have to have a rethink as to if I want it to become a regular thing."

"Just get that mouth down on it and I can assure you that I will leave you in no doubt."

With that Tom got down to work on George's tool and was soon taking a sizable delivery into his mouth. Yes, it was clear that George wanted Tom as his boyfriend, it had been the greatest load that he had taken into his mouth the whole evening. They were just sealing things with another kiss when Clive entered spoiling their fun.

"I take it seeing that neither of you are now sporting a hard cock that I haven't entered at the wrong time. Sorry to have to break things up but it is nearly eleven o'clock and George hadn't you better be getting off home now before your mum starts wondering where the hell you have got to."

"I guess that I had really, although I would prefer to stay round here for longer. Tom, thank you for today I have really enjoyed it and once we have both got dressed then as long as it is alright with Clive we will have to exchange phone numbers so we can arrange to meet up again very soon."

"Would that be okay with you Clive, if George and I exchanged details?"

"As long as when you are going to have sex next that you have it here so I can at least watch you fucking each other, unless you will allow me to take part."

"I think that George won't object to there being the three of us involved will you George?"

"As long as we do get some time with it just Tom and me if that is alright with you please Clive. I know that it is your house and that in me asking it is being a bit on the cheeky side."

"Well who am I to stand in the way of a budding relationship. By the way George one day Tom might tell you the reason why he ended up being round here today to start off with, and why he allowed things to even get started."

Tom realised that Clive was not just going to allow things to drop and that he would forever use the fact that Tom had murdered his own brother to his advantage.

"I guess it puts a whole new meaning to the phrase snuff videos doesn't it Tom, with the film that you have starred in?"

Tom chose not to answer because he knew that if he had said exactly what was going through his mind at this point in time then Clive would have ended up making that phone call to Marcos, the boss.

"So what sort of film was it that you starred in then Tom, I didn't realise that what will become my new fella was a celebrity."

"I'm sure that Tom will get round to telling you in the not too distant future, we might even all sit down here the one evening and watch him in his star roll. What do you think Tom, do you reckon that George would like to see the film that you starred in?"

Tom knew that he was expected to answer and did, but it wasn't the answer that Clive expected him to come out with.

"I think George would prefer watching your films, having said that if we watch the one you are talking about Clive through till the end then he will even see you coming into shot towards the very end."

"So you were in the same film then were you Clive? You kept that quiet, you've never told me that you have done any film work."

"I think Tom is winding you up a bit, I just went on afterwards to clean up the mess that had been made, didn't I Tom. You had made one hell of a mess and then came crying to me to come and help you clean it up."

"Something like that Clive, but I think that I did make it worth your while if I am not mistaken."

Tom although being a little careful with what he was saying was enjoying himself in making Clive feel not quite as cocky as he had been when first bringing the event up to George. Tom knew that if allowed then Clive would walk all over him. It was then that Tom thought of something that he could do the next time he was to come over here and have sex with the two of them. Not that he wanted to do anything that might spoil what might be ahead for him and George, but he did need to try and even things up between himself and Clive.

Once dressed and before leaving George did three things, he exchanged contact details with Tom, he then kissed Clive on the cheek, then the final thing that he did before leaving was to go and give Tom a full on kiss on the lips right in front of Clive. George had realised that Clive had tried to make Tom feel uncomfortable with his comments and had decided that by giving Tom a kiss like he was it would piss Clive off in quite a big way. Kiss finished he went on his way back to his parents' home.

"Well Tom that has been quite a last twenty four hours for you. Started the day by shooting your own brother in the back of his head, then getting your arse kicked at squash, followed by you getting it fucked by not just me but a couple of dildos. And that isn't mentioning the fact that this time yesterday you thought that you were straight, and now not only have you decided that you no longer want to be bothered with females, that you are now already aiming to get into a relationship with a guy. What a difference a day can make."

"I must admit that it has been a hell of a time. Talking about Gavin what time were you thinking of us heading over to Coventry? I will need to pick up the van from where I parked it a few streets away and I'd like to check out just to see how things are so we, or I, have got enough time to get the place clean before the delivery arrives in the morning."

"I guess that we might as well head over there soon, do you fancy a quick coffee before we get on our way and then once drunk we'll make a move. Have you got something to wrap the corpse up in so if neighbours do see us then they will not be able to tell what we are loading into the van?"

"I went and bought a couple of tarpaulin sheets this morning. I thought that I'd use one to wrap Gavin up in and the other I would line the van with."

"If we just use a sheet then nosey neighbours might still be able to tell what it is, I'll tell you what I have got an old rug down the shed I'll go and get it."

"Thanks Clive, I had thought that something like a rug would have been ideal but when I was looking in the shops for one big enough they were all well over a hundred pounds. Gavin has had more than enough money out of me while he was alive and I wasn't going to spend that sort of money on him now he is dead as well."

"There really was no love between the two of you was there?"

"Yes, Gavin used to love me just as long as I gave him enough money for him to get his next fix. As for me though he was just a pain in the backside."

"Well seeing how you took that dildo up there earlier then I guess that Gavin needed to be really big to make it painful for you."

"You know exactly what I was meaning Clive, he was just a total user."

With that they made their way through to the kitchen so Clive could make the drinks.

"So can I ask how you got to become so friendly with George then Clive?"

"You can ask by all means, my daughter was living here until eighteen months ago and about two years ago George and her started to get together a bit. That was until George realised that it wasn't girls that he was really interested in. Well in the couple of months that they had been together I had got to know the kid quite well and ever since he has been popping round here once or twice a week. From what I can make out he hasn't had any real boyfriend before, so if you intend to get it together with him then I'll warn you here and now I won't see the lad being hurt in any way if you know what I am saying."

"I assure you if we do get together hurting him is the last thing that I have got on my mind, and that is both emotionally and physically."

"Just make sure that you don't because I consider George as being like a son. I am not too sure though that I am happy with him getting into an affair with a murderer though, the lad could do a hell of a lot better. Having said that though Tom I have always got on with you and other than what happened last night I would have considered you to be the ideal match for him although at the time you were totally straight. Today has worked out exactly how I had planned it to."

"What do you mean by that Clive? That today has worked out
how you had planned?"
"Well I know George has been dying to get a boyfriend but you
see he is quite a shy guy, believe it or not he never goes out to
find himself anyone. When I got you round here and started
getting you to do things I was hoping that you would get to enjoy
things more than you thought. I'll admit though that it did come
as a shock to find that you were so willing to do whatever you
were asked."
"I can assure you that it came as a bigger shock to me than it did
to you. I had never thought for one moment that I could have
enjoyed having any sort of sex with another guy let alone have
got as much pleasure from it as I did. Even now with us just
talking about it there is a stirring in my jeans."
"Well if you are that eager to get more then I suppose that you
can always have another go at sucking my cock for me while we
wait for the coffees to cool down enough for us to drink them. I
still have a spare beaker that you can use when you are about to
shoot after you have taken my load down that throat of yours."
Tom had by this time come to terms with the fact that he just
loved taking a cock in his mouth and also liked taking it's
produce. He went over to where Clive was stood and having
dropped to his knees started undoing Clive's trousers before
taking the semi hard cock into his mouth. Five minutes later they
were drinking the coffees, Tom having tasted Clive's latest load
as well as having used a beaker for his own produce.

Chapter 5

Twenty minutes later Clive was dropping Tom off where he had parked the van and then the two vehicles were driven round to the house.

No sooner were they through the front door Tom was checking to make sure that there had been no change from how he had left things earlier in the day. To his relief now the floorboards had dried out there was no sign of any staining. In addition, where he had moved the body to was still looking as though his aim of keeping any further blood from reaching the flooring had been achieved.

"Well I must admit Tom that you seem to have done a bloody good clean up so far, and I can't see that there will be that much here for us to do other than just to get rid of the body. Before we start getting him wrapped up you were saying earlier how he had fucked you over several times in the past by promising that he would repay you only never to come up with the goods. So basically he fucked you, am I right?"

"I guess you could say that and in quite a big way as well."

"In that case Tom I think that before we get rid of him that you have just about got time to get your own back. With it having been a good half an hour since you last shot your load am I right in thinking that you could get it hard again now if you tried?"

"I have never had a problem in that area, I can normally go again after just twenty minutes."

"In that case Tom I think you had better get your own back on that big brother of yours. I'll help you to get his trousers down and then I want to see you fuck him like he has fucked you in the past."

"You have got to be kidding Clive, you are saying that you want me to get my tool up his arse although he has been dead for over twenty-four hours?"

"I don't want you to Tom, I am telling you that is what you are going to do if you don't want to see a copy of that film getting into other people's hands."

What Clive was ordering him now was way beyond what he was prepared to do. This was his older brother after all and he was dead. Yes, he had enjoyed it earlier when he had got his cock inside George's backside but to put it in his dead brother's that was extreme.

"So what are you waiting for then Tom, you have already told me quite clearly that you are able to get it hard again so I suggest that you start getting on with things."

As soon as Tom had completed the task that Clive had set him he ran upstairs to the bathroom where he threw up in the toilet bowl, before getting soap and water and washed his member to try and remove the thoughts from in his head. It then dawned on him that the camera would have captured what he had done and again had his head over the bog and was sick for a second time. He then realised that Clive had been standing in the doorway all the time and was clearly getting enjoyment out of seeing Tom in such a state.

"So I guess you didn't enjoy doing that then from your reaction Tom, you surprise me, this afternoon I got the impression that you were up for just about anything. Now once you have finished puking up I think we had better start getting a move on otherwise neither of us are going to end up with any sleep before we have to get up again."

"With what you have just made me do I think that getting any sleep will not happen for me, if I do doze off I am pretty sure that I will have nightmares."

"You'll be alright once we've got rid of him. Now have you thought anymore as to where to dump the body?"

"I haven't, have you got any ideas?"

"As it happens I know just the right place and I know that in the past there have been four bodies dumped there that have never been discovered, so it will probably be one of the best places for us to use."

It was ten minutes later when Tom started up the engine and pulled the van away from outside the house. With there having been the two of them getting Gavin into the back of the van had proved quite an easy task and now all he had to do was to follow Clive's directions until they reached the dumping site. Tom was trying his hardest to put the thought of what he had done to his brother just half an hour ago out of his mind, though failing in his efforts.

"Will you make me a promise please Clive? I know from what you told me when I was round at your place that everything that happens in the house is captured on the cameras and is automatically recorded on your computer. Can I please ask that you erase what took place just now because that is one thing that I will have enough difficulty coming to terms with without knowing that you have got it on disc."

"Don't worry on that score Tom, I might be a nasty bastard at times but I assure you that just as soon as I get home it will go from all records. I just made you do it as a punishment for what you did. You should have just knocked Gavin out cold and then taken him somewhere in order to finish him off and not have done it in the house. If you had been caught then it might have been my head up for the chop as well as yours. Now if you take the next right then you'll see a dirt track on the right, it leads down to a disused gravel pit that nobody ever goes near unless they are wanting to dump things. I bet within a couple of weeks there will be that much stuff having been dumped here that your brother will be buried a few feet down."

The rug and sheet accompanied the body and after a quick check that there was nothing left in the rear of the van they closed the back doors and got on their way back to the house in order to do the finishing touches to the clean-up. It was half one when they had ditched the body in the pit and within an hour Clive was heading for his car and left Tom to head back to his own flat.

"By the way Tom, if you are having difficulty sleeping then just think about your time at mine instead of what happened at the house. I reckon if you can do that you'll end up falling to sleep

with both a smile on your face as well as a rather stiff cock
knowing you. I'll see you back here in a few hours."
Once in his flat Tom got showered and then headed for his bed.
Clive had been proved right, he thought about not just what had
taken place round at Clive's but also on how things could develop
between himself and George, and very soon he was falling asleep
having got quite a firm member inside his boxer shorts.
It felt as if he had only been asleep for a short time when he was
woken by the sound of his alarm ringing. He desperately wanted
to just turn over and have a few more hours under the quilt but
forced himself to get from in the bed and ready himself for work.
All he hoped was that Clive wouldn't bring up what he had done
to his brother in the early hours of this morning.

"Morning Tom, I hope you managed to get a decent night's sleep
after everything, and before we go any further there are two
things that I need to say. The first is that I have destroyed all
recordings of what you did this morning, the second is that I am
sorry for what I made you do as I have realised that it was going
way over the top. And I am not just saying that Tom, I really am
sorry for having put you through that. Now that as far as I am
concerned is the very last time that the matter will ever be raised."
"Thanks Clive. I think that even with it not being brought up it
will be something that will stay with me till the day I die."
"As I say, I am sorry for having made you do it. Now everything
is all sorted out and besides there being a slightly damp patch on
the floorboards nobody will ever know what has gone on here.
There was one other thing that I needed to inform you about."
"What's that?" Tom asked, almost fearing what might be said.
"Nothing to get worried about unless you have decided that you
don't want to be gay after all. When I went out to the car this
morning to head over here there was a certain young man waiting
for me. He asked me to tell you that if you were serious about
wanting to get to know him better then he isn't doing anything
tonight and had already told his mother that he might be staying
out for the night."

"So does that mean that you want me to come over to your place after we have finished here at ten because it will be a bit late. Besides, I have got to take the van back first thing in the morning before I have to be in here."

"Well I will leave things totally up to the two of you as to where you spend the night. I consider that I owe you after what happened and although I would like to take part as I did yesterday if you just want to pick him up and bring him back to yours for the night then I won't have a problem with that happening."

"Thanks Clive, what about me phoning him later and asking if he can make his way over here for when we finish. That way it will save the best part of an hour in me having to go all the way over there to pick him up in the van."

"Why wait till later on, I am sure that George is sat with his phone in his hand just waiting for it to start ringing. From the way he was talking this morning I think that he has already developed a soft spot for you. If you want and as long as the two of you will be able to control yourselves why don't you ask him if he wants to come over earlier on, then you'll have time to talk here when we haven't got any customers in the house."

"Are you sure that won't create a problem? Does he know what we do here?"

"He knows, and you know sometimes I take some weed with me, well when I do it's because George has asked me to get him some. He knows about the house and what we do, and I know that there isn't a problem with it either, he is a good lad and will never go talking about what goes on even if he does become a regular here. You never know, if we carry on increasing our sales as we have been then I might even be able to persuade the hub to allow me to get a third person working here if you know what I mean."

"Fuck me Clive, I only met the guy for the first time yesterday, from the way you are talking you'll have us married by the end of next week."

"Well there did seem to be something between the two of you, I could tell that when he gave you the kiss before he left. I noticed

that you both kept your eyes fixed on each other's while you had
your tongues down each other's throats."

"You weren't meant to be watching that closely Clive, I must
admit though there was something that was there from within the
first hour of meeting him."

"Are you sure that it wasn't just a case of by then you had got that
cock of his in your mouth?"

"Well besides that. So what is the earliest I can say for him to get
over here if I ring him now?"

"Whenever you like just as long as it isn't before we have had a
chance to get the delivery put away."

"We'll have that done within the next half an hour as long as it
arrives on time. Are you meaning that it is okay with you if he
spends the whole day here?"

"As I say, as long as the two of you can behave yourselves then I
have no problem with him being here whenever he wants to be. I
will say though that you know what some of our customers are
like, if they get one hint that there are any gays here then they will
find somewhere else to get their gear from like yesterday. When
George gets here I will be making that very clear to him as well.
If I see the two of you even looking at each other in that way
when we have got customers here then I will not be happy."

"I understand what you are saying and I don't want it to become
public knowledge at this stage myself that I am now gay. Be
assured that I won't allow anything to happen between us while
we are open for business."

"Tom that isn't what I said, if there are no customers in the house
then within reason I don't care what the two of you get up to, but
when we have company you both need to control yourselves."

"Thanks Clive, we will. I'd better make that call then. It might
turn out that he has got plans for the day and won't be free till
later anyway. Or he might not want to come over here at all and
just want me to head over with you at the end of the day."

"I think that even if he has got plans he will change them as soon
as he hears that you want him to come over here when he can."

Tom phoned and it was clear that George was waiting for the call
as without it having had a chance to ring a second time he was
answering his phone. They had only just started talking when
there came a knock on the front door, it was the delivery.
"George, I need to get to work right away but if you want Clive
says that it's cool with him if you come over here and spend the
day at the house with us. I take it you know where it is."
Having heard that George both knew exactly where it was as well
as him heading straight out in order to catch a bus over the call
was concluded.
The order had all been put away under the relevant floorboards
well before opening time which was at ten o'clock and Tom
found himself looking at the time on his phone every couple of
minutes.
"Tom, you really have got it bad. For God's sake give George a
ring and ask him where he is and how long he will be before
getting here. I can't deal with seeing you looking at the time
every ten seconds."
"I'm not looking at it every ten seconds at all Clive, I think it is
more like every five." Tom laughed.
By half ten there was still no sign of George, Tom wasn't going
to call him again as he didn't want George to feel pressurised in
any way. It was now Clive who would be the one who made the
call, he too was getting a little concerned as an hour and twenty
minutes was more than enough time for him to have arrived. He
didn't answer which only helped to fuel both Clive's as well as
Tom's concern.
Just after Clive had tried to call George for the second time there
came a knock on the front door and expecting it to be one of the
dealers Tom went and answered it to find George on the doorstep.
"Don't tell me that you two were worrying about me. Morning
Tom."
  "What's taken you so long. I thought you would have got here
half an hour ago, or were you not in such a rush to see me?"
"If you allow me to get inside I'll show you just how keen I was
to see you. By the way I hope you had a good sleep last night

because I somehow think that you won't be getting much tonight."

Tom closed the door once George was inside and as the visitor went to take Tom in his arms in order to give him a kiss Tom stopped him from doing so.

"Before we do any of that sort of stuff I had better point out the house rules here. When there is anyone in the house other than us two and Clive then we have to pretend to be totally straight. And that means not only no touching but also not making any comment or even a look that might give the game away. Now I've told you the rules and with only Clive here at present come here." With that they kissed each other on the lips while embracing one another.

"So Tom, two questions for you, what time is your lunch break and where abouts is your flat?"

"As regards a lunch break we don't officially have such a thing we just grab something as we go. With respect to my flat you will have just walked past it as you came up the road. I live about fifty metres further down towards the city centre."

"Bloody hell that is handy for work isn't it?"

"That is exactly why I got the place, as with this line of work you never know when you will be needed to come in."

"So when you said that you don't have a break does that mean that you will be working all the way through till ten tonight?"

"Well both Clive and I have got to be here till then but it doesn't mean that we will be working all that time. We got the delivery first thing this morning and got that all put away before we opened up. Now it is just sit around waiting for knocks on the door. When you turned up I was half expecting it to have been one of the dealers."

"That's a point are we allowed to smoke in here because if we can then I wouldn't mind buying an eighth of resin so I can have a couple of spliffs while I wait around for you to finish."

"Are you trying to say that just being with me isn't good enough?" Tom laughed as he pulled George closer and gave him another quick kiss.

"Where is Clive hanging out or is he busy with a customer?"

"You will find him sat in the lounge waiting for you to put in an appearance. I think he was just giving us space to say hello to each other."

They went through to the lounge and started talking but were soon interrupted by one of their regulars knocking wanting quite a sizable order, saying that he had never known trade as good, and that he would be back again later on in the evening to get more. When Clive and Tom were putting together the order that he wanted now they could not believe that he wanted more later on as with what he was taking now it was more than he'd had any previous day.

As soon as the guy had left Tom asked Clive if he thought that they would have enough stock here to see them through till Wednesday morning when they were due to receive their next delivery. Clive thought that they might just about scrape through but decided it wise to give the hub a quick ring just so they were prepared in case he needed to phone through an order at the end of today.

Having come off the phone he informed Tom that there would be no problem as regarding getting the order delivered, however if they needed one it would leave Tom in a tight spot. He had to return the hire van between eight and nine in the morning and if they were getting a delivery he'd have to be back at the house before half eight at the very latest.

"If needs be I will have to make sure I am down there for when they open and then get a cab back here. There is no way that I can afford to shell out another eighty pounds for the extra day."

"I guess that we'll just have to see how the rest of the day goes, but can't you drop it round before they open and just drop the keys in through their letter box?"

"I could but they like you to be there so they can check the vehicle over straight away with you and then as long as there's no damage then you get your deposit back. If I just leave it there then I think I might end up losing the deposit because they will find something wrong with it if you know what I mean."

"I take it that it is a bit of a dodgy company from how you are talking."
"Well I know of three people that have been ripped off by them but they are the cheapest around which is why I used them. Until I get my next wage I am a little on the tight side with the extra cost of me moving flat so every penny counts at the moment."
"If you get really short all you need to do is ask and I'll sub you some until pay day without a problem."
"Thanks Clive but I am trying not to have to come cap in hand to you if I can avoid doing so because if I do then I'll end up short again next week."
"Well now you have got yourself a boyfriend you'll need every penny, they work out the same as having a woman in tow."
"Talking about George I'd forgotten he was here, he will be wondering what is keeping us."
 With that they went through to the lounge to find George fast asleep on the settee.
"I think he is just getting some sleep in because he knows that with sharing your bed tonight that he won't be getting any later on."
"Clive I bloody well hope we get some as over the last couple of nights I think I am already short of sleep to the tune of about eight hours."
"You know full well that with George in bed beside you there will be very little sleeping going on if any."
"Did I hear my name?"
"You did sleeping beauty, have you had a good kip then?"
"Did you just call me sleeping beauty Tom?"
"I did, why do you ask?"
"Is that how you see me then, as a real beauty, I knew you quite fancied me but I didn't expect you to be using those sorts of words about me."
"Well George you must know that you are one hell of a good looking guy which is why I was surprised when Clive told me that you hadn't got a boyfriend. That is why I didn't waste time because someone with your looks will soon get snapped up."

"You sweet talker you, are you trying to get into my trousers or something?"

"I don't think that I'd need to sweet talk you for that to happen for one moment. You love it just as much as I do that is why you were waiting by Clive's car this morning to ask him to give me the message."

"Okay, I think you have made your point, and I bet you never had any problem getting a girl when you used to be that way inclined. I bet they were queueing up for you."

"Well if it wasn't for the hours that I put in here then I think I would have had a bit of a choice if that doesn't sound too cocky."

"We'll leave your cock out of it until after you close this place and you show me where that flat of yours is. By the way have you got a single bed or a double?"

"I've got a feeling that you will be keeping me that close to you that it wouldn't matter either way, but as it happens I have got a four foot wide one which is in between a single and double."

"That should give us room to move round without falling out."

"Anyway George Clive is here and it isn't really fair the two of us talking between ourselves and ignoring him. So what shall we talk about? But be prepared for the conversation to be halted at a moment's notice. As soon as there is a knock at the door then we will be leaving you on your own again. And next time can you get a bit of sleep in for me please otherwise tonight you are going to be wide awake and I'll just want to sleep."

"You may want to sleep Tom but there is no way that I am going to let you until we are both well satisfied with the amount of sex we have had and I take some satisfying."

"I noticed that yesterday but I think I'll cope with keeping up with you." They both laughed then turned their attention to Clive.

"So what have you got planned for next Sunday then Clive, do you fancy having a couple of visitors pop round for the afternoon and evening, as long as I can get Tom to come over?"

"You know that you are always welcome if I am in. I will be doing my usual trip to the squash club but will be back about five at the latest so if the two of you want to come round after that then you are both welcome. And Tom, shall I get a stock of beakers in because if funds are that tight for you then we can always fill a few, or at least you can. Which reminds me, they are coming round this evening to pick up the four that you used so I'll have some money for you in the morning."

"What, so they pay up there and then and you don't have to wait for it to be tested or anything."

"We aren't dealing with the NHS you know, no when they collect the money is always handed over without delay."

"And here was me thinking that I wouldn't see any of it for weeks if not longer. That is good news."

"I thought that would put a smile on your face when I told you. So who's going to guess how long it will be before the next knock on the door, I think we will have another visitor in about fifteen minutes."

"I think it will be sooner than that Clive, I will say ten. What about you George are you going to guess?"

"Well seeing it is my first ever time here it would be pure fluke if I guessed right but I would say that you'll have a knock in no more than three minutes from now."

They all made a note of the time and waited. It was three minutes and fourteen seconds when the knock came, much to the delight of George.

The remainder of the day was quite busy for both Clive and Tom, which allowed George plenty of time to sleep on the settee, much to Tom's disapproval. He knew that the more sleep George got during the day then the less he would be able to get tonight. Not that he was going to complain unless it became a daily habit and then Tom knew that in no time he would have bags developing under his eyes.

Although they were busy the time still seemed to drag by for Tom, he was looking forward to finishing for the day so he could show off his flat to George.

By nine o'clock it was quite clear that they would have to put an order in for delivery tomorrow morning which was something that Tom was really hoping that they could have avoided doing.

Even if George hadn't been stopping over for the night he had still got to get the van back before he started work. Now it would mean that he would have to leave home by half seven at the very latest and with not finishing till around half ten tonight it would restrict the free time that he would have.

"Is there no way that we could get the delivery to be made a little later than normal. We both know that we can have it away in less than half an hour so even if it didn't get here till half nine we could still have it stashed away before opening time?"

"Tom I know that it will leave things tight for you but with us always having had the deliveries early then if I ask now then there may well be questions as to why we want it later. I don't think that either of us would like to have to explain the reason behind the request."

Tom was not all that happy but he could understand totally what Clive was saying. He would have to get the van back to the hire company early and just leave it there and hope that he would get his deposit back. At least he would be getting the money from his sperm donations, which would be a big help. He would also need to come up with a reason for him having hired the van, as he was almost certain that George would quiz him on why he had it.

"Have you got any idea as to what I can tell George is the reason for me having the van Clive, obviously I'm not about to tell him or anyone else the real reason."

"Well didn't you tell me the other day that you hadn't unpacked all of your boxes yet. Just tell him that you only got them to the flat over the weekend and hired the van in order to move them."

"Why didn't I think of that, it's an obvious explanation. Anyway had we better get counting what we need to get ordered otherwise it will be getting on before we get finished."

"Tom I know that you are just itching to get George back to yours and in bed but I will not allow your personal life to interfere with work. We will put the order together at ten when we close up and not a minute before and if you don't like it then I'll tell George that he can't come over during opening times."

"Okay Clive, I only asked because I think that all the dealers have already been here for the last time today. I can't think of any of them that are still to turn up."

"As I say we will do it when we lock the front door, but if we are all sorted by then it will take no more than ten minutes before I get it phoned through. It isn't as if it will take an hour."

"You're right Clive, I'm sorry that I asked."

Tom was really beginning to get annoyed, other times it would have been Clive who would want to get away as fast as possible but today he was just being awkward. Tom wondered if this was going to be the norm from now on. Would Clive just make things as difficult for Tom as he could, knowing that he had got such a hold over him. He could see himself losing his temper before long if Clive continued the way he was, and although it would be justified Tom knew that there was no way that he could allow himself to say anything that might get Clive really annoyed. Okay so he had said that when he got in that he had destroyed the one lot of recordings, but he had still got the main one that could see Tom either dead or in nick.

They both went through to the lounge for the last half an hour before the ten o'clock cut off point only to find George asleep again.

"I think he must have got his eight hours in while he has been here Tom so at a guess you will be doing no sleeping tonight if I know George. If he is up for it then you can guarantee that there is no way that he will allow you any sleep no matter how much you might need it."

"Well I guess that I might as well leave him asleep until we are ready to go."

With the two of them talking it was enough to get George stirring from his slumber, and as soon as he had woken up sufficiently he asked if there was any dealer in the house. When Clive told him that there wasn't and that they would probably not be getting anyone else tonight George then got up from the settee and having gone over to where Tom was standing took a hold of the front of his jeans.

"In that case then Tom it won't be that long before you have to start getting this thing working, have you any preference as to what happens first because I had a thought. Before we go from here if Clive is feeling randy then he might as well have a bit of fun before we leave. I bet you wouldn't object to him shagging you while my cock is in that mouth of yours would you? What do you think Clive, would you like a bit of fun before you head off home?"

"And here was me thinking that you would want to have Tom all to yourself for the whole of the night."

"What do you think Tom, do you like the idea of having Clive deep inside you while you suck on my cock?"

"I guess I am happy to go along with whatever the two of you decide You both know that I love having one in both ends at the same time, but I did think that you would be keen to check out my flat George."

"We've got all night Tom, besides once Clive gets inside you then we both know that he will have shot his load in there within fifteen minutes so we can still be back at yours by about eleven."

"Don't you want anything to eat then George because I was thinking of stopping off at the takeaway on the way home."

"I'll be chewing on that cock of yours most of the night if I have my way and I think that you will also give me plenty to drink from it as well."

"Have you told Tom yet what you have borrowed from me George?"

"Now you've spoilt my surprise, I wasn't going to tell him until much later on this evening."

"Go on then George, what have you borrowed from Clive, let me guess the mask and pants."

"No Tom, if I am going to take a piss in your mouth ever again I will do it the same way as Clive did last night so I can watch it."

"In that case then I can only assume that it is one of the dildos."

"Wrong again, it is no good you guessing because it is something that you haven't seen yet but I am pretty sure that you will enjoy it when we get round to putting it to use."

"So you're not going to tell me then?"

"No, that won't be used until much later in the night. Before that comes out of my bag I will have given both your mouth and backside a real good seeing to and I hope that you will have done the same to me. I have spent most of the day dreaming about what we can get up to tonight and I reckon that it is going to be good fun."

"Don't forget that I will need to get at least a bit of sleep."

"Well you had better make sure that you tire me out then is all I can say to that."

On the one hand Tom really couldn't wait to get George back to his but he was now thinking that tomorrow he would end up really pissing Clive off because he could visualise himself falling to sleep between having people in the house. Either that or just yawning all day long.

George was watching the time tick down and as soon as it got to just a minute before ten he then suggested that all three of them readied their cocks so as to not waste any time. Clive put him right in his place.

"George you randy git, you will have to wait for a few minutes because although the door is just about to be locked Tom and I have still got work to be done before anything else happens."

"Sorry, I just thought that once you closed up that would be it for the night."

"Not quite George, Clive and me have got to go round the house checking what stock we need to get ordered but it won't take much more than ten minutes so you won't have to wait too much longer before you get my mouth round that dick of yours."

With that George was once again left on his own in the lounge while Clive and Tom went and got the order together.

"If you are going to shag me which room are we going to use because I assume that you won't want to do it in any of the ones that have got cameras in them."

"I hadn't thought about that Tom. I guess if we did it would be another film that we could watch round at my place. But I think if we are going to do something like that then I would want to get a shot of you taking that big dildo up your arse. I think that for tonight we can do it in one of the rooms upstairs."

By this time they had checked all the stock and with Clive getting his mobile out in order to make the call Tom put his hand onto Clive's jeans to see if there was any sign of life down there just yet. There hadn't been but with Tom still rubbing it through the material it was soon growing.

"I'll go and get George so as soon as the call is finished we can get straight down to business."

The house closed for business and by just quarter past all three of them had got their trousers down round their ankles and all had got very firm dicks. There wasn't a minute wasted, and it was not long before Tom had got one dick up his backside and another in his mouth. He just couldn't get enough of it. The harder that Clive worked his dick in and out of Tom's backside the harder Tom worked on the member that was in his mouth.

"Clive, are you anywhere near shooting your load yet because I think that Tom would really love it if we both shot at the same time. What do you think, fill his arse and his mouth together."

"Well if you want that to happen you had better be very close to doing so because I can tell you that I won't be long at all." Clive answered.

With a bit of discussion between the two of them they managed to fill George's request and feeling the one load entering his backside and another filling his mouth Tom knew what was about to happen. He had just got his hands down quick enough onto his dick in order to catch his own load in the palm of his left hand. Although not quite being able to retain it all as it had exited the end of his dick with such force.

As soon as he was sure that there was no more to come out of George's member he then straightened up as Clive withdrew from within Tom's backside.

"So George I have just taken your first load of the night, do you want to deal with this?"

He lifted his left hand up so George was able to see that it was well full of his produce.

"It would be rude of me to say no." With that he started licking it up out of the palm of Tom's hand and when he had got a decent load retained in his mouth he then brought his face up to Tom's and went to kiss him. As Tom responded with the kiss he found his own mouth being filled with what had seconds ago been in his palm, their tongues again started working each other's mouths. "Well guys sorry to interrupt but now I have done what George wanted I think I will be getting on my way, and I suggest the two of you head off as well otherwise if anyone from the firm comes past they will wonder why we are still in here."

After having secured the house they were on their way, Clive heading for his home in Warwick and the other two walking down the road to Tom's flat.

Chapter 6

"Well that was a good starter for this evening Tom, I think you enjoy it when you have a cock in each end at the same time don't you?"

"I do but if being honest with you I am really looking forward to it being just the two of us all night, but I will have to get some sleep."

"I know you will need to and I was just saying what I was in front of Clive because he intends me to keep you awake all night. That was why he got me to come over for the day. Don't let on that I have told you but I wasn't waiting by his car this morning at all, I was up but still in my bedroom. Clive came round and asked me if I wanted to come over for the day and then offered to bring me over with him if I got ready in time. Well on the way over here Clive suggested that I go and grab breakfast in one of the cafes in the city centre and then when I got a call I was to make my way here. His idea is that for the whole week I stay here and sleep in the house during the daytime so at night I will be awake enough to ensure that you get no sleep at all. What he doesn't realise is that I can sleep solidly for twelve hours a day so sleeping tonight won't be a problem for me, especially if I am in your arms."

"So am I right in thinking that Clive is trying to deprive me from getting any sleep whatsoever all week?"

 "That is his plan and please don't let on to him that we are getting sleep every night. If you can keep up the impression all week that you are getting increasingly knackered then he will think that I am doing exactly what he wants me to do."

"So what is his idea then, because if I was to go the whole week without a wink of sleep I would be like the walking dead by next weekend."

"He hopes that by Sunday you are that knackered that you will not wake up no matter what is taking place. He wants to find out

if when you are fast asleep if a dildo or a dick goes up your arse if you will still get a hard-on."
"Even I would be interested in knowing if that does happen. I'll tell you what seeing as you have had a fair bit of sleep throughout the day if I go to sleep with my back towards you then once I am well away then try it out if you think you can get it inside me without waking me up."
"If I am going to be shagging you then there is no way that you will be asleep for long, that I can assure you."
"Anyway this is my place, I'm up on the second floor but the place has got real good sound proofing so those in the flat below won't get to hear what is going on above them."
"They would if I had brought that big dildo over and tried shoving it up your arse without any lube on it."
"Your right there, I think they would end up phoning the police because I would be screaming that loud that they'd think I was being murdered."
Having made their way up the stairwell Tom was opening his flat door. As soon as it was open he pulled George inside and shutting the door behind them took George in his arms and started kissing him on the lips while at the same time beginning to undo his visitor's shirt buttons.
It was less than five minutes after they had got through the door that they were both totally naked and lay on the bed together, not bothering with pulling the quilt over them as it would only end up on the floor anyway.
"So who's shagging who first then Tom?" George asked with an air of expectancy in his voice.
"Well I guess seeing as I took you up the backside yesterday it must be your turn to show me just how good you are at filling me."
"But are you meaning filling it with my dick or do you mean with what will be coming out of it?"
"I guess that it will be both, but unlike yesterday there really is no hurry as we've got all night."
"And here was me thinking that you wanted to get some sleep."

"Well I guess that we can do a bit of that later, but I for one want to enjoy having you in my bed with me tonight."

"Don't forget what Clive has got planned. He is intending that I stay over here all week and that I am not allowed to let you sleep at all."

"Well that is just stupid of him, he knows that I have got to be awake with the customers otherwise mistakes can start happening."

"Work's finished for the day. Well the one type of work is finished, but you had better be ready to work hard for the next couple of hours and then as long as you have worn me out enough I might just let you get some sleep."

"Well with you next to me then I am not too sure that I will want to sleep anyway. How about once we have shagged each other we just lie here together and talk. It would be good to get to know each other other than just sexually if you know what I mean?"

"I do Tom, for starters I want to know all about this film that you had the starring roll in, was it a sex film by any chance?"

"What makes you think that it was anything to do with sex?"

"Because you have got one fit body and your dick is fucking lovely."

"And how do you mean that then George, when it is up your arse or when it is in your mouth?"

"I'll tell you what I am more than happy to have that thing of yours in either hole just as often as you want it to be there."

"You George are sex mad, has anyone ever told you that?"

"Yes, you just have. But I wasn't the one who started getting either of us undressed just as soon as the door was shut was I? So I am the first guy that you have had in this bed then but I bet you have had loads of girls in here haven't you?"

"Not as many as you are probably thinking, I don't go out and bring a different one back here every weekend if that is what you think. In fact I haven't had one person here since I moved in four weeks ago."

"That has got to have been by choice because with your looks I bet the girls queue up to get a chance of being shagged by you."

"That George is now well and truly a thing of the past, and as far as I am concerned I would be more than happy if you are the only person that comes here to spend the night ever."

"Part of me gets worried when you start saying things like that because I have never been in a relationship with a guy. Yes I have had sex on more than one occasion but it has always just been a bit of fun."

"So do you mean by what you have just said that you just want us to have fun then and not be partners as it were?"

"That Tom is not what I said. All I meant is that at the moment we don't know a thing about each other really other than that you know that I am gay and that you were totally straight up till you ended up round at Clive's yesterday afternoon."

"And that young man is why I said that once we have had a bit of fun then we can just lie here in each other's arms and talk. I hope then by the time morning comes to have done enough to have convinced you that you want to get to know me one hell of a lot more than just sexually."

"I must admit that from what I have seen so far then you won't have to do much else before you hear me saying that I want us to be an item. You seem like a really nice and genuine guy,"

"I'll be totally up front with you, there are certain things that I have done in my life that I am not proud of. One day I will reveal all to you before we get too heavily involved because there are things that you ought to know about me."

"Well that can wait, now let's start having some fun and then in a bit we can talk while we both recover enough before going for it again."

Tom didn't raise any objection to George's suggestion and was very soon feeling his guest's dick entering his back passage, and it was only seconds before he was aware that he was experiencing its full length within him. George just couldn't stop himself from really going for it and the harder he worked on shagging that arse the more he knew that not only was Tom loving it but that he would not be able to last that long before making a deposit inside Tom.

"Sorry about this Tom, I know that you said that you wanted me to take my time in you but I am loving it that much I just know that I will not be able to stop myself from shooting my load in next to no time."

"Well if it is anything like when I felt it happening yesterday then I will be following you very shortly, the question is where am I going to deliver mine when I feel you shooting yours inside me?"

"If you can just hold back for a few seconds I'll get my mouth round it for you. I'm sure you would prefer not to get the sheets messy this early in the night, we have got to sleep in them, unless you are intending to change the sheets before we try to get some sleep that is."

Tom did not need George to tell him when he was making his delivery as Tom could feel it pumping into his rear end. The warmth of it gave him a sensation that was like nothing else, and he knew that as soon as George got his mouth in position he would be delivering one hell of a load into George's mouth.

"I hope that you have built up a good thirst while you have been shagging me George because I think that I will be delivering quite a bit into that lovely mouth of yours."

As soon as he was confident that he had delivered as much as was there for now George pulled out and then wasted not one second in getting round the front of Tom. Having got his head in place he was soon taking the full length of Tom's member deep into his mouth. Just as George had not been able to hold things back Tom was exactly the same, and no sooner had the mouth got in position it was receiving all that Tom had got stored up. As he felt it leaving his body he knew that George would have to be working hard to avoid any of it escaping. George kept his mouth in place for quite some time and when he eventually deemed it time to come off it Tom's member had already started to go limp.

"Well I don't know where you got all that lot from Tom, but it felt as if I was taking gallons down my neck."

"That George is because I enjoyed what you had been doing to me so much. To be totally honest with you that was one hell of a lot more enjoyable than anything I had inside me yesterday."

"I'll let you into a secret now, I don't normally do that, well never. That is the very first time that I have ever shagged a guy. Was it alright for you because I know I didn't last long."

"George I can assure you that if it hadn't been as good as it was then there is no way that you would have had to take as much as you did in your mouth. As I just said, that was better than anything that went up there yesterday and I am not just saying that either."

"Where's the bathroom Tom because I want to go and wash this dick of mine because when you have shagged me then I expect you to be taking mine in your mouth. With it having been up your backside then it won't be very nice for you to have it in your mouth."

"If you want to wait for about fifteen minutes if I come through with you then I might push you into the shower and start shagging you in there while you get washing that dick of yours. I think that if it isn't hard by the time you start getting the soap round it with me inside you then it won't take long before you have something bigger down there to wash."

"I've never had sex in a shower before, what's it like?"

"I wouldn't know George, neither have I but we will soon be finding out, that is if you want to. Don't get me wrong in any way I am not trying to get you to do anything that you are not comfortable with."

"I know that, your name is Tom not Clive. It's only him that uses anything that he can get over you in order to have total control over what takes place. Is that how you started doing the sex thing yesterday Tom, has Clive got a hold over you as well?"

"When you say as well, does that mean that he is blackmailing you into doing stuff that you don't want also?"

"You don't think that I would go round there twice a week and wank into a beaker while he watches if he hadn't do you. I know that he gets good money for what I put into those beakers but however much he gets I know it must be a lot more than what he hands over in my direction."

"Well he told me that he gets five hundred pounds a time, I don't
know how true that is but he has told me that I will get half of it."
"He's a bigger bastard than I thought in that case, because the
wanker only gives me thirty quid a time. I knew that he would be
getting good money for the stuff but didn't realise that it was that
much."
"As I say George I only know what he has told me. So do you
mind me asking what sort of hold he has got over you then. Don't
tell me if you don't want to or if you are not ready to."
"Well I guess if we are going to get it together then we had better
start off the way we mean to go on. I never think that any
relationship can last long if you can't be totally honest and open
with each other. It's when you start keeping secrets that things
start going all wrong from what I have seen."
Tom now realised that if he was going to allow this friendship to
develop into what he was hoping it would then he was going to
have to tell George about what he had done to his own brother.
The question was how would George be able to handle a truth like
that?
"Did you know that Clive has got cameras hidden in nearly every
room in his house Tom?"
"No, no idea. I know we have at the house down the road but that
is for security reasons. Why the hell has Clive gone to all the
expense of getting them fitted at his home?"
"Quite easy, so he can film anything that goes on round there and
then he edits it all and creates quite a little show. When he was
saying about you being in a film I thought that he was meaning
that he had got you filmed doing stuff round there."
"Well with what took place yesterday afternoon I guess that he
has got some footage to work with now. Do you think that is why
he got you to come round and why at the end of things he left the
two of us in the lounge together?"
"I hadn't thought of that but I guess it would give him some real
good footage to play with, and he won't have to doctor it so much
to make sure that he doesn't appear in the film that he puts
together. He did the same with me about two years ago, and he

made a really good film of me having sex with this other guy who was at least mid-thirties. At the time I was still under age and he threatened to show it to my parents if I didn't do exactly what he told me to do."

"So being perfectly honest then George, when you have been going round there in order to fill a beaker or two tell me has Clive been filling them as well?"

"Don't ever let on that I have told you this because he will make my life hell if he finds out. When I go round there it is only me that ever fills the beakers, not that Clive doesn't shoot his load every time I do but he never uses the beakers. He earns his money from mine by the sounds of things."

"So would I be right in thinking that he either shoots his load in your mouth or up your backside?"

"It's always up my arse, you see he reckons that I am totally shit at doing things with my mouth."

"Well from what I have experienced with that mouth of yours then he certainly is talking out of his backside if he says that. Over the years I have had quite a few different mouths go down on me and I'll tell you right now that you do a pretty good job, otherwise you wouldn't have to take as much down your throat as you do if you weren't any good at it."

"Thank you, you sweet talker you. Perhaps it's got something to do with the fact that I like having yours in my mouth but have never really liked the fact that I have to take his otherwise I'll be in the shit with him."

"So he has got a film of you having sex when you were under age and at a guess he has now got another film there of the two of us having fun. I can tell you now that if he has got one of us then he will have one hell of a hold over me because I will lose my job if it gets back to the main man that I am gay."

"You are kidding me of course."

"No, if top man finds out that I am gay then I will be out of a job straight away."

"What, when he is that way himself. Why do you think that Clive has got the cameras fitted up in his place?"

"Am I reading things right? Are you telling me that the top man is gay and that he knows that Clive has got the cameras set up. Next you'll be telling me that Marcos has seen the film that you starred in."

"That Tom is exactly right, what's more I have even met the guy. The one evening when I was at home Clive phoned me up to get me to go round his. When I got there Marcos was sat in an armchair in the lounge and it turned out that he had seen the film and wanted to know if I looked as good in the flesh."

"I don't believe what I am hearing. So Marcos is gay and after he watched the film of you and this other guy he then wanted to meet you."

"He didn't just want to meet me Tom."

"Are you saying that you had to strip off in front of him so he could see all of you then?"

"Well that was how things started but having seen me without any clothes on he then wanted me to get mine hard so he could have a good look at it. Well by the time I left there I had been shagged by both of them, and I'll tell you one thing Marcos has got quite a big dick on him."

"So if Clive filmed us at it yesterday then do you think that he will be showing Marcos that as well?"

"I doubt it somehow, from what I was able to gather he is into youngsters, that is why he never comes back round when I am there now. He considers that I am now too old."

"So it wasn't just on the one occasion that you met Marcos round there then."

"No, it became quite a regular happening until I started getting too hairy for his liking. Clive even got me to shave on a regular basis so that Marcos would keep interested in me. Once he saw that I had got hairs under my arms as well as some growing round my backside then that was it. Not that I was at all unhappy for it to come to an end I can tell you."

"So is it just Clive and Marcos that you have had to have sex with while round at Clive's then, or are there others that he uses you to please?"

"There was another guy on the one occasion, but I didn't even get to know his name. I got the impression that he had come up from London in order to check me out but I'm not certain of that."

"What do you mean by that George, that he'd come to check you out?"

"I don't know for sure but I think that it is another line of business that they run. I think they find youngsters and then after they get a good enough hold over them they then sell them off to this guy from London. When I was there this guy from down London said to Clive that I wasn't as young as he is normally fetched all the way up here to see. I wasn't supposed to hear but I got the impression from what was said that he comes up here every now and again to fetch boys to take back down with him."

"So if what you are telling me is right then Marcos isn't only into the drugs business he also runs a child prostitution network in a way."

"I don't know if he puts any of them to work himself or if he just sells them on once guys like Clive have found them for him. Just think if Clive had got his claws into me earlier then by now I might be down in London and having to do God knows what and for whoever."

"So you think that if you had gone down there you would have ended up being some sort of sex slave then."

"Well he doesn't want them to look young for them to go down there to do the cleaning round his house and the cooking does he?"

"Bloody hell George, this is turning out to be a hell of a last few days."

"So are you going to tell me what Clive has got over you then seeing as I have told you what I have?"

"I will George but you will probably want to get dressed and out of here as fast as you can, and I wouldn't blame you if you did. All I will ask though is if I tell you that you please don't say a word about it to anyone, and I mean anyone."

"Fuck me Tom, this sounds serious."

"It is George, now have I got your word that it stays between the two of us even if we don't end up together"

"I told you what I did because I trust you not to tell anyone else about what he has got over me, and I didn't ask you to promise me that you wouldn't talk about it."

"You're right and I'm sorry for having asked it's just that with what I am going to tell you you'll see that it is one hell of a lot more serious than what you have just told me, but here goes." Although not quite believing it himself Tom then told George everything about what took place at the house the other night with his own brother. He emphasised the fact that if he had allowed Gavin to leave with what he was carrying then Marcos would have made sure that Tom was no longer around.

"So by the sounds of things you weren't given any option by your brother so had to do what you did and as a result Clive has now got it all recorded in detail. So that was why he got you to do the things that he did yesterday?"

"That's right George, now if you want to leave and head back to Warwick then I totally understand and if you trust me I will even run you back because I have still got the hire van."

With that George pulled Tom across the bed to where he was lying and having wrapped his arms round him started kissing Tom on the lips. This time though for Tom it was saying a hell of a lot more to him than the previous kisses they had till now. It confirmed to Tom that George wasn't intending going anywhere.

"Well now we've established the fact that you will be staying the night what do you think about us going and grabbing that shower then?"

George got straight up off the bed and taking Tom by the hand told him that he needed to lead the way.

"I guess Tom that we are both in the same place, Clive has got us both at his beck and call and there isn't a lot that we can do about it."

"Oh but you are so wrong George. We have got one real big thing that if we can do it right then it will put us firmly in the driving seat to my thinking. You are openly gay and although I haven't come out as it were I have accepted the fact that I prefer guys to females. With Clive though he maintains that he is straight. That is how we can get our own back on him."

"I don't quite understand what you are trying to get at Tom."

"Well he has got films of both of us that ensures that we toe the line with him and do whatever he wants us to. I have got one thing on him at the moment but I think that by the end of the week we both might have enough on him to even things up a bit."

"You'll have to explain what you mean because I don't know if it is me just being thick but I can't see what you are getting at."

"Clive has got what I did at the house all recorded, well I downloaded all the footage of him helping me remove the body in the early hours of this morning. If I save that then I have one thing over him. The other thing that I was thinking is if between us we can get him to have sex with us in one of the rooms at the house where there are cameras then I can download that as well. If we get footage of him participating in gay sex then that will even things up."

"No it won't Tom, are you forgetting that Marcos already knows that he has sex with lads?"

"I wasn't thinking of threatening to show Marcos the film, I was thinking more along the lines of threatening to get a copy of it to his daughter. I bet she would want nothing more to do with him if she knew what he got up to."

"Now that Tom is one hell of a brilliant idea. I used to go out with her for a while and I just know that she would go absolutely ape shit if she found out something like that about her dad."

"The question is though are you still in contact with her, or at least do you know how you could contact her if needs be?"

"Yes, although we split up, whenever she pops round to see her dad she always nips round to my place to say hi. Although Clive doesn't know that she still has anything to do with me. He told me that I was never to talk to her again after I had chosen to get a boyfriend rather than his precious daughter."

"There you go then, and how would you feel about her seeing her father shagging your backside?"

"Well she knows that I am gay anyway and she also knows that I love taking it up the arse so I'm not too bothered on that score. Besides, it would be worth any grief that she might give me if it was to put an end to Clive ruling my life."

"In that case George we will have to work on that during the week but now I think that we have done more than enough talking and I for one am just gagging to get my tool up that beautiful backside of yours. Let's get that shower."

They had got in the flat just after half ten and George considered that Tom had earned some sleep by two in the morning, having set both alarms for seven they went to sleep cradled in each other's arms. Tom had already told George that he needed to take the van back in the morning and George had said that it was no problem and that he'd go with him.

All day on Tuesday Tom was trying his best to make the yawns that he was doing seem convincing to Clive. George had made a point of telling Clive as soon as he had arrived at the house in the morning that he hadn't let Tom get as much as a wink of sleep all night. Tom even asked Clive if he could take George home when they finished for the day, as then he might be able to get some sleep. It was a suggestion that he didn't want Clive to agree to but he thought that it would only help the pretence that he was getting increasingly tired. George for his part told Clive that the sex had been that good all night that he just couldn't wait to get Tom back in bed for another all nighter.

The day seemed to go fine for both Tom and George, Clive seemed content in the fact that he had got the other two under his thumb and saw no reason at present to use the fact in order to achieve anything. As far as he was concerned he was in control and that was the way it was going to stay.

When it came to close on closing time George started touching Clive up on the trousers with the hope of getting him eager to have a bit of sex before he headed off to his home in Warwick. Him and Tom desperately wanted to try and get something really incriminating on film over him and there was no time like the present.

"So Clive, I know that you shagged us both on Sunday. Then last night you did it to Tom so it's got to be my turn to receive your dick inside my arse tonight hasn't it before you go. I'm sure if I ask him nicely then Tom won't object to having me shoot my load into his mouth while you are shooting yours inside me."

"I thought that you would want to save yourself for when you got Tom back to the flat, we don't want you getting tired as well and letting Tom get some sleep now do we?"

"I have been sleeping nearly all day again Clive so I really won't be needing any tonight."

"In that case George I might just be tempted to get my tool stuck right the way up you, I haven't got any lube here though so it will have to be just spit."

"That's alright Clive, I'm sure that with all the use you have put it to over the last couple of years that I'll be able to handle it."

George had already been told by Tom that sound was also recorded as well as visual and was making a point of getting as much said by Clive as he could without it sounding too obvious that he was trying to trick Clive into anything.

As soon as the front door was locked and with them not needing to put together an order again till tomorrow George seized his opportunity and got straight on his knees in front of where Clive was standing in the front room. He wanted to get Clive so aroused that he didn't bother saying that they needed to head upstairs before allowing anything to develop. Before Clive had a chance to raise any objection George had not only undone Clive's trousers but had already got the member between his lips and was working on it well, although it was something that Clive had always said that he was crap at doing. In no time at all Clive's dick was as firm as it gets and with George knowing as much now lowered his own trousers and pants while still having Clive's member in his mouth. He wanted to give Clive no chance to hold things up until they made their way upstairs and into a room where there was no camera.

Tom came back into the lounge having ensured that everything was secure for the night and as soon as he saw the state of play

realised that George was playing a blinder. With Clive being so
aroused as he clearly was it looked as though they would be
getting down to business right where they were. Tom had worked
out where the camera was in the room and subtly guided George
to take up his position in a way that would ensure that they got
Clive's face in shot as well as being able to catch on film exactly
what he was up to.

Their plan came together and in no time Clive was inserting his
tool deep into George's rear end. Tom got on his knees in front of
George and took the dick into his mouth. For Tom it was not an
issue if he was seen taking George's member into his mouth as he
would openly admit that he just loved doing so to anyone that
chose to ask.

Just as with the previous evening as soon as Clive had shot his
load that was it he was in a hurry to get off home. With them all
leaving the house at the same time Tom knew that he would be
able to save the required piece of footage before Clive would get
home and had any chance of deleting it.

Once in the flat Tom and George viewed the tape of the day and
having fast forwarded it till the relevant time they both smiled as
they watched the footage on Tom's smart phone.

"Well George all I can say is well done you. I really didn't think
that he would let anything happen while we were downstairs. He
must think that we are that thick that we weren't going to try and
get our own back on him in any way. He is either that thick or just
that cock sure of himself. Now I know that you are gagging to get
me into that bed of mine but do you mind if we spend a bit of
time transferring this onto my computer. The last thing I want to
happen is for Clive to get home and delete it before I have got it
saved."

"That Tom is perfectly fine with me, not only am I really happy
that your idea seems as if it might just pay dividends but being
with you is nice without us having to have sex all the time."

"All I hope is that Clive didn't do such a good job that you don't
want anything from me tonight because I would just love to show
you how much I am really getting to like you."

"Tom, don't worry on that score, besides when I get mine in
either your mouth or up your arse I will show you that I am really
getting to like you too."
No sooner had Tom managed to do all that he wanted with the
footage the display showed that a third party was gaining access.
Tom immediately shut his phone down so Clive wouldn't be able
to see that he had been online to the site.
"Bloody hell George that was close. Just think, if we had got
straight down to business when we got through the door then we
would have missed our chance of getting it transferred onto the
computer."
"I didn't think that it would be the very first thing that he did
when he got in though, did you?"
"I had a funny feeling that he wouldn't leave it on there for long
because you can never tell who else will be able to gain access to
the recordings. He must have broken every speed limit on his way
back home in order for him to be there already though, we only
left the house about fifteen minutes ago and it normally takes
twenty minutes for him to get home from here."
"Do you think that he might suspect that we are up to something.
I must admit that I was overly keen on getting inside his trousers
than I usually am. He normally has to tell me to do it rather than
me doing all the running."
"To be honest George it doesn't really matter what he thinks. We
have already got the footage saved and that my friend is all that
matters."
"You just said 'my friend', I thought you would have said my
boyfriend."
"From what you were saying last night I thought that you wanted
to play things slow. I can assure you that is the only reason why I
haven't referred to you yet as my boyfriend."
"In that case I must be more of a girl than I thought because they
say that girls are allowed to change their minds, not fellas."
"So does that mean what I think it does then George? Are we
going to give it a try at being an item?"

"No we are not going to give it a try Thomas at all, we are going to succeed if I have anything to do with it."

Needless to say it was gone two in the morning before they got to sleep, having confirmed the fact to each other that they were both happy with forming a relationship.

With Tom not having to be at the house early with no delivery due it meant a later start. In addition, the fact that Clive had come good with the money from his sperm donations Tom suggested that they both go and grab a cooked breakfast at a little café that he uses from time to time. A suggestion that George was happy to go along with, he would tell Clive that he had to practically force Tom to get out of the door as all he wanted to do was to get some sleep.

 Over a full English breakfast each they discussed how they were going to go about informing Clive that he was no longer the one that was in control and that now they had got something very firm on him, in fact two things. There was no way that he could ever use the footage of Tom shooting his brother dead without himself being put in the frame as an accessory to the fact and aiding with the disposal of the body. As regards to any footage that he had on them having sex then that was no big deal for either of them, but if it came to Clive's daughter's attention that her own father shagged blokes then that would be a different thing altogether.

"Tom, I know that Clive is intending for us both to go over to his on Sunday afternoon for when he gets back from the squash club. How about we get a copy of the disc and take it with us, then when he says about us watching a porno we could say that we have brought one with us that we think that he would be interested in watching."

"The only one snag with that idea is that I know that he has got a gun ,and if we put him in a position like we are going to then is he likely to use it on either of us?"

"No Tom, not with what I have got in mind. You aren't the only one that can come up with some good ideas and I think that you will like what I am going to say. Before he starts getting really uptight with what he is seeing I will tell him that there is a copy of it in the post to my house, and if I am not there to intercept it when it arrives then my parents will get their hands on it. He will know that if they were ever to see the footage then my dad would soon put one and one together and know that Clive has been at it with me ever since I started going round there. That means that my dad would twig onto the fact that Clive is into having sex with underage lads.”

“That is a really good idea and should ensure that he does nothing to you which is the main thing.”

“He won’t do anything to you either, can you transfer the other footage onto the disc as well so he sees himself helping you get rid of Gavin’s body. That should give us both a guarantee that he doesn’t do anything stupid.”

“I like your thinking but if he sees that on the disc then he will know that I have told you about what I did to Gavin.”

“And? I’ve just thought, can I have a copy of the two discs anyway please Tom?”

“Why would you want a copy of the other one George? Surely you just having the one of what Clive got up to with you tonight will be enough to keep you safe.”

“Yes, but if I have got a copy of you doing the stuff with your brother then I will have a hold over you as well. If you ever try and ditch me then I will use it in order to keep us together.”

“And what makes you think that you will ever have cause to use it? Aren’t you forgetting that it was me that wanted us to become an item while you were the one that was holding back.”

“I guess that you have got a good point there, but when you come out then I can see that I will have competition. There will be as many blokes that want to get a part of you just as there were girls when you used to bat that side of the fence.”

“If, and I say if that is the case then they will just have to carry on wanting, as far as I am concerned we are together and when I am in a relationship of any kind there is one thing that I don’t do and that is play around.”

“You say that now but what about in a few months’ time when you have got bored with me?”

"That George is something that will never happen. As far as I am concerned I am more than happy with the boyfriend I have got and all I want to do is to get to know him a hell of a lot better than I do at the moment. Just out of curiosity what do your parents think about you being gay?"

"They are really cool with it, so much so that they keep hassling me saying when am I going to get myself a proper boyfriend. I think they will be chuffed to bits when I tell them that I have actually got one and that he is really nice."

"Well that's good to hear, I thought that if they got wind of you getting into a relationship then they would then try and make things difficult."

"No, they will be the opposite and I bet it isn't long before they start asking when I am going to move in with him."

"So when are you, just so you know how to answer them when they do get round to asking?"

"I guess that will depend on when I am asked to, won't it Tom?" The way that George had said it left Tom wondering if George was actually waiting for the invitation. He thought for a moment before making his next comment because he didn't want to appear as if he was trying to push things along too fast for George to handle.

"Well as far as I am concerned if you are going to be stopping here all week anyway then you might as well bring your stuff over, if you know what I am meaning? But it is up to you but you are more than welcome if you would be happy to."

"So are you asking me to move in with you or what Tom, come on spit it out."

"And I thought you would get insulted if I spat it out."

"You know exactly what I was meaning, if you want me to move in with you then I had better hear you ask me."

It was now clear to Tom that George was just waiting to be asked and he didn't disappoint him.

"So when are you going to head over home and pick up your stuff then George?"

"You still haven't asked me Tom, come on let me hear you say it."

"Bloody hell George, are you going to move in with me or what?"

"Well I guess that is the closest I'll get to being given a proper invitation. I will have to think about if I really want to make that sort of commitment at this point."

"Sorry if you think I was being a bit pushy. I was just thinking that if we are going to have a good go at building a real bond between us then if you were to be over here living with me then we would get to know each other a lot deeper than if you just stayed over occasionally."

"Well I've thought about it Tom and I guess that tomorrow I can pop back and grab a few more of my clothes to see me out till the weekend. Then when we are finished at Clive's on Sunday you can come round to my house and help me pick up the remainder of my stuff."

"Does that mean that I will have to meet your parents?"

"Yes it does. They will want to meet you anyway because if they don't then I know what they are like they will worry themselves crazy wondering what you are like. You don't have to worry though, they don't bite."

Tom was well pleased, not so much in the fact that he would be meeting George's parents but rather that George was more than happy for them to meet him. There was also the added thing, George was moving in with him. Only been gay for a couple of days but already had got a boyfriend who was going to move into the flat with him.

"You do realise something George, before now I have been with the same girl for over six months and never even given it a thought about her moving in with me, I have only known you for a couple of days and look at what is happening."

"I'll take it as a compliment then that I must be better than any girl that you have been out with in that case."

"If you don't know that already then I am pretty sure that you will soon get the message."

They were just happy talking and getting things sorted. They were happy being in each other's company.

"So if you are going to head off back to Warwick tomorrow then what do we tell Clive. He will wonder why you are going there."

"If he asks me then I will tell him that we have really hit it off and that in future if he wants me to make any sperm donations it will have to be when we both go over there to visit him. If I am moving in with you then he'll find out soon enough anyway so we might as well tell him straight off. Besides, I have just decided that I might as well go over home today and get my stuff."

"I have got a funny feeling that he will not be at all happy."

"As if I care about what he thinks, as long as we are then that is all that matters to my mind."

"You're right of course George, and he did say to me the other day that he wanted you to find yourself a decent boyfriend which was why he got me over to his, or at least that is what he said. There again we have already established the fact that you can't really believe a word that comes out of his mouth."

"Let's get on our way otherwise you will be late for work and don't you go falling asleep either."

"George, I am on such a high about you moving in I think that no matter how tired I might be getting to sleep is going to prove quite difficult."

Chapter 7

When Clive turned up at the house the Wednesday morning to find George was not there he was quick to ask Tom what was happening. Tom had hoped that George wouldn't head home till later then he would be able to be present as well when Clive heard the news. Here goes Tom thought.

"He has gone back to Warwick in order to pick up some of his gear just to tide him over until the weekend."

"I thought that he brought enough with him to last till the weekend when he came over here on Monday'"

"Well the more stuff he brings over here during the week will mean that he won't have as much to bring back here on Sunday."

"So am I right in thinking he is intending to stop over at yours again next week as well?"

"Not just next week Clive, we are getting on that well that this morning we agreed to give it a real good go together and as of Sunday he will be moving in. Well I guess in a way that isn't quite right, he already has, as good as."

"And you didn't think of asking me if it was okay for that to happen?"

"I thought that you would be pleased after what you said the weekend about wanting to see George with a real boyfriend. Well I guess your wish has come true."

"I'm not at all sure that I am happy allowing the situation."

"Well I'm really sorry if you don't approve but we have really hit it off well and it is something that we are both really happy about."

"Aren't you forgetting something Tom. I have the final say in regard to what you get up to."

"Sorry to be the bearer of bad news but you haven't quite got the hold over either of us that you thought. Or at least after last night you certainly haven't got the hold that you did have. You see you were not quite quick enough getting home and erasing the recording of what took place in the front room after we locked up."

"Exactly what are you telling me Tom?"

"You aren't the only one that knows how to download recordings of what takes place here and using them to your advantage. It makes some real interesting viewing seeing you shagging George's arse right in front of the camera. And with the light on then I am sure you will remember just how clear the images are as well. Now who would you most hate to see get a copy of that tape?"

"If you have made a copy of what took place then I suggest that you hand it over to me right now if you don't want to see me get really annoyed."

"I'm sorry to have to inform you but I didn't make a copy, we actually did four. One of which is just from the early hours of Monday morning and it shows you quite clearly helping me get rid of Gavin's body from in this room. The other three include that as well as you shagging the arse off my boyfriend. Oh and by the way Clive, from now on that is a privilege that you will no longer be enjoying. And you had better find someone else to use that dildo on as well because my arse is now reserved for just one thing and that is for George's use only."

Clive now didn't quite know what to either do or say, the saying like a rabbit caught in headlights expressed how he was feeling at this point. Everything that he had worked so hard to achieve could easily end up all for nothing if those tapes got into certain people's hands.

"You have gone really quiet Clive. I would have thought that you would be asking who we had got in mind of sending the other copies to. We did think about sending the one to Marcos but then I would be in the shit as well, and George nor myself want that to happen. Then we thought who else would react the most from seeing what you get up to behind closed doors and between us we came up with a couple of ideas, your daughter being one of them."

Tom could see that Clive was now very red faced and was
actually relishing the fact that as things stood it very much
appeared as though it was him and George who were now holding
all the trump cards.

"You wait until George gets here and I tell him about what you
did to your own brother. I am certain that once he hears that you
are a murderer then he will run a mile."

"I am really sorry to disappoint you Clive but I am afraid that he
already knows all about what I did. You see we are both of the
same opinion and that is that you don't lie to friends let alone
your partner. I am just wondering if George has posted the one
copy yet or not, I know he was going to before heading back
here."

"Who's he going to post it to?"

Clive was now really getting concerned. From how he was acting
Tom was almost certain that Clive thought that there would be a
copy being sent straight to his daughter.

"Well if I were to say that George was posting one to your
daughter then that would mean that we really hadn't thought
things through very well. Once your daughter has seen it then
George and me lose all our power over you. No Clive, he is
posting it to someone that will not ever open it unless something
happens to either George or myself. If you like, it is our little
insurance policy just to ensure that you don't think of trying to do
something stupid as I know that you would live to regret it if you
did."

It was at this time that their conversation, if you could call it that,
came to an abrupt end with the sound of knocking on the front
door. It turned out to be one of their big customers which pleased
Tom as it would mean he would be in the house for the best part
of an hour, by which time George may well have arrived back.
As they started sorting out the order the dealer passed comment
that Clive was not his normal talkative self to which Clive didn't
attempt to make any sort of reply.

"He's alright, it's just that when he woke up this morning he had
a real sore throat and as a result he is trying not to make things

worse by talking too much. It's nothing to do with you, he hasn't been saying that much to me either. In fact I think it fair to say that I have been doing most of the talking since he got here, which I think is a first."

Tom was really relishing things. He had got Clive on the back foot and while the dealer was there Tom knew that there was no way that Clive could say much. It did however enable Tom time to think up how he was going to progress things. He had already decided that he was going to inform Clive that last night both George and he had a good few hours' sleep together in his bed, or should he say in their bed, with George now living there. Tom wanted to think of something else that he could hit Clive with that would ensure keeping him off balance. He then had a thought that if there was any way that he could pull things off then it would mean that the end result would be perfect for him, although in no way perfect for Clive. He waited his time until eventually the dealer had received and paid for his order and was heading out of the door.

"So Clive, tell me have you ever thought of asking Marcos if you could have a change of scenery?"

"Are you kidding me, are you trying to suggest that I ask to be moved somewhere else?"

"Well you must get bored with having to travel between Warwick and here twice a day especially when there are six houses that are all much closer to where you live. I am sure that if you spoke to Marcos he would be able to find a space for you in one of the houses closer to your home."

"Do you really think that I am going to give this place up after all I have done to get it so profitable."

"Don't you mean all we have done to get it like it is. I believe I get on just as well if not better than you with most of our clientele. There is one good thing though Clive, when you do move you can assure Marcos that I am more than capable of running the house here. What's more I even have someone lined up to take over my roll once I have taken over from you."

"You are being serious aren't you, you really do think that I am going to move and leave this place to you and that useless twat George, he wouldn't last here ten minutes with the type of people that we get coming here."

"You say that but he has put up with you for the past couple of years so if he can do that then I am sure that he can handle things here. If you are referring to the fact that he isn't very good with figures then I already know about that but I will be here to sort out all the money side of things until I have helped him get more proficient at maths. Now have you got any particular house that you would like to take over. I did hear that there is one in Leamington that isn't doing as well as it should, and with you being that brilliant I think Marcos would love to get you in there to do your magic."

Clive just hadn't got a clue as to if Tom was being deadly serious or if he was just winding Clive up for the laugh, one thing that he did know though was that there was no way that he intended moving anywhere.

"Sorry to disappoint you Tom but there is no way that I am going to be asking Marcos for a transfer so I'm afraid that if you hate working with me that much then you had better quit, and you won't need to work your notice either."

"Now you know that isn't about to happen. Can you recall what you told me the other morning about you being a nasty bastard at times. Well I have got news for you Clive, you are not the only one who can make people do things against their wishes. Now there is another avenue that I could go down, I could make a few more copies and deliver them to your neighbours. I think then it won't be just a case of you asking to be transferred locally but I think your life would become that unbearable where you live that you would want to move well out of the area altogether."

It was at this point that there came another knock on the front door and on opening it Tom saw that it was George, carrying two very full backpacks.

"Have I missed anything?" George asked before the door was shut behind him.

"Well I have been having a real good talk with Clive while you have been getting your gear. Now initially he didn't seem at all happy with you moving in with me but I think I have made him understand that we will do what we want and not what he allows. Then we moved on a little and I am just trying to point out to Clive that it would be very much in his own interest if he were to speak to Marcos and request a transfer to one of the houses closer to where he lives. Unfortunately at the moment he doesn't seem to agree with me but I think it is only going to be a matter of time before he comes round to my way of thinking."

"So Clive, I bet it came as a real shock to find out that I am moving in with Tom, and an even bigger one when you found out that neither of us give a toss about what you might think or say about it. By the way you are quite photogenic, you ought to see the recording from when you were shagging me. I know that you deleted it just as soon as you got home so didn't have a chance to see it yourself. If you want to I am sure that we have the odd copy floating around for you to borrow. I guess you'll be quite interested in seeing just what others will if you don't start doing what Tom tells you to. You seem to be forgetting that you have had me running round after you for two whole years, always fearing what you might do. Well now Clive you will start to understand what I have had to put up with and we'll see just how much you like it. Now when was it that you were intending making that phone call to Marcos to see if you can get a move to somewhere more local to where you live."

It now became clear to Clive that it hadn't just been Tom mouthing off but it was obvious that the two of them had talked at length about what they were going to do. It also became quite clear to Clive that if he didn't do as he was being instructed then those tapes would be posted out, George would make certain of it even if Tom had second thoughts. Clive had never really trusted George, which was one of the reasons why he tried offloading him down to London in the first place.

"So Clive, George asked you a question, aren't you going to answer him because that would be very rude of you if you didn't, and I don't like people that are rude to my boyfriend."

"You two really do think that you can get away with this don't you?"

"Well they say two minds are better than one and you have got away with it where George is concerned for the last two years, so on that going then I think that George and I will be okay for a good four years on that score. Now do you need me to remind you of the number you ring if you need to speak to Marcos because I have got it in my phone's memory if you do."

Part of Clive wanted to call their bluff but the thought of his daughter ever getting a copy of what had taken place the previous evening was consuming him to such a degree that he pulled out his mobile phone from within his trouser pocket.

"Oh by the way Clive please don't go anywhere while you make that call because I want to hear what you say to Marcos and I am sure that Tom is just as keen at hearing what is said."

"In fact Clive, I'll go one better than what George has just said and put the phone on loud speaker so we are able to hear what the top man has to say on the subject. Not that I don't trust you it's just that I don't trust you. Now loud speaker, and don't beat around the bush and say quite clearly that you want a change of venue to work out of."

Both George and Tom stood there listening to the conversation between Clive and Marcos. Tom was really pleased that he had suggested that the phone be put on loud speaker as he had just heard Marcos say that there was an opening at the very house that Tom had referred to earlier in Leamington. If Clive were to move there then instead of him having to travel about thirty miles each day then with it being in the neighbouring town it would mean less than ten miles a day.

The two of them listened closely to hear how Clive answered the one question that Marcos asked him. Marcos had asked what he thought of Tom and as to if he would be able to handle running the house without Clive being around. Tom almost burst out laughing when he heard Clive replying to the question. He said that he thought that Tom would find things quite tough to start off with but was sure that within no time he would soon be getting to grips with things. In addition Clive pointed out the fact that there was someone that both him and Tom had known for some time that he was sure would be able to be trained to take over Tom's roll within the house. By the time the call was finished both Tom and George were well pleased, however there was one person present who was far from being happy with the situation.

"Now Clive, I really don't understand why it is that you are looking so glum. Just think that from next Monday you will be in a completely new house with new customers to meet and get to know. Plus, with the house currently doing so bad then it will give you a real good opportunity to earn yourself some brownie points with Marcos when you start working your magic and get the place taking serious money like it should be."

"You may have got me moving but I promise you both here and now that I will get you both back and when I do you will regret ever having crossed me."

"But Clive, I will just point out that there will always be a copy of that disc somewhere safe and if anything unpleasant ever comes in either George's direction or mine then believe me when I tell you that the tape will be made quite public. It won't just be a case of one copy being sent out to your daughter. Now from what Marcos said with it being Wednesday now and with you having got a busy week ahead of you didn't I hear him say that if you felt that I would cope without you being here then you could take the rest of the week off. Well Clive I will be perfectly alright here without you so I'll say goodbye then."

"And I'll say the same but just before you go am I right in thinking that the invitation that you gave us to pop round on Sunday is now withdrawn, because if it isn't then Tom and I will bring a disc over for you to watch. I'd like to see it on a television as so far I have only seen it on Tom's phone. I bet on a real big screen like you've got it really does look as though you are enjoying yourself."

"Go to hell the pair of you." Clive said as he grabbed his coat and made his way towards the front door.

"We don't want to go there we are trying to get away from you. Now fuck off and don't slam the door on your way out."

"Right then George before I make a phone call do you really want to have a job working here. You know that if the place ever gets raided by the old bill then you are likely to be banged up for quite some years."

"Well if the place gets raided and you are banged up then I might as well be because from how I am seeing things at the moment if I couldn't get to be with you then it would be like me being in prison."

"And now who is it that is doing the sweet talking. You silver tongued devil you."

With that Tom phoned Marcos in order to inform him that as he had suggested to Clive he had chosen to walk out of the house and that Tom was now running things. He assured Marcos that there was no way that it would affect trade as he had always got on well with all of their customers. Tom went on to inform Marcos that he believed that he'd already met the person that Clive had referred to as being an ideal candidate for taking on the vacant position that Tom's promotion had created. When Tom told Marcos that the intended new addition to the staff was going to be George the boss' immediate reaction was that he was no more than just a kid. To this Tom pointed out the fact that by his understanding it had been a good couple of years since he had last met George and since then he had matured well. Marcos was happy for Tom to have George in the house as long as he felt that he was up for the job. Again Tom assured Marcos that if he hadn't been sure that George would be fine carrying out the duties asked of him then there was no way that he would have put his name forward. With Marcos being happy for Tom to run the place as he saw fit the call was drawn to a conclusion.

"I was waiting for you to ask him how much of a pay rise you were going to get with you now running the place, also will I automatically be on the same money that you were on until today?"

"George, I don't know if you have a clue as to how much either Clive or I used to get paid but I am pretty sure of one thing. When I tell you just how much we will be bringing in between the two of us then I know for a fact you will be shocked."

"Well I guess that it must be pretty good money because not only have you got a nice flat but the house that Clive lives in must be worth a fair bit."

"I think that when we have got settled together then we could easily start looking for a much better place to live than the flat. How do you fancy living in a detached property somewhere, but it can't be too far from here because I need to be close by."

"Is the money going to be that good then that we'll be able to afford a real nice place?"

"Believe me when I tell you that you will be earning one hell of a lot more than most eighteen year olds do. And as for me, if it went through the books then I would have to start paying higher rate tax."

"You have got to be kidding, that doesn't come in till you are earning somewhere in the region of a hundred grand a year does it?"

"I think it is slightly more than that but I assure you that I am not joking. You will be on five hundred a week for the first few weeks, while I train you up."

"I thought that with what I did already that it was enough to keep a smile on your face."

"George I was talking about training you up on this job not what happens in the bedroom. If I had been talking about that then I am sure that you know a hell of a lot more about having sex with fellas than I do."

"The way you say that it sounds as if I have been a right slut and go with anyone. I'll let you know that I can count on just a couple of hands the number of guys that I have been with, well almost."

"I didn't mean any offence when I said that George but let's face it I have only been at it for just a few days where with you there is two years' experience for you to refer to. No, with the job here there will be quite a bit that you will need to learn. The first thing is that I will have to introduce you to all our customers, but you won't have a problem with any of them unless they find out that we are an item, then there might be one or two that try to make life difficult for us."

"So I guess from that there are some that are homophobic then, what will they do if they do find out?"

"I don't really know, it might be that they will have no problem with things, after all as long as they can still get their requirements from here there shouldn't really be an issue for them. I know that there are at least three of our regulars that supply to the gay scene, one of which actually works in one of the gay venues of a weekend."

"So other than being introduced to the customers what else will I need to learn?"

"Everything George, the pricing, what stocks we need to carry, how to place orders and of what. Then there will be the real interesting part for you."

"What's that, and don't say when we close up at the end of each night and get you back to your flat."

"That wasn't what I was meaning, I was thinking that you will enjoy counting out all the money that we take so it is all ready for when the delivery arrives to be taken back to the hub. If I had been thinking of after we close up then it would be a case of us going back to our flat, not mine."

"That will take me some getting used to. I will automatically call the flat yours because that is what it is really as you had it before I came onto the scene."

"Well once you have brought the rest of your stuff over then it should feel more like your home to you, or at least I hope it does."

"Well they do say that home is where your heart is, so with you being there then it shouldn't take me too long to get calling it our place."

"You soppy git you. Anyway while we haven't got any customer here I might as well start showing you where everything is stashed and how to lift each of the floor boards up. Initially you will find that there are some that take some lifting if you are anything like when I first started here. Do you know what all the different substances look like even and what weights we sell them in?"

"I know what cannabis resin looks like and skunk of course, other than that I must admit that I am not too sure. With cannabis I know that you sell it in weights of a teenth, an eighth, quarter, half ounce and an ounce."

"That is how you buy it as the end user, but we don't bother with anything small here, that is up to the dealer to cut it up to the sizes that he wants. We only supply in full ounces and you'll see that most of the guys will take a fair few ounces at a time."

"That must work out to be loads of money. I can pay ten quid for just a teenth so I am trying to work out how much that works out to be an ounce."

"Our dealers don't pay anywhere near what you would pay as their customer. It depends on exactly what they are having and how much but they can pay somewhere in the region of a hundred an ounce."

"Even so if they take, let's just say five ounces then that is still five hundred quid on the one sale."

"George I think that you are in for one hell of a shock when you see just how much money comes into this place every day. We are not talking hundreds but thousands and that is just from some of our better customers. When Dave gets here you'll see him pass over somewhere around eight grand at a time."

"So does he just come here once a week then with him taking that much at a time?"

"No George, he can come twice a day on some occasions. He doesn't actually work the stuff at street level himself but instead he has got quite a little team that do all of that for him."

"So just how much comes through this place every day then Tom, ten thousand or more."

"If I were to tell you that last Saturday we had our best day yet
and that when we counted everything up it was not too far from
being a hundred."

"What a hundred grand in just the one day?"

It was quite clear to Tom that George had got very little idea as to
just how much money changed hands on the local drug scene on a
daily basis. He will have quite an awakening ahead of him, Tom
thought to himself.

Tom was just about to start showing George round the house in
order to reveal all the places where the various products were
stored when there came the first knock of the day on the front
door since Clive had walked out..

"Well here we go then George, are you ready to meet the first of
the guys?"

"I guess I am, all I hope is that they all end up liking me
otherwise it could affect your takings, and Marcos will soon tell
you to get rid of me if that starts happening I know."

"George what is there to not like about you. Now don't forget,
they are not to get any idea that we are an item, or at least not
until they have got used to me being the boss round here and are
happy with you being my number two."

With that Tom opened the door and stood on the doorstep was the
person that he had just been talking to George about.

"Morning Dave, I was just talking about you. This is George and
he will be working here with me from now on. Come on in and
let's get the door shut."

As soon as Dave was inside he started asking loads of questions.
Where was Clive? How come he had moved on to pastures new,
as he had always appeared happy running this place. Was George
to be trusted to keep his mouth shut even if he got a tug from the
old bill? Tom had heard the same sort of stuff asked of himself
when he had first come onto the scene but within just days he'd
been accepted as part of the house.

"You'll find that George is a good guy, and once he has learnt
everything then I am pretty sure that even if I wasn't here he
would be able to get your order together for you without having

any problem. I don't think that it will be too long before he is trying to tell me how to do things round here if I am not mistaken."

With that Dave accepted the facts as they had been put to him. As long as he was still able to get his supplies from the house and wouldn't have to start paying more for them then that was the main thing that concerned him. Happy with things Dave now passed a piece of paper over to Tom, on it were his requirements for now but he was quick to say that he would be back again later on. He went on to ask Tom if he could be as fast as possible because he had got to take his wife to the doctors and wanted to get the stuff out to his guys beforehand. Tom left Dave with George in the front room while he went round the various rooms in order to get the list filled. As he went he was working out the prices and without having to use a calculator worked out that the total amount due was just shy of eight grand, or seven thousand eight hundred and fifty pounds to be exact.

"Go on then Dave, I know you will already have worked it out, how much does this lot come to then?"

Dave said the exact amount that Tom had worked it out to be and George just stood there totally gob smacked as he watched the money being counted out. This was just the first customer of the day and from the last couple of days of being here he knew that the front door was knocked about twenty times during the day if not more. Even if all the rest only spent half as much that still works out to be getting on for the eighty grand mark if not more. It was now that he realised that Tom had not been joking about the amount of money that passes through the house.

As soon as Dave had got his stock he left.

"Well George what do you think of Dave, he's a pretty good lad but I'll tell you one thing there is no way that I would want to cross him. From what I have heard he can be a real nasty bastard if you get on the wrong side of him. Did you have a decent chat with him while I was putting his order together?"

"Yes, he was saying that if it didn't work out for me here then I was to get you to contact him and he would sort out work for me to do for him. I thought that was pretty good of him seeing as he had only just met me for the first time."

 "Well I can't see you ever having to take him up on the offer but he is one of the few that I would be happy with you working for. He looks after his guys and doesn't take the piss out of them. He pays them all pretty well from what I have heard and I know that if he found out that you were gay then he would have you serving up pills in one of the gay clubs in no time at all."

"So he is one of the guys that you were talking about that supplies the gay scene?"

"To be honest when I mentioned it earlier I had forgotten that Dave works some of them as well but he only does a few of the clubs and the rest he leaves to the other guys, as they were supplying the pubs before Dave even started trading. You will find that there is quite a loyalty between most of them. One thing that I haven't mentioned up till now and it is really important as well. Whenever anyone comes here for an order then you stay with them in the lounge while I put it together, and if there is a knock on the door while there is already someone here then answer it and ask them to come back in fifteen minutes. We never have more than the one dealer in the house at any one time."

"Can I guess why that is Tom before you go ahead and tell me. Is it because they don't want any of the others knowing what they are buying from here."

"That George is exactly the reason. If they want to discuss things away from here then that is fine by me but it doesn't take place here. Now if you come with me I will show you where we stash all the money and then as long as there isn't another knock I'll show you where everything is."

Tom had shown George where the money was stored and had revealed to him where both the cannabis resin was stashed as well as the green. He was just about to take him upstairs to show him where the serious drugs were when there came another knock.

It was gone three in the afternoon before Tom had managed to show George where all the products were stashed. As they had gone round Tom realised that they would have to put an order into the hub for delivery in the morning otherwise they would run the risk of running out of certain lines.

"So have you been keeping count of how much money has come into the house so far today then George?"

"I think that so far it is just over thirty grand isn't it?"

"I know that you have already told me that maths isn't your strong point but it is something that is really essential in this line of work. Now don't get me wrong, I am not getting heavy with you in any way but the more you practice then the better you get at it. Now so far we have taken in forty seven thousand five hundred pounds exactly. Now if you can remember that then whenever anyone else comes then try and keep a mental record of what has come in. will you do that for me please George?"

"I can do but don't expect me to have it dead on at the end of the night, because I really am that bad, especially with these sorts of amounts. Until today I had never even seen what a grand in cash looks like let alone what has been handed over to you."

"George it won't take long before it means nothing to you. I can remember when I first started I kept thinking what I could do with that sort of cash but what you have got to say to yourself is that it isn't yours so it is pointless filling your mind with those sorts of dreams."

"While we are on about money you said earlier that I would be earning five hundred a week while I am on trial but you didn't say how much I would then be on once I have proved myself."

"I never mentioned anything to do with you being on trial, I said that you would be on five hundred while I trained you up. Once I am happy with your abilities then I will let Marcos know and you'll probably find that he will pop round in order just to test you out on a few things. As long as you give him the answers that he wants to hear then he will sanction you going onto full pay as a number two."

"And how much will that be then Tom, about six hundred a week?"

"No, it will be a nice round figure that even you will never be able to forget."

"Are you meaning what I think you are? Are you trying to tell me that I will be on a grand a week once I have proved myself?"
"That's right George, not bad money for an eighteen year old, which you will be by then."
"Well if I'm going to be earning that much can I be really rude and ask how much you will be on, or don't you want to tell me."
"If I told you that I will be on twice that amount until I have proved that the house takings aren't going down what would you say?"
"Well Marcos certainly won't double your money when you have gone through the initial period like he will be with me, that's one thing for certain."
"You are wrong there George, each house has an allotted five grand wage allowance, you will be getting one of the five and as long as I am doing a good job then I will get the remainder."
"Excuse my French but fuck me, no wonder you were so eager to get Clive out of here. So overnight your earnings have doubled and then in a few weeks' time they will double again, that's unreal. I thought that I would be on somewhere like three hundred a week and that if you were lucky that you would be getting about five hundred for having all the responsibility. I never dreamt that the job paid anywhere near as good as that. So can you just remind me what that figure was of today's takings and then I will really try my best to keep a mental note of how much it is by the end of the day."
It was clear to Tom that George had suddenly decided to put his all into learning the job and proving himself in the shortest period of time. Tom also knew that George wouldn't be just doing so in order to secure better money for himself, but also to ensure that the house was a success and that he didn't end up letting Tom down.
"One of the main reasons why the pay is so good is because if we ever did get raided then running a place like this comes with it a very long prison sentence. If you like it is the same as getting danger money when you do a risky job, here though it isn't your life that is in danger it is your freedom."

"I get that Tom and I know if the place did get raided and then when questioned by the police if I ended up telling them too much then my life would be in danger."

"That is something that I urge you never to do. It will be a lot better spending a few years behind bars than to piss Marcos off because you would be dead in a very short time after talking to the police. Having said that though in the last four years there has only been four of the houses raided and two of those were because of the guy working in the one was in a pub one night and having had a few drinks started talking too much. What he didn't know was that there just so happened to be a couple of off duty coppers standing within feet from him and they were listening to everything that he was saying."

"So other than that there have only been two really in four years, and from what Clive has said there are about fifty houses in total aren't there?"

"To be quite honest with you George I don't know exactly how many there are but I think you wouldn't be far off if you are just talking about the ones that are supplied out of the Birmingham hub."

"Are you trying to tell me that Birmingham isn't the only hub that they operate?"

"They have got one of a similar size up in Manchester somewhere and then another in South Wales, but from what I have heard that one is nowhere near as big."

"So if we say that there are about one hundred houses in total. And that only two of them have been raided over a four year period then, if my maths are right, it works out to have a probability of it happening of just half of one percent a year."

"And what was that you have been saying about being useless at maths, I consider myself to be pretty hot with figures and you working that out in your head is impressive. So were you just pretending to be stupid earlier or what?"

"Do you mean the forty seven and a half grand that has passed through your hands today?"

"So you knew all along how much it was then, so why did you ask me to tell you the figure again if you had already got it logged in that head of yours?"

"I thought that you might think that I was showing off when you first asked me how much the house had taken earlier if I had got it right. That was why I said somewhere in the region of thirty grand. I wasn't too sure if I was supposed to know the details. Also with what the various guys have had I have got a rough idea as to how much they pay for what, but at the moment I am not going to say what I think the figures are until I have seen a few more transactions done. I think by the end of today I should be able to name quite a few of the prices as long as you are charging the same to each of the guys."

"You are a clever little fucker on the quiet. I can see that I will have to watch my back otherwise you will want my job in a few weeks' time."

"You don't need to watch your back Tom as I will be doing that every time I shag you."

"So come on then George, why do you pretend not to be very good where maths is concerned and what other mysteries are you hiding about yourself?"

"I don't really know, I think it was going back to my first school and that the teacher always kept going on about me being so clever, and as a result I started having a real hard time with the other lads. They were always calling me stuff like being teacher's pet and saying that I was a right creep. As soon as I started secondary school I just started pretending that I wasn't very good with numbers and it just became a habit I guess."

"So in other words you are probably not just better than I am at maths for you to be so convincing then you are one hell of an actor as well."

"I thought you were going to say that I was a convincing liar."

"You did manage to get Clive to believe that you were no good at maths and not many people get one up on him, despite all his faults he is a pretty good judge."

"Yes, but he believed that I actually enjoyed it when he was shagging me for the last two years."

"Well I must admit that when a dick is up my arse to a large degree it doesn't matter who it belongs to as long as it hits the mark. It isn't as if you have got to like its owner."

"There is that to it but with me I knew that I was having to let him shag me otherwise I would be in trouble, that takes away all the enjoyment I guess."

"I understand what you are saying and all I hope is that you never get to that stage with me, thinking that you have to have sex with me in order to keep your job."

"Don't you worry on that score Tom, if you start getting boring then I will just have to go out and buy one of those huge dildos to put some life back into you."

"As long as you buy some lube at the same time that is all I will ask."

"If you stop making my bedtime enjoyable I might just forget to use any lube in order to teach you a lesson."

"Let's hope that we never get to that stage. Changing the subject back to work have you noticed that we haven't had anyone knock the door for ages. It must be a good half an hour since the last guy left and this time of day they are usually queueing to get their stocks."

With that Tom went through to the front room and had a look out of the window. It soon became quite clear why they hadn't had anyone knocking. Parked right outside the house was a marked police car without anyone sat in it. Tom immediately knew what was happening. Clive had got a few friends on the force and Tom was sure that he had arranged for the car to be parked there in order to try and fuck their takings up. That way Clive would be able to get his house back if Marcos decided that Tom was not the right man for the job after all.

"The sly bastard, Clive has only arranged for a squad car to be parked up outside of here. Well he isn't going to get away with doing that."

"What can you do about it Tom?"

"Quite easy, Marcos has got police eating out of the palm of his hand at a much higher level than Clive has. I am going to phone him and ask him what the score is."

Without saying anything else to George at this stage Tom called Marcos and informed him of the cop car being parked immediately outside of the house. On hearing it Marcos told Tom to leave it with him and if it hadn't gone within fifteen minutes that he wanted Tom to give him another call. As soon as the call was ended Tom shared what was going on with George before turning his attention back to his phone and making a second call.

"Clive, I know what you have done getting the filth car parked up outside, and I just thought that I would warn you that Marcos is on the case, and when he finds out that you arranged it you had better watch your back. I think very soon Marcos will be withdrawing the offer of you running that house in Leamington or any other place, it will be difficult to run a house when you are no longer breathing."

Without giving Clive a chance to answer he hung up.

"Well I think that should get Clive worried if anything does."

"Do you think that Marcos will find out who was behind it being parked up outside?"

"Well if he does then we might as well do away with the recordings that we have got of Clive because they won't be of any use if Marcos does find out that Clive was behind it."

"Do you really think that Marcos would have Clive killed just because of it?"

"I don't just think that he will, I am absolutely certain that is what will happen. If you think about it why would Clive ask for a car to be parked there? It tells the police quite clearly that there is illegal activity going on here of one kind or another. If they have been keeping an eye open as to who approached the house and then turned back then the police would soon realise exactly what the place is used for. Having said that there is no need for you to start getting worried because I know very well that the police are not going to be raiding this place even if they do know what goes on here."

"How can you be so sure Tom?"
"For the simple reason that Marcos has just told me so while I
was talking to him on the phone. I told you that he knows people
quite high up on the force and if Marcos is relaxed with things
then there is no need for us to be anything other than the same. If
Marcos thought that the place was likely to be raided he would
have told me so I could get everything together ready for it all to
be collected. You see if there is a real risk of one of the houses
being visited by the old bill then it is stripped of all stock within
an hour."
"So are you trying to tell me that if the place is going to be raided
then Marcos knows about it well before it actually takes place?"
"That is about the bottom line George. Why do you think that the
statistics are so low, what was it half of one percent?"
Although Tom had been talking to George he had also been
keeping one eye out of the window in order to see if the police car
was being approached. As soon as he saw someone unlocking the
front driver's door he was outside like a shot. George for his part
just stood there looking through the window wondering what
Tom would be saying to the copper.
After just a very short conversation Tom was soon coming back
into the house.
"What did you say to him Tom?"
"I just told him that if he didn't want to get into grief with some
very senior bosses of his that in future when he gets a call from
his mate Clive that he tells him where to go. I think he got the
message. Now though you watch we will end up being as busy as
hell from now till closing time. They will all have been keeping at
a safe distance while that car was where it was."
"It must have been there for the best part of an hour, so does that
mean that we will have to stay open later if guys are still to turn
up?"
"That is one thing you will learn about this business and the main
reason why I only live just a couple of hundred yards away from
here. If our customers need stock then as long as it doesn't
become a regular occurrence we try to accommodate them. Today

it hasn't been anyone's fault other than Clive's why they haven't already been and got their orders so it would be out of order for me to say to them sorry but it's ten o'clock so you'll have to wait till tomorrow."

"I hear what you are saying and with us being paid so well I have not got any problem even if it means us staying open until midnight."

"George, I have got a problem with that. You have got two bags there that need to be emptied and I have got one in my trousers that needs to be as well."

"You, Tom, are sex mad. That reminds me, while I was going over to Warwick to get my stuff I thought about something you said earlier. When we were talking about the dealers finding out that we were an item at the one point you said 'not until they have got used to the way things now are' or words to that affect. What did you mean by that?"

"Well there is no way that I intend hiding the fact that I am in a relationship with you for a minute longer than I need to. Once everyone has got to know you and everything is running as it should be then I intend telling them all exactly how things are. At the very worst we might lose a couple of the smaller dealers but that won't be too much of an issue."

"So you are prepared to risk losing customers in order to tell them."

"I am not going to try and hide the fact for a moment longer than I need. I will have no problem in letting them know that I have fallen in love with another guy."

"Bloody hell Tom, run that one past me again. Did I hear right, did you just say that you have fallen in love with another guy?"

"You heard exactly what I said, there is as much wrong with your hearing as there is with your ability to do maths."

"I know we are getting on really well but isn't it a little premature saying stuff like that Tom?"

"Well it might be for you and I am not expecting you to turn round and say the same to me but I know where I am at and I know what I am feeling. You George have turned my life upside down and there is something about you that has reached into the very core of me."

"Bloody hell Tom, you'll be writing poems soon coming out with that sort of stuff. Mind you the way things are going I honestly don't think that you will have to wait too long before you hear me saying that word to you but I am not quite there yet."

"That George brings joy to my ears. I was thinking as soon as I had said the word that I might have been getting too deep for you to be able to handle. For a split second I imagined those bags of yours heading back to Warwick without even being opened."

The conversation was cut short by a knock at the door, the first of the dealers that had been waiting for the coast to be clear before coming to the house. From there on all the way through till just turned half eleven it was one endless flow of customers. George had been doing a good job of letting the guys know that they would have to pop back later but that they weren't to worry as the house would stay open until the last guy had got his order.

"Well that was all a bit manic George, well done by the way you seemed to control the flow really well, and it went smoother than if I had been doing the job."

"That was probably because you turn the customers round faster than Clive always did from what I have seen of him. Sometimes he would be talking to them for ten minutes before even taking the order out of their hand, even if it was clear that they wanted to get on."

"Right, I think that is just about everyone sorted out for today. Before we go any further I will just give the hub a quick call to tell them that I am running a bit late but will be phoning through an order within the next half an hour, just so they know what is happening. Then we need to go and see what to order and after that is the part that I think you will enjoy, the counting of all the cash.

"I believe that it will be ninety three thousands, two hundred and eighty pounds if I am not mistaken."

"Well George I will have to take your word for it because I have
been that rushed that for the first time ever since starting here I
have actually lost count myself."
"I might have got it slightly wrong because there were a couple of
the dealers that you were sorting out that I could hardly hear what
was being said between you with everything that was going on."
"We'll soon see when we count up, but let's get the order done
first. If you lock the front door we will start in the back room and
the cannabis then once that is done we'll move upstairs."
With that they worked their way through the various rooms until
Tom was confident with the order that he was going to place. He
was well pleased, as it was even bigger than the one that they had
placed the other day and to his thinking it was probably the
biggest order that the house had ever put in. He did wonder
though, if George had got the figures right then there shouldn't be
quite so much needed. Tom phoned through the order then the
two of them started counting out all the cash ready for when the
delivery arrived first thing in the morning. It soon dawned on
Tom as to why there seemed to be a discrepancy between what
George had said the takings were and what he had ordered.
"I have just thought George, you need to add eight thousand, five
hundred and thirty quid onto that number you said. When Dave
came round here the second time he went round with me getting
his order together and you wouldn't have heard how much it was
as we did the deal upstairs."
 "Did you say this morning that Saturday had been the best ever
day here and that you were just shy of one hundred grand?"
"That's right, why?"
"Because Tom, if I have got the sums right, with adding Dave's
order to it then today the house has broken the hundred grand. I
make it one hundred and two thousand eight hundred and ten
pounds. If I am right."
"Well we are just about to find out. If I count it then if you would
be as good as to double check everything for me then as soon as
we both agree on the end figure I think we can then close up shop
and call it a day."

It only took ten minutes before George had proved to have been dead right with his calculations. They had broken the hundred grand for the first time ever.

"Sorry about this George but I have got to make another phone call before we call it a day."

With that Tom phoned Marcos. Clive had been told by the top man a couple of weeks previous that he wanted to know immediately if they ever achieved breaking through the magical figure and Tom was very pleased to be able to phone Marcos up on his very first day in charge. Marcos was well pleased and although Clive hadn't informed Tom of it Marcos had told Clive that if they did achieve it then there would be a ten grand bonus for them. It was going to be heading in Tom's direction and would arrive with the order first thing in the morning.

"We're in the money George. We're in the money big time."

"What are you on about Tom. I know that you are now on much better money than you were this time yesterday and that I have now got a job but what are you getting at?"

"Ten thousand pounds bonus is what I am getting at George, we have got a ten grand bonus for having hit the hundred thousand pounds, and it will be arriving here with the order first thing in the morning."

"In that case Tom, can I suggest that we stop off at that takeaway that you were on about Monday night in order to get some food to celebrate. I am absolutely starving."

"If you had said I could have got something delivered here during the day, that is what we usually do when we are busy."

"The way things were I would have had to eat it while talking to one of the dealers and the only chance of you having got it down your neck was if you ate while putting the orders together."

"I wondered what you were going to say then when you started talking about me getting something down my neck, I thought you were talking about what will happen just as soon as we have finished eating supper."

"I thought that tonight we would skip sex and just get straight off to sleep. I have noticed that you have been yawning one hell of a

lot throughout the day, and I am getting a bit on the tired side not having slept on the settee most the day like I was doing."
"Let's go get some food and then see what happens after we have eaten. I have got this funny feeling that by the time we have finished stuffing our faces with food that we will want to have a dessert if you know what I mean."
With that they locked up and headed home, via the Indian takeaway.

Again it was about two in the morning before they got off to sleep. Before doing so they had decided that first thing in the morning they would be heading into the city centre in order to look for some additional furniture for the flat. It had become quite clear that if George was moving in then they needed to get another set of draws and a wardrobe as with Tom only having limited cupboard space they would need more. George pointed out that they had a delivery arriving first thing. They decided that they would have to make do with what they had until Sunday at which time they would have more time available to go out shopping. With the extra ten grand it meant that Tom wouldn't have to wait until pay day before he could afford to buy the additional furniture which was something that he thought that he might well have had to do. They both slept well.

Chapter 8

By the weekend George had proved to Tom that he was quite capable of doing the job, although it had taken Tom a good three weeks to get to the stage that George was at already. It was as they were locking up on the Saturday evening that Tom told George that first thing on Monday morning he would be giving Marcos a call. When George enquired as to why Tom informed him that in his opinion the pay rise was now due, although so early after having come onto the scene.

"Are you having me on Tom. I know that since we spoke I have been getting the takings right but I don't know if I am ready to be tested by Marcos."

"I thought that you said that he tested you out on a number of occasions when you were younger."

"I didn't mean in that way, and I hope that what took place back then doesn't make too much difference when he does get to see me again."

"The boss is okay, don't you start worrying on that front. I admit that I didn't have a clue about the other stuff until you told me about it the other day but as regards to working here he is fine with it otherwise there was no way that he would have allowed me to have you here from day one."

With that they made their way home, where after a quick bite to eat it was to bed and after just half an hour of enjoying each other's company they both fell fast asleep wrapped in the other's arms.

Sunday morning they spent going round various furniture stores until they found the additional furniture that was needed. Then in the afternoon they headed over to Warwick where Tom would be meeting George's parents. To say he was a little nervous of doing so was an understatement, he was as worried as hell.

They caught the bus over and throughout the thirty-eight minute journey all Tom could talk about was asking George what he should say and if there was anything that he was to avoid bringing up.

"Tom just be yourself. They already know about what job I have got and that you are not just my lover but are also my boss. When I told them that they did ask if you had made me move in with you as part of the terms of my employment."

"I hope that you put them straight on that one right away. If you remember you had already been home and grabbed some stuff before you got the offer of working for us."

"Tom, will you just chill out please. You are beginning to get me worried now as to if they are going to approve of you. No, I'm only joking on that score. Remember what you said to me when I spoke about the dealers not getting along with me, you turned round and said, 'what is there not to like'. My parents will like you almost as much as I do."

"I've just thought, just now you referred to me as your lover, well to be a lover then doesn't there have to be love involved?"

"Well I did tell you the other day that I didn't think that it would take me too long before I caught up with you on that score."

"So go on then George, spit it out and say exactly what you mean."

"You are just dying to hear me say that I love you aren't you Tom? I can tell."

"Well I have made it no secret that you have stolen my heart."

"You will just have to wait is all I can say to that."

"You mean just like I have made you wait to get your birthday present from me. I was amazed that on Thursday you never uttered a word about it being your eighteenth and I was determined that I wasn't going to bring it up unless you had first."

"I thought that you had forgotten all about it Tom, so you have got me a birthday present then? Tom, dare I ask if it is something that you will be giving me once we get into bed later?"

"No George, we'll have sex as and when the mood takes us, there is no way that we are only going to have fun in that department twice a year on just our birthdays."

"So what have you got for me then Tom?"

"You'll find out later, but we can't spend hours with your parents as we'll need to be back at our place and ready to go out by half six at the latest."

"So I take it from that you are taking me out for the night, what is it a guided tour of all your haunts from when you were a straight guy?"

"We are going out for a meal at what I believe is the best restaurant in Coventry, and that is being paid for out of the bonus that we got for hitting the hundred grand."

"Don't you mean the bonus that you got and not what we got."

"George the house runs best when there is team work and whereas if it had been Clive running things he would have probably pocketed the lot and not even told me, I will not do that. The ten grand is our money not mine, we've already spent some of it on the furniture that is being delivered early Monday morning and the meal tonight is coming out of it as well. Consider that as a birthday present from Marcos if you want."

"So if that is Marcos' present then what have you got for me then?"

"You, young man will just have to wait and see. All will be revealed later."

"Go on Tom, at least give me a bit of a clue."

"No George you will just have to be patient and wait."

By the time Tom and George had arrived back in Coventry along with eight bags of George's belongings it was close on six o'clock in the evening, so much for only a quick visit to George's parents and old home.

"I think that both my mum and dad are quite happy with me moving in with you, although they reckon that we are moving a little on the fast side considering we have only known each other for just a week."

"I know they think that we are both being a bit rash but if you feel the same towards me as I do to you then in my mind why wait?"

"You say that but I haven't heard you say that four letter word today Tom."

"You mean the one that starts with 'L' and ends with a 'E' and has an O and V somewhere in between?"
"That's the one."
"Well some things just don't need to be said, and besides, they say that actions speak louder than words."
"And what do you mean by that then Tom, or are you just talking about when we get to bed later?"
"All will be revealed but for now though we had better get our act together because I have booked the table for seven which means that we will just have to leave the unpacking of your bags till we get back in. By the way have I told you that we need to be at the house by eight in the morning because we have got a delivery due and it can arrive any time between eight and half nine. That means that we can't have a ridiculously late night unless you want us both to be knackered at work tomorrow."
"Are we going to walk into the city?"
"No I'll order a taxi to pick us up at half past which gives us thirty minutes in which to get ourselves ready, which should just about be long enough for us to both get showered and changed."
"Only if we shower separately, if we both go in there at the same time I know that you just won't be able to resist getting up to something."
"You say that as if it is only me that enjoys having sex. Unfortunately though and as much as I would like to time does not allow anything like that to take place. I guess if you had wanted that then we would have had to leave your place earlier."
"Don't you mean my old place? It did seem funny saying goodbye to mum and dad knowing that I won't be seeing them for some time. I guess that we won't have a chance to get over there again until next Sunday at the earliest."
"I reckon so, but from what your mother was saying about you being a dab hand in the kitchen I can't wait to see what food you start dishing up."
"As long as you don't mind straightforward English food then I am happy to cook but don't expect anything flash. My mum taught me everything that I know about cooking, and as you

might have guessed from the conversation this afternoon, they don't like any of this foreign rubbish. I think if I had ever cooked them something like a curry I would probably have ended up wearing it over my head."

"It has got to be better than what I manage to put together, that is why I eat takeaway food so often, it tastes better."

With that it was deemed that they really did need to get a move on. George went through for a shower while Tom phoned through for a taxi to pick them up at half past, just twenty-two minutes in which to get ready. As soon as George emerged from the bathroom with just a towel round his waist Tom needed to look in the other direction because he just knew that there was no way that he would be able to stop himself from removing the towel.

"What's the matter Tom? Are you frightened that this might happen?"

As Tom looked round to see what George was meaning the towel was removed revealing not just the whole naked body but also one that was displaying a very erect member.

"I'm sorry George, as much as I would love to I am going to have a quick shower myself."

"Are you sure you don't want me to come in there and wash your back for you?"

"If you come in with me then there are two things that will happen. Firstly it won't only be my back that you will want to be washing, and secondly we will not be ready for when the taxi arrives."

"I know, I was just wanting to see how good your self-control is, and by the looks of the front of your jeans it appears as though you haven't even got a stiffening down below."

"I can assure you that it will be when we get back from the restaurant, but as I said we can't be too late getting to sleep."

With that Tom went to get his shower while George sorted out some clothes from in one of his bags to wear for the evening. They had only just finished getting ready when the sound of a car's horn was heard from outside signalling the arrival of the

taxi. They headed straight out, Tom picking something up from
out of a draw as they went.

"What was that you just grabbed Tom, was it some cash for
tonight?"

"No the money is in my back pocket. It is just something that I
thought that I might need to take with me tonight that's all."

"Well it wasn't big enough to have been your gun so what was it
then?"

"You George are a nosey sod at times, do you know that?"

"It has been said a few times but we have agreed that we will not
have any secrets between us, so come on then what was it?"

"Will you do me a favour please and just wait until we are eating
our meal before you ask me again?"

"I hate suspense but seeing as you have asked me so nicely then I
guess I will have to."

"Thank you George. Now I guess you have never been to this
restaurant that we are going to but you'll find that they have two
totally different menus. They not only do a full English style line
of food but also Chinese. The head chef married a Chinese
woman about five years ago and for the last three she has been
overseeing that side of the kitchen. I'll tell you one thing for
certain that it is the best Chinese food that I have ever tasted. She
believes in keeping it all original to their own country's methods
and style and is nothing like you buy from the average takeaway."

"I take it from that you will be eating Chinese then, you don't
have to use chopsticks do you as I have never managed to master
using them?"

"Most people that eat in there do tend to but it isn't forced on you.
When I first tried to use them I couldn't handle picking anything
up with them at first but you would be surprised at just how quick
you can get used to eating with them."

After what had been no more than a ten minute taxi journey they
were very soon being seated at the table that Tom had reserved
for them. As they were shown to there place in the restaurant it
soon became clear to George that Tom had informed the
restaurant that it was a belated birthday meal. There was not just a

birthday card from the restaurant on the table addressed to George but there was also a wrapped present.

"Tom, it's quite clear that you have eaten in here on a few occasions before with them all recognising you, but are you a real regular here with them having done me a present and a card?"

"I have been here on quite a few occasions and it was quite funny when I phoned up to book the table and told them it was to celebrate a birthday. They wanted to know what the young lady's name was so they could do the present. When I said that it was for a guy by the name of George and that he was someone very special to me the phone went dead for a few seconds. I think by the time the call was finished they had realised that it was a boyfriend that I was bringing here and not a girlfriend as it always has been in the past."

"So do I take it from what you just said that you have come out of the closet to them here?"

"I guess you could say that. What's more I felt really good about not hiding the fact that I would be dining with someone far more special to me than any of the girls that I have ever brought here before."

"That reminds me, what was it that you shoved into your pocket as we left the flat? You did say that you would tell me when we got here."

"No George, what I said, as I am sure you will remember was for you not to ask me until we have got our food. As yet we haven't even looked at the menu, although I know exactly what I will be ordering."

"Do you always order exactly the same thing then, don't you like trying different things?"

"I do and if you want Chinese can I suggest that between us we get the Chef's special for two. It will be a whole selection of different dishes and the great thing about doing it that way is that if there is something there that you don't like there is always plenty of other things to get stuck into."

"I will go with the expert's recommendation as I have never even stepped foot into a Chinese restaurant before let alone one as up market as this place is. I feel a little underdressed as most of the male customers are wearing collars and ties.”

“There is no reason at all for you not to feel relaxed, there is no dress code and you are quite welcome to eat in here in just a t-shirt and jeans if you want. That is one thing that I really do like about the place, it caters for all sorts as long as you can afford to settle the bill at the end of the night.”

With that Tom grabbed the waiter’s attention and having placed an order for food also requested that the drinks that he had ordered while booking the table be brought out.

Very soon after a bottle of champagne appeared at the table along with ice bucket and two flutes.

“Bloody hell Tom, I have never even tasted champagne and I’m not too sure if I will like it or not.”

“George, this is your night and if you find that you don’t like it then just tell me and I will get something else brought you in its place. I want tonight to be just right for you.”

“I am still itching to know what you picked up from out of the draw earlier.”

“I can see if I don’t reveal what it was that it will get in the way of you enjoying your meal. All I hope is that it doesn’t put you off your food when you find out.”

With that Tom reached into his pocket and placed a small box on the table directly in front of George. “Happy birthday darling”.

“Fuck me Tom. I know that we are getting on really great but I don’t need to open it to know that it is a ring case. Hadn’t we better wait for a while before we start thinking of stuff like getting engaged?”

“You idiot! If you open the box you’ll then see exactly what it is and having spoken to Clive the other day he informed me that it was something that you have always wanted, so I hope that it meets your approval. And if it doesn’t fit then we can get it adjusted no problem”

With that George opened the case to discover that it was indeed something that he had always wanted. With him having Irish heritage he had always wanted to be in a deep friendship with

someone where a cladder ring would be relevant. He was now
with Tom and from the way things were looking then he had
found that person. He picked the ring out and tried it on until
happy with finding a finger that it fitted spot on. It just so
happened to fit the best on the third finger of his left hand.
"Do you realise which finger you have got that on George?"
"I do now you have asked, but it fits better on this one than on
any of the others, do you think that the ring is trying to tell us
something Tom? The Irish do say that cladder rings have got
hidden powers."
"George if that is right then in the not too distant future I guess
that you will have to get it altered so it fits on a different finger as
that one will have other rings going on it."
"Thank you Tom, it's just what I have always wanted. I feel like
giving you a kiss but I guess that I had better wait until I get you
back inside the flat before I can do that."
"Why wait, if that is what you want to do?"
Tom couldn't believe what he had just said. He had virtually told
George that it would be okay for them to kiss right now if that is
what George wanted to do.
"If I thought for a moment that you were being serious Tom then
I would be out of this seat and round that side of the table kissing
you right now."
"So why the hell are you still sat down then?"
George could not quite believe what he was hearing coming out
of Tom's mouth. This was one of Tom's regular eating places and
it appeared as though he would be quite happy for George to go
and give him a kiss.
"You really do mean that you would not have a problem with me
coming round there and giving you a kiss. If you are quite sure
that it won't create you any sort of problem then I would love to."
"In that case stop being a silly arse and get round here."
George did as he had wanted and was soon kissing Tom on the
lips for all in the restaurant to see and Tom responded to it. For
Tom to allow this to take place it spoke more to George than

anything else, and once he had returned to his seat he then had to pass comment.

"Tom, I know that you have used that four letter word in my direction a couple of times and now I believe that it wasn't just words. For you to have allowed that to take place then I believe that you really have fallen for me in a very big way."

"Well George, when I said that I loved you it wasn't just words."

"That now is quite obvious from what has just taken place and I think it is about time I levelled with you and told you that I think that I am falling in love with you too. I know that if my parents heard me saying that then they would without doubt tell me to stop talking rubbish because we have only just met. If they did then I think I would have to ask them if they have never heard of the saying love at first sight."

The conversation was interrupted by a procession of plates and bowls being brought out to the table, each containing a different dish.

"Tom, this might sound crazy but what do we do?"

"Well I guess that there isn't really a right and a wrong way to eat this sort of meal as it seems as though it is acceptable to handle things just how you want. For me I just take a bit of a variety and once I have got more room on my plate I add something different. But as I say there doesn't seem to be any right and wrong way. I have watched various people in here to see how they deal with it and nearly everyone has taken a different approach. So I guess just tuck in and I hope that you enjoy it."

With that they both took a selection from a number of the bowls and started eating. George with the aid of conventional English cutlery while Tom was using authentic Chinese implements.

It was an hour and a half and the best part of three hundred pounds later when they got up from the table in order to get the taxi that was now waiting for them outside.

Once in the back of the cab it was George who spoke first.

"I know that it is really expensive to eat there but can I ask a favour, can we keep it as somewhere we go to when we are celebrating something special please? The only reason why I say

that is because I just think it would be nice to be able to say that
every time we have eaten there is for a specific reason."
"I'll go along with that. All I hope is that we have cause to go
there again in the not too distant future in order to celebrate our
next special occasion."
"That's a point, when is your birthday?"
"It was last month, but that wasn't exactly what I was thinking
about."
"I know you weren't, you were on about us going there when we
celebrate the fact that we have got engaged, and if I am right then
I don't think that it will be too long before we eat in there again."
Tom could not believe his own ears. He knew exactly how much
he had fallen for George but with what his partner had just said it
implied very strongly that George too was getting similar
feelings.
"So am I to make out of what you have just said that you don't
think it will be too long before we have cause to go in there again
then?"
"Well when you placed the ring box on the table and I jumped to
the idea that it contained an engagement ring then it got me
thinking. I have been trying to work out what I would have said if
that was what the box contained."
"And have you come up with any answer then young man?"
"I think that if it had been a proposal then I think that the ring
wouldn't have stayed in the box."
"I'd love to have seen your parents faces if they had been here to
hear what you have just said. For me though you have just
rounded off a perfectly good night in the best possible way that I
could imagine."
"No Tom, that comes when we get back to the flat. I think that the
sex between us tonight is going to be something very special, it
won't be a case of having sex it will be a case of making love."
"And what was that you were saying the other day to me about
me writing poetry?"

"Okay, so I was just a couple of days behind getting to the same place that you were at. So when do you think that we will be eating there again then Tom?"

Tom knew exactly what George was saying in his roundabout way, he was asking Tom just when was he going to pop the question. Tom for his part thought that he would turn the tables. "Well when you do get round to asking me George I know exactly what I will be saying in reply, so I guess it is down to when you are ready to ask me the question."

"You sly sod you. That has just put the ball in my court."

"There is nothing sly about it George, you know that if I thought that you would have said yes then that box would have contained a different ring. As far as I am concerned I am ready to make that sort of commitment to you right now, but if you are not ready just yet then there is no way that I intend putting you in a difficult position. When you feel that you are ready the answer will be waiting for you but I am not intending to try to rush you into something that you are not entirely comfortable with."

"Will we be able to book a table for four next Sunday so I can invite my parents along to celebrate with us?"

"Are you meaning what I think you are because if so you had better ask me the question first."

"You know exactly what I am saying and besides, I don't need to ask the question because you have already given me the answer."

They had got back home and Tom still had not managed to get George to actually ask him the question, although having said that he wouldn't book the table for the following weekend unless he had been asked directly.

They had arrived home just after ten in the evening and by midnight they were both fast asleep, knowing that they had an early start in the morning with the delivery expected. Both slept soundly wrapped in each other's arms.

They were at the house just before eight o'clock the Monday morning and very soon after they had got there so did the delivery. The guy delivering informed them that they were to expect a visitor very shortly, and when Tom enquired for more details he was informed that Marcos was due anytime now. This threw Tom, he hadn't phoned the boss yet to inform him that George was ready to be tested and Marcos didn't normally visit any of the houses unless there was a problem. Tom was just seeing Dave, the delivery guy off when he recognised the boss' car pulling to a halt. He waited in the doorway for Marcos to get out of his car and approach.

Chapter 9

"Morning boss, this is a bit of a surprise, I wasn't expecting to be seeing you today. Shall I get George to put the kettle on?"

"Morning Tom, I don't think that a drink is required but there is definitely a need for us to have a talk."

Tom was already beginning to panic. Had Clive gone and talked about everything to Marcos, and if so what was going to be the outcome? They went inside and Tom showed Marcos through to the lounge. George for his part was stood in the hallway not knowing if he was supposed to go into the lounge with them or not.

"George, I think that initially you can wait out here, but I think that you will need to get involved before long so don't go far." Marcos informed him.

As Tom and Marcos entered the lounge Marcos made sure that the door was closed firmly behind him before the two of them took a seat.

"So it all happened in here then Tom. I must say that you have done a good job of cleaning up. If Clive hadn't told me what had happened then I would have been none the wiser."

"So Clive has told you about what happened here on Saturday night then I assume. I am really sorry Marcos but my stupid brother gave me no option than to take the action I did."

"Well as it happens there doesn't appear to have been any fallout from what took place so although I don't approve of you doing the deed in the house it seems as no harm has come from it. Now I know that your brother was an addict and that they will do just about anything in order to get their next fix but how did he know where to find the gear?"

"He has been here a couple of times with his old dealer and when Clive has been putting the orders together then sometimes he had the customer going round the rooms with him. It was through Clive doing that Gavin knew exactly where to find what he wanted. When I collared him on his way out he was carrying that much it had got to have been the best part of ten grands worth of gear."

"Tom, I am not here to listen to your excuses. I am here because I want to know exactly what has been going on over the past week or so. Clive phoning me up out of the blue like he did wanting to be moved to a different house set alarm bells ringing. Then when he arranged for a police car to be parked out front it became clear that there was something going on between you and him. Now I want to know what exactly has been taking place. I know that there is no problem with any of your customers as the takings would reflect if there was something amiss on that front."

"I'm not going to lie to you Boss. Clive thought that he would forever have a hold over me having recorded what had taken place that evening. He got me over to his place the other Sunday and made me watch the film that he had got of what took place. The bottom line Marcos was that he then thought that he had got me under his thumb and for the first twenty four hours or so he had. I can go into detail with you if you want me to but I evened things up a bit and as a result Clive took the decision that it wouldn't work for us both to carry on working in the same house."

"Okay then Tom, I hear what you have told me and to a degree I understand, but why was it Clive decided to move and not yourself?"

"Quite simple if being totally open with you Boss, I gave him no choice."

"Now I am really curious. Tell me more."

"Well he had recorded the footage from when I murdered Gavin and was using it to dictate everything. As a result I thought of a way to get one over him. He helped me get rid of the body and before he had a chance of deleting the footage I had saved it onto disc. That brought me about even because there was no way that he could then either go running to the police or tell you without himself being involved. That still was not quite enough to have over him so between George and myself we came up with a plan

of what we were going to do. I believe you are aware that George
is gay and that Clive used to abuse him from before he was of age
to have sex. Well it turned out that with the hold that Clive had
over me he thought that he could get away with doing the same to
me. Well to cut a long story short until the Sunday after I had
done the deed with my brother Clive forced me to have gay sex
with him. I will add that until that point in time I was totally
straight and the thought of having sex with another guy was the
furthest thing from my mind. The end result was that I actually
enjoyed the whole experience and Clive got George to come
round in order for them both to take advantage of me. Well
George and I instantly hit it off and I guess the rest is history."
"Well thank you for your honesty Tom, I had a feeling it must
have been something along those lines but needed to make sure.
Unfortunately, I couldn't get all the details out of Clive before we
said goodbye."
"When you say Goodbye, that sounds final. Have you sacked him
by any chance?"
"Not in the way that you are thinking Tom. When I found out that
it had been him behind the police car being parked up outside
here I needed to have a serious talk with him. Well it turns out
that reading between the lines there was so much ill feeling
housed by him towards you that I needed to ensure that things
were stopped right there and then."
"I am probably going to sound really naive in asking what I am
about to but does that mean that Clive is no longer with the
organisation?"
"He is no longer breathing let alone being part of things any
more. With him having got the police involved with this place
then there was only ever going to have been the one outcome. I
thought that you would have known that from the outset."
"I guess I was just hoping that it hadn't had to go that far. Alright
me and Clive didn't exactly see eye to eye on some things but I
still would not have wished him dead."

"Well as far as I am concerned he got exactly what he asked for. Now changing the subject a little has George told you anything about me."

"Again I respect you too much to start lying to you. Yes he has told me about what happened a couple of years ago but believe me boss that it will never be spoken of by me other than between the three of us. I don't know if you are aware of the fact but as of yesterday George has moved in with me and we are not only together but although it is all very fast we are getting on really well. Having said that though none of our customers here have any idea as to me having turned from straight to being totally gay let alone that I am in a relationship with George. That was something that I was going to be asking you about."

"What, so you were going to ask me if it would be alright for you to let our customers know that you two were together."

"I guess so. Please don't get me wrong, we don't mix business with pleasure and there is no way that I intend things between the two of us to affect the takings here for one moment."

"I'll put all my cards on the table Tom and then we will all know exactly where we stand. I have no problem with you and George shagging each other if that is what you both want to do. That is entirely up to the two of you. What I will say is that in addition I have no problem who knows that you are together on the one condition, that the takings here don't suffer as a result. If you want to make it public knowledge then I respect you for it in a way but if it means the takings here start dropping off then you will both be out of the house in an instant. Do I make myself clear?"

"Perfectly Boss, and there is no way that I will allow that to happen and thank you. I'll be honest with you Marcos I think that me and George will be together for quite some time and the thought of having to try and hide the fact that we are together in more than just work wise would have done my head in. I get on well with all of the customers that use us and there are a couple that I am not too sure as to how they will take the news but with all the others there will not be an issue. Regarding George I ought

to tell you that I was intending contacting you today because he
really has picked up the job fast and I think that even you will be
shocked with what he already knows about things here. I know
you always give new guys a test before you put them onto full
pay and I firmly believe that whatever you ask him you will hear
the right reply.”
“You say that but from what I can recall there was one really
huge stumbling block that he would have to address first before
anything.”
“If you are talking about the fact that he is no good with figures
then that was what I thought until he revealed the fact that he has
no problem in that area at all. It was something that he had grown
up pretending so he had an easier life at school. It turned out that
he is by far better with maths than I am and I thought that I was
pretty good with numbers. Each day he has got the total of the
day’s takings spot on.”
“Well in that case let’s get the youngster in here to see what he
has to say for himself. But before we do that I ought to tell you
that as of today you will be on full wages with the takings here
not having been affected with the departure of Clive.”
“Thank you boss, I thought that I wouldn’t go onto full rate for at
least a couple of weeks if not longer.”
“You should know by now Tom that I am a firm believer in
rewarding those that prove themselves to me and you have
already done that. To have killed your own brother in order to
have protected my stock is good enough for me. Now do you
want to grab George for me and then as soon as I have spoken
with him then I will get on my way in order for you to get the
delivery all away before you open up.”
With that Tom went to find George and found him up in one of
the bedrooms putting the new stock away.
“Marcos wants to see you George, and before you start getting
nervous there is nothing wrong. In fact far from it.”
On the two of them entering the lounge Tom thought it wise to
inform Marcos of what George had been doing while him and the
boss had been talking.

"Marcos, you know what you were saying about you having to get on your way to allow us time to get the delivery away, well George here has already done it for me."

"So George, now we both know what has gone on in the past but that as far as I am concerned is history and not to be discussed. Tom has already informed me that you have told him everything but I would hope that you trust each other enough for you both to be totally open with each other and I have no problem with that. Now Tom tells me that instead of you having real difficulty where numbers are concerned that is not the case, is that right George?"

"It is boss, it has just been something that has been with me for so long that I always just carried on pretending to be a bit thick at maths. You can test me if you want and I believe that no matter what you ask that I will come up with the right answer if that doesn't sound too cock sure of myself."

With George sounding so confident Marcos gave him a few fictitious orders to work out the value of, and with George having got the total figure worked out faster than even Marcos could achieve, even with paper and pen, the boss was satisfied that there was no problem in that department.

"So George, Tom has been telling me that you are now an item, now how do you think that things would be able to carry on here if you were to split up?"

"It isn't going to happen Marcos so it's not worth me even trying to give you an answer to that question. I appreciate that we have only known each other just over a week but it has been love at first sight for both of us and we have started things off as we mean to go on. There are no secrets between us, which is why I had to tell him about what had taken place a couple of years ago. I also trust Tom enough to know that it won't go any further no matter what. He has also told me about things that have happened in his life that he felt that I should be aware of."

"Am I right in thinking Tom, that you have told him what we were talking about?"

"Marcos, George knows all about what took place here the other Saturday night with my brother. As George so rightly said we have started off the way we intend things to go on and have nothing hidden from each other."

"Right, I am happy with everything here and as of today you are both on full pay. Now before I go George is there any chance that I can shag you just for old times' sake?"

"I would prefer it if you didn't please Marcos." Tom interrupted,, not happy with what his boss had just suggested in the slightest.

"Good man Tom, that was the reaction that I was hoping to hear. I assure you that I only said it in jest, besides, I am sure that George will have told you that he is now far too old for my liking."

"The only reason why Tom dived in so rapidly then boss is that he was frightened that I would be getting something that he wouldn't." George laughed.

Having taken a quick glance of his watch Marcos prepared to leave, before doing so though there was one large bombshell that he would drop on then before he went.

"Tom, I know that you have only got a small flat along the road. Why don't the two of you try and work out how you can stash all the stock downstairs here and then if you did that then nobody would ever need to go upstairs here, so your private area wouldn't be violated."

"Are you saying for us to move in here Marcos or am I miss understanding what you just said?"

"Well if the two of you did move in here then there would be much more room for you both than with the place you are currently in Tom. Besides which it will give the house better security with you living here, especially with you now having to carry greater stock levels."

"Do you mind if I don't take you straight up on the offer Marcos as I think that it is something that George and I should talk through before I commit us to anything."

"Do as you both please but the offer is there. Now I really do need to get on my way because there is a house in Leamington that should have been getting a new boss running it from today but that is not going to be happening now."

"Have you got shut of Clive then?"

"George I'll tell you all about it after Marcos has left as he needs to get on his way and he has already wasted time here."

"On the contrary Tom, I have not wasted any time here. I am really pleased with the way you have got the takings up and on how things are running here. As long as you bringing certain things out into the open doesn't effect things too much them I will not have a problem."

"Just one question though Marcos, when the two of us get hitched do you want an invite to the wedding?"

"Bloody hell George and I thought that it was Tom that was rushing things a little. Are the two of you getting on that well then that getting wed is something that you have already talked through?"

"It is Boss, but you didn't answer my question, will you come to our wedding?"

"As long as there is some decent grub laid on at the reception then it would be rude of me not to."

"I think that with the money that you are paying us there shouldn't be a problem with us getting decent caterers in to do the food side of things."

Tom was really relieved that there appeared to be nothing bad between Marcos and George with what had taken place between them in the past and that they were able to just leave history behind. He was also very pleased to hear George talking about them getting married so openly as it eased his fears that he was rushing George a little.

With Marcos having left the house and with there still being the best part of half an hour before they were due to open Tom decided to bring up the conversation that hadn't quite been concluded from the previous evening.

"So George, are you going to give me a reason to try and book a table for four at that restaurant then or what?"

"I thought that we had decided on that last night."

"No George, the way things ended was that I had said that before I was going to phone them then you would have to ask me a certain question, and as yet I haven't heard you ask it."

"Bloody hell Tom, are you going to get engaged to me next weekend or what?"

"If that is you asking me to then the answer is yes."

"In that case I suggest that as soon as the place opens you had better get booking that table."

"I think before I give them a call you had better check that your parents are free and that they will come. It might be that they think we are rushing things to such an extent that they say that there is no way that they will come along."

With that George pulled his mobile out of his trouser pocket and started making the call.

"I know full well that they will give me grief about it but I am pretty sure that they will still come even if they think we are being too hasty."

By the time George had finished making the comment to Tom the call was being answered.

Tom stood there listening to George's side of the conversation and it was clear that his mother was giving him a tough time, but it soon became apparent that they would be coming along.

By the time George had finished the call to his mother Tom was already on the phone to the restaurant in order to try and book a table for four the following Sunday evening.

"Well that's the table booked. You'll have to phone your mother back and tell her that the reservation is for seven o'clock and that if they are happy for us to arrange it we will organise a taxi to pick them up from their house at 6:15pm which will give enough time."

"I know that my dad will automatically expect to drive over."

"Well if he does that then it could spoil the evening for him because he will be thinking about not having the next drink because of being over the limit. If we organise a taxi for them then they will have no excuse not to celebrate by having more than just the one drink."

"I'll phone my dad up tonight when he has got back from work and tell him that the taxi is already arranged and that he hasn't got a choice. I know that if I just say that we will arrange one then he will tell us not to bother and that he will drive."

"That's all sorted then. Now I think it must be about time that we took the bolt off the front door and get ready to receive our first customer of the day."

"There is one problem that I have got though Tom."

"What's that?"

"When do I get paid because somehow I have got to buy you a ring before Saturday and until I get paid I haven't got any money."

"What day last week did you start working here George?"

"I think it was on Tuesday after I had been over to Warwick to pick my stuff up. Why?"

"Because young man we take the previous weeks wages out of the Monday takings. So on my reckoning you will have five hundred pounds due tonight."

"That isn't right Tom. I was on five hundred a week which is six days and I only did four and a half so that works out to be £375."

"Who's the boss here George?"

"You are of course but if you pay me for the full week then if Marcos picks up on it then he will think that you are manipulating things in my favour because we are an item. I don't want us to give Marcos any reason to think that we aren't doing things exactly right."

"I hear what you are saying George but I can assure you that Marcos would say exactly the same thing, the firm doesn't bother with half weeks, or docking your wages if for some reason you have to have a day off to go somewhere important. Everyone in all the houses get treated the same and if you have worked more than fifty percent of the week then you get the full week's wage."

"In that case Tom as long as we don't need a delivery tomorrow morning can we go into the city centre because I think we have got rings to buy?"

"As long as we don't need a delivery I can't see any reason why not George, now why don't you put the kettle on and make us both a drink while I go and unlock."

"There is something else that we need to discuss though sometime during the day Tom."

"I know there is, are we going to move into upstairs here?"

With that George headed for the kitchen in order to make them both a drink while Tom unlocked the house. In the twenty minutes before having the first knock at the door they had been talking through the possibility of moving into the place and were both of the same opinion that with upstairs having four bedrooms they could convert two of them into living areas.

"So why are you talking of only changing two of the rooms from bedrooms then George and not three?"

"I just thought that if we kept a spare bedroom then we could have visitors stay over if the occasion arose."

"There is no way that can happen. I know that Marcos would immediately be on our case if we were to do that."

"It was a bit stupid of me even thinking it, I had overlooked the fact that we are sitting on thousands of pounds worth of illegal substances."

The day went as smooth as it could have and Tom even plucked up the courage to tell three of their regular customers about him and George being an item.

Dave had received the news really well and had told Tom in no uncertain terms that although he himself was totally straight that he had always thought that Tom could do a hell of a lot better than the girls that were normally round him. Dave had gone on to wish them both all the best and went as far to say that when the happy day came round that he would be pissed off if he were not to get an invite to the wedding.

It was after the front door had been locked that George asked Tom if he had been keeping a record of what they had turned over for the day.

"To be truthful now I am confident that you will be I haven't been bothering. At a guess I would think it must be getting on towards the hundred again, but I am sure you are just about to tell me exactly."

"Well I think that going into the centre in the morning will not be on the table because I am pretty sure we will need a delivery tomorrow."

"I'd guess at about ninety, possibly just over."

"You are way out Tom, I make it one one four fifty five."

"You're being serious as well aren't you? I knew we had moved some gear but didn't think we had broken the hundred grand again. If you are right then we had better see what we need to get delivered in the morning because we will no way have enough here for another day if it carries on like it is."

"And what was that Marcos was saying about being concerned about the takings dropping when the guys started finding out that we are shagging each other."

"Don't forget though George that I have only told those that I thought would be cool hearing it. There are three that I have got a feeling will not be coming back here once they hear the news. Okay they are only small players but between them they do shift getting on for a hundred a week and that is a hit that will show in the figures."

"But it isn't like them changing from going to Sainsbury's and moving to Tesco's is it. They can't get this stuff from anywhere."

"George I think you would be shocked if you knew just how easy it was for guys to find alternative suppliers. Don't fool yourself for one moment that we are the only ones in the area that they can buy the stuff from, I know that there are at least another two houses not too far away that they can buy gear from."

Tom went on to enlighten George that there were other houses in the locality that could fill any gap that developed. Admittedly the gear was generally not of such a high standard and to Tom's knowledge the prices were slightly higher but if any of their customers really took offence that they were gay then they would soon change.

"I think that you are worrying about nothing Tom, If our gear is better and cheaper than they would be stupid to go somewhere else just because of our private lives."

"You may think that but once it becomes general knowledge
about you and me then I think we will lose at least two or three
regulars."
George thought differently and they agreed to disagree and wait
to see just what happened over the following few days.

Everything was going fine both at the house and with their
relationship. They had discussed at length as to if they were going
to move along the road and make their home in the upstairs of the
house but as yet they had still not come to a final decision. Yes,
the place would be a lot bigger than what they had got at the
moment but if they were ever to be given the sack then they
would then become homeless overnight. With the fact that
Marcos had already told them quite clearly that if the takings at
the house were to drop because of their private lives that they
wouldn't remain there it was something that they were in no hurry
to rush into.
It was eight o'clock on the Thursday morning when Tom's
mobile started ringing, waking the two of them up. Tom answered
it, still half asleep.
In a milli-second he realised that it was the boss on the other end
and knew straight away that for him to be calling so early that it
could only be spelling bad news.
Tom lay there listening to what Marcos was telling him saying
very little in reply to what he was hearing. It turned out that
Marcos had been informed by inside sources that the tip where
Tom had dumped Gavin's body was going to be the focus of a
police search as of nine o'clock this morning. Marcos asked Tom
outright if that had been where the body had been dumped.
Having informed Marcos that it had been it was the next comment
that Marcos came out with that set the alarm bells ringing and at
quite a loud volume.
"Is there anything there that could possibly link Gavin's body
back to you Tom? If so then I suggest that you tell me right now
so I am able to get someone in to cover the house because if there

is then I strongly suggest that you get miles away from here and keep your head down."

"The answer to that Marcos is that I don't really know. Do you know how long DNA traces can remain out in the elements because I think that would be the only way that it could be tracked back to me?"

"So what you are saying is that there could be a trace back."

"As I say Marcos if DNA can still be found then there might be a chance because obviously I handled not just the body but the carpet and sheeting that we covered it with."

"Right Tom now think hard before you answer the next question, at any time while you were handling your brother's body did you cut yourself? The reason I ask is even if DNA cannot be found then if there are any blood deposits on him that are not his then that will give the police a good solid lead as to the murderer."

"I honestly can't think that I did cut myself and I'm pretty sure that if I had I would have remembered."

"Okay then Tom, let's leave things as they stand for the time being and we will just have to wait and see what transpires."

"Just one question Marcos, do you know if the reason behind the police search at the tip is directly related to Gavin or could they be investigating something else?"

"I don't know the answer to that and to a large degree it doesn't matter. If they find Gavin's body there, which they will then they will automatically investigate into how it got there and who was responsible. With it only happening a couple of weeks ago I would think that they will soon be able to identify the body. With you being his brother then they are bound to be coming in your direction to ask questions even if they don't think that you were behind his murder."

"You don't think that Clive could be behind the police interest in the site do you?"

"That I don't know Tom. I do know that he had a very deep rooted dislike for George and you after what had taken place but as to if he had put any sort of safety net in place if he were to disappear then I have not a clue. Anyway as I say stay there and open up as usual and as soon as I hear anything then I will let you know."

Marcos hung up leaving Tom to start explaining the phone call to George.

"So from what you have just told me then it sounds as though you will be pulled in by the police just as soon as they can confirm the identity of your brother. What happens then?"

"If I knew the answer to that one George I would gladly tell you but I don't. All I do know is that if there is any way that they can find my DNA at the scene then I will have some very big questions to answer."

"I heard you mention to Marcos about if Clive was behind the police interest at the tip, what did he say about that?"

"He is as much in the dark as we are on that front. Yes he does get inside information as to what the police are up to but I don't think that they will give him all the details, and if Marcos had started asking too many questions then it would have pointed to the fact that he knew something about it."

"I can understand that but where does that leave us?"

"You mean where does that leave me. There is no way that you will be dragged into things because at the time that it happened I hadn't even met you. I can't help but think that Clive must be behind it in some way or another."

"If you think back to when we first put the recordings together of him we told him that we had got a couple of people looking after a copy and if anything happened to us that the recordings would become public knowledge. Do you think that he did the same before Marcos got him taken out of circulation?"

"Well if that was the case then I would have thought that by now the police would already have paid me a visit. If they had got a copy of the recording then they would not have had to wait until they had discovered the body before they dragged me in."

"Just one question though Tom, I know that you haven't been living here for long, would the police know where you are now living?"

"I would have thought so because I have notified the council as well as both the electricity and gas suppliers that I now live here and am responsible for the bills."

"In that case then I think that we are worrying about nothing. I bet you the police had received information about something completely different that has been dumped there."

"That George does not matter in the slightest. Even if they are going there looking for something completely different when they discover Gavin's body they will start a murder investigation."

Although it was still quite early there was no way that either of them were going to be able to get back to sleep and with things as they were sex was not on the menu either. As a result they both got up with George heading straight for the kitchen in order to cook them both a full breakfast.

Almost as soon as they had sat down at the breakfast bar Tom's phone started ringing for a second time this morning. He looked at the caller display and saw that it was from one of Marcos' numbers, he answered it fearing the worse.

It was Marcos calling to inform Tom that he had received further information from his inside sources and that the police were going to the tip on a completely unrelated matter from what had been told him. It still didn't mean that Tom was in the clear but it did imply that it hadn't been anything to do with Clive, so Marcos thought that Tom had got nothing to worry about.

"But what if there are traces of my DNA found on Gavin?" Tom asked his boss, still very concerned.

"He is your brother so of course there will be DNA matches but they will not be able to prove anything, so if I were you I would just relax and if the police do make contact then just sound surprised and deny any knowledge of his death."

With Marcos having hung up on him again Tom started making his way into the kitchen in order to bring George up to date with developments. He had only just reached the doorway when there came a loud knocking on the front door downstairs. Tom went straight to the window that overlooked the road and saw that there were two police cars parked up blocking the road and with lights flashing.

In an instant George was at his side and was also looking out of the window.

"I guess they are here to talk to you Tom, what are you going to tell them?"

"I don't know George. I'll go down and open the door but you stay up here. If you see that I am going with them then can you phone Marcos up straight away so he can arrange for someone to be at the house with you this morning until I get back."

Tom didn't wait for George to give him any sort of reply and was heading down the stairs. George carried on looking through the window to try and see what was happening. To his displeasure he saw Tom being led out to one of the cars handcuffed. The next thing he was aware of were four officers entering the flat through the door that Tom had left ajar.

"And you wouldn't happen to be George Sharp by any chance?" The leading officer enquired on seeing George.

"I'm George why?"

"I have a warrant for your arrest."

"Why? What am I supposed to have done?"

"Accessory to murder for starters, and we have a warrant to search the flat. So if you sit down right there and keep your hands where they can be seen."

With George doing as instructed he watched as three of the officers went rummaging through various cupboards and draws.

"I'm glad you are here because we were going to take a trip over to Warwick to pick you up just as soon as we had finished here." The officer informed George.

George's only interest at the moment was in watching to see what the others were doing. He knew where Tom kept his gun and when the one policeman went to the cupboard in question he soon called over to the officer that had been addressing George.

"I've got it Sir, it's in here."

Just as in the movies George watched as the gun was picked up with the help of a pencil so as not to contaminate the weapon. It was then dropped into a clear polythene bag but not until after the chamber had been sniffed.

"It doesn't smell as it has been fired within the last day or two."

"Well from the time and date on the film it probably is still the weapon used as it would have been at least a week ago when the incident took place."

Having discovered what they were after George was now taken out to the other car that had been parked outside and once in the rear seat it pulled away.

At the police station both Tom and George went through the initial searches before being put into separate cells while waiting for duty solicitors to become available, at which time they would both be interviewed. Tom for his part had got nothing that he was really able to say as it immediately became clear that they had received a copy of the recording of Tom shooting his brother and as such there was nothing that he could say that would have helped. With George though he was standing by the fact that he had not even met Tom at the time of the shooting so therefore how could they accuse him of being an accessory to the fact. His solicitor had told him to keep to the same line of defence as it was the truth.

"Right then Mr Sharp perhaps you would like to explain this then." The interviewing officers said as he started a disc running on the TV monitor in the room.

George watched in horror as he saw both himself and Tom talking to Clive, during which Clive had asked if George knew that he was shacking up with a murderer. The film was from the house and was at the time that both Tom and George had basically forced Clive to phone Marcos.

"So are you still telling me that you didn't know anything about the shooting because from this I would say that you are lying through your teeth."

"Can I have some time alone with my client please?" The solicitor intervened.

Very shortly it was just George and his brief in the room.

"I asked you if you knew about the shooting and you told me no. now at the time I did say that I needed to know the truth otherwise things might go wrong. Now I have got a really big problem. You have already lied under caution and as such it will not go in your favour. I am afraid that no matter what route we take there will be no way that you are going to walk out of here shortly. If you had told me everything then we could have approached things from a different angle and as a result I could probably have got you bail, but now that looks very unlikely."

"I am sorry for having lied but I had forgotten all about that conversation that we'd had and didn't think that there would be any way that they could ever find out that I knew for certain."

"Well we'll see what we can do Mr Sharp but as I say I think that you getting bail will not be an option, and you will probably be held until your court case comes round."

"And what exactly is likely to happen?"

"Initially you will be up in the local magistrates court tomorrow, morning, but with the gravity of the charge against you it will be referred to Crown Court straight away."

"Why will it have to go to Crown Court?"

"Because Mr Sharp you will appear before a judge and jury and when found guilty the sentence will be such that a magistrates court would not be able to proceed. You see Mr Sharp you are probably looking at somewhere in the region of a five year sentence which is far greater than a magistrates court can issue on anyone."

"So just because I was told after the event of what had happened I will be sent to prison for five years?"

"That isn't exactly what I said. The sentence will probably be for that long however with you being so young and with the fact that you have a clear history the sentence will more than likely be reduced to something along the lines of three years. At a guess you will have to serve half of that period in prison and then the remaining eighteen months out on licence during which time if you commit any offence you will be immediately returned to prison to serve the rest of the sentence"

"And what is likely to happen to Tom?"
"Of course I cannot discuss another case with you officially however what I can say is that first degree murder can have as much as a life sentence depending on the circumstances and if it had been a pre-meditated act."
"His twat of a brother was a drug addict and Tom court him steeling a load of stuff in order to feed his addiction. If Tom had allowed him to have just walked away with the stash then it would have been Tom's body that the police would have been looking for."
"Well the police did inform me that they thought that your partner did run some sort of drug operation locally however they haven't been able to get any evidence to support their thinking. Now if Tom were to tell the police where the drugs are being dealt from then that might well go in his favour. Or if you were to tell me then perhaps I can do a trade with the police on both of your cases. You never know the police might see getting that property raided as such a big thing for them that they may well be prepared to reduce the charges against you both."
It was now that George remembered one of the first things that Tom had told him when he was first offered the job. Tom had told him that if the shit ever did hit the fan then George would be far better off spending time inside rather than opening his mouth to the police regarding Marcos' operations.
"Well if Tom does have anything to do with the distribution of drugs then it is news to me. I have only known the guy for less than a couple of weeks but if he was a drug dealer then I would have thought that I would have witnessed something that would give your comment some sort of credit. Did the police find any illegal substances in our flat because if they did then Tom must have hidden them well as I have never seen anything in the place."
"To my knowledge after the two of you were brought in then police sniffer dogs were used and from the information the police have given me there were no drugs found."

"They weren't found simply because there aren't any there. As I say I have only known Tom for a few days but if he was anything to do with drugs then there would have been no way that I would ever have moved in with him. I hate drugs."

"There are a lot of people who don't take drugs that supply them I can assure you, so that is not a very valid point that you have raised."

They continued talking until the solicitor pointed out the fact that the police would want to continue their interview. He pointed out that it was up to George as to how he wanted to progress but it was the solicitor's advice for George to come clean as it would go in his favour when in court.

"Just one question, has Tom admitted to the murder because if he hasn't if I tell the police that I knew then it will be dropping Tom right in it."

"With the evidence that the police have on him it would have been totally stupid if he had tried to deny that the incident had taken place. I don't know and don't need to know if you have seen the footage but there is no way that there would be any point in Tom denying that he did kill his brother as the evidence is so strong."

"So are you telling me that Tom has admitted to the police that he did it then?"

The solicitor again avoided answering the question directly which led George to think one thing.

"He hasn't admitted it has he. I thought that the solicitor was supposed to be on the accused person's side and here you are trying to trick me into dropping my boyfriend right in it. I don't know how any of this stuff works but I do know one thing and that is that I want a different solicitor appointed to represent me. As far as I am concerned you are clearly working on behalf of the police rather than either me or Tom."

"I am not in here representing Tom I am here to represent you, and my advice is that you tell the police everything you know otherwise you will be spending some years inside a prison."

"Don't threaten me. As I have said I do not want you to be
representing me, now can you organise for me to be allocated a
different solicitor because I think I have said all that I intend to
you."
With that the solicitor accepted defeat and very shortly after
George was being taken back to the cell to wait until there was a
different solicitor available.

Chapter 10

Both Tom and George were detained at the police station until the following morning where to both of their surprise they were each informed that they had been allocated a new solicitor who would be speaking to them prior to them being taken from the police station to the court.

When Tom met the new brief it transpired that he had been taken on to represent them both by an unknown person, and the brief was able to inform him that all expenses were being covered, also that from his thinking they would both be given bail. While he was talking to Tom he did say that with George there would probably not be any bond money to be found but with Tom's offence being of such a serious nature there would without doubt be a financial sum required to secure his bail. It was on hearing this that Tom immediately thought that with him having very little in the way of savings that he would end up having to spend the time between court cases in prison. It was to his joy that the solicitor informed him that all expenses on that front would also be covered. Tom could only think of one person that could be behind the newly enlisted solicitor and to his mind it had to be Marcos.

When it came to George meeting the brief the information given him was very much the same as had been told Tom with the one big difference, the solicitor let it slip that he had been taken on by a female. This really did throw George as the only one that came to mind was his mother and there was no way that his parents would have been financially able to take up the costs involved. Although he did try and get more information the brief was being very tight lipped as to who was paying him.

The two of them were taken to the court building in separate vehicles and held in cells until their time in the dock came. As had been predicted they both were referred to Crown Court and would be notified of their appearance dates in the coming days until which time they were given bail, Tom with having a twenty thousand pound price tag linked to his. Although George had been through his appearance before Tom had been brought up from the cells the solicitor instructed him to head straight off home and that as long as Tom got bail then he would be along not too much later. George had wanted to go in and listen to Tom's case being heard but the brief advised very strongly against him doing so.

By early afternoon George entered the flat and was shocked to find it in such a mess, it was clear that the police had carried out a very thorough search of all rooms and had not bothered to tidy up after them. As he made his way round the flat he noticed that Tom's computer was still in place and by the look of things the police hadn't bothered looking at it. He then checked the draw below it and was relieved to find the two discs still present. Okay the police had been given a copy of Tom actually committing the murder of his brother but if they had got hold of this one they would also have seen sexual acts taking place between Tom, himself, and the deceased Clive. It was on thinking about Clive that he wondered how the police had got a copy of the recording. As he started working on getting the place tidied, returning things back in draws and cupboards there were two, three things that were going through his mind. Who had been the female that was behind the new solicitor? How had the police got the recording? But the most important of them all was how was Tom getting on and would he be returning home?

George had to wait until just turned half past four before he heard anything regarding his partner, and it was the news that he was hoping to hear. He received a call from the brief who informed him that Tom had just that moment got into a taxi and should be back home within no more than fifteen minutes. It wasn't until the call was over that George first started thinking about if it was worth him sticking around or would he be better off just packing his stuff and making his way back home to his parents. At the end of the day from what the solicitor had told him there was no way that Tom would be on the scene once his court appearance at

Crown came. Something else came to mind that he hadn't given a thought, what was happening with the house down the road? Would Marcos have got replacements in running it or would he have just pulled all the drugs out of there and closed the place down. If the police knew about the shooting then there was a good chance that they would also have been told as to where it had taken place. He wished at this point in time that Tom had got a television because then he would have been able to check out the local news to see if anything about the case was being reported. George also wished that last time he replaced his mobile that he had saved up and bought one that had got internet facilities on it rather than just having the basic one that he had. He was still deep in thought when he heard the front door shutting.

"So you were given bail then."

Tom had only just walked through their flat's door when the comment hit him.

"Yes, but whoever is behind the solicitor has had to put up a huge load of money as assurance. How are you anyway? I have been worried sick about how you were doing and was praying that you didn't end up saying anything about the house and Marcos to them. I take it that you haven't said anything to either the police or the solicitor?"

"I remembered the first thing that you taught me Tom, and that was that it would be better for me to spend time inside than open my mouth regarding the operation."

"So where do we go from here then George, I guess that the brief has told you that I am pleading guilty and that I am likely to go away for quite a few years."

"He hadn't told me that you had entered a guilty plea but from what he had said it sounded as though it would be pointless for you to have tried denying anything. That recording was so clear there was no way that you could have convinced a blind man that it hadn't been you that had pulled the trigger."

"So as I just said where do we go from here George?"

When Tom had walked through the door he had hoped that he would have been greeted with a hug and kiss but with George keeping his distance Tom was thinking that it was obviously all over between the two of them.

"I was just thinking the same thing when you came back. It did cross my mind if I would be better off heading back to Warwick and back home, that is if my parents want anything to do with me now I have got into this mess."

"And it is all my fault George. What can I say because the word sorry simply isn't enough to make up for what I have got you mixed up in."

Tom was on the verge of tears. He knew very well that George was just an innocent party in all this yet at the end of the day might well end up having to spend at least some time in prison purely as a result of them getting together.

"The saying 'shit happens' springs to mind but it isn't as if I didn't know about what had gone on between you and your brother. If you had kept it a secret from me then there would have been no way that I would still have been here. As it is I knew what had taken place and if being fair to you it was me that decided to stick around. No one forced me to fall in love with you Tom it was just something that happened, and now I don't know quite what to do."

"Can I ask you something please George?"

"Go ahead, I'm listening."

"Can I come over there and give you a hug and a kiss please?"

"I don't know Tom, at the moment I just don't know what I want to happen from now on. Don't get me wrong I wasn't lying when I said that I love you and I know that you love me too, but if we keep together then it will be even harder for us both when you have to go inside for years."

It was on hearing George's reply that the tears started flowing, initially just from Tom's eyes but he was soon joined by George doing the same. It was only now that their true feelings were being allowed to be shown that they drew close to each other and embraced. There was no attempt to kiss from either party but as far as Tom was concerned at least while they were hugging there was a chance that things between them might survive.

"I would do anything to change the situation George but it is what it is and I guess that at the end of the day it is a decision that you have to make without me trying to influence you."

"Has the solicitor said anything to you about how long you are likely to get?"

"Well the duty solicitor was talking about me looking at a minimum of twelve years and having to spend a good six at the very least inside, the new guy though thinks that he will be able to get it right down to below ten. He did say that he was hoping to get me facing no more than eight years with just half of them actually being locked up. He did point out though that a lot depends on the judge at the time. He said that with my brother having been a drug addict that it would work in my favour as the jury would be sympathetic towards me having to come to his aid for the last few years. From the way he was talking it sounds as though he is going to approach it that I had been pushed to the limit by Gavin and that when I pulled the trigger I was not in a stable mental state. He asked me a few times if I have ever been under the doctor for any sort of mental health issues."

"And have you?"

"Not for years. I did go through a spell some years ago of getting really depressed and at the time my family doctor referred me to some sort of shrink that did actually seem to help at the time."

"So when you say depression just how bad were you, was it at the stage where you were thinking of doing the ultimate?"

"You mean was I feeling like taking my own life, I guess that there were occasions where I was that down but as I say that was years ago and I haven't suffered from the same for what must be well over five years now."

"When you first started talking about it and saying that it was years ago I thought that you were talking about when you were just a kid, I didn't think that it would have been just five years ago. Did you tell the solicitor that it was so recent?"

"Yes he knows and he even asked for me to sign a document to allow him to get details from my doctor. That is what makes me think that he is going to say something along the lines that at the time I wasn't of a sound state of mind."

"I think they call it diminished responsibility or something along those lines. If he does go down that route though is there not a risk that you get sent to some sort of institute for the mentally unstable instead of prison?"

"Well if you stick around here then you will be able to ask him that tomorrow because he will be coming round to talk to me about eleven o'clock."

"You say if I stick around, I guess that is something that we both have got a say in. not only have I got to want to stay but you have also got to want me to."

"George I'll tell you right now that there is no way that I want you to leave, but as I said earlier it has got to be your decision."

"I haven't got a clue why, but I guess that I might as well stick around to see how things go."

"I hope it is because you love me. If you want I will sleep in the armchair until you have decided exactly what you are wanting. I am not about to try and force myself on you."

"If you are going to be sleeping in the armchair then I might as well start packing my bags now."

"Does that mean that you want me to be in bed with you then?" Tom asked, unsure of what George was actually saying and frightened of jumping to the wrong idea.

"If I wanted to spend the nights on my own then I would have packed my bags and have gone by now instead of having spent the last three hours tidying this place up. You would have died if you had seen the state that the police left it in. one good thing though is it doesn't look as if they have touched your computer and I checked to make sure that the disks are still in the draw and they are."

"How bad was the place then if you have spent three hours cleaning up?"

"If I said that at least half the contents of every draw and cupboard were strewn across the floor I wouldn't be exaggerating. It was a right mess."

"I wish I had been here because I would have taken some photos of how they left it and asked the solicitor to put in an official complaint."

"Oh yes and that really would have been good, the last thing I think you need to do is to start pissing the police off otherwise they might really go to town when it comes to you being in court. Wouldn't it be better to try and keep as much in their good books as you can?"

"I suppose you are right. Changing the subject have you had anything to eat because I haven't had anything accept a single cereal bar first thing this morning, and a cup of what they said was coffee but it was more like dish water."

"Eating has been the last thing on my mind. All afternoon there have just been the same three questions going round and round in my mind."

"And what were those?"

"How you were getting on, how did the police get the recording and the other thing that is bugging me is who is it that has got us the solicitor?"

"Well I think that I have got the answer to all the questions or at least I can guess. As for how I am doing I am dreading my time inside but at least my worst fears haven't materialised. The recording was probably left with someone for safe keeping and when Clive disappeared then it was forwarded on to the police. And as for the solicitor I would guess that Marcos is picking up the tab."

"That was exactly what I thought at first until the solicitor let it slip that he had been taken on by a female. The only woman I know that would care about me enough to get a top class brief fighting my corner would be my mother, but there is no way that she would be able to afford one so it can't be her. I just haven't got a clue as to who it could be unless it is one of your old flames."

"You have got to be joking on that front, none of my ex's would piss on me if I was on fire. If it isn't Marcos then who the hell could it be?"

"As I said I can't think of any woman that would get involved."
"And the solicitor wouldn't tell you who it was only that it was a woman?"
"That is a point he didn't say it was a woman he said that it had been a female. I wonder?"
"What George, do you think you know who got him us?"
"Well I do know of someone that would be able to put their hands on the sort of money that we are talking about and at a guess she has just come into loads of money as well."
"You have totally lost me, is it someone that I know?"
"If it is the person that I am thinking that it is then she must have hated her father even more than I thought, either that or she thinks a hell of a lot more of me than I realised."
"Come on then George, the suspense is killing me are you going to tell me or what?"
"Well I might be barking up the wrong tree entirely but I have got a funny feeling that Samantha is behind it all."
"And who the hell is Samantha when she is around?"
"Clive's daughter and the girl that I was shagging before I realised that I was more interested in my own sex than females."
"What, you think that Clive's own daughter has come to our aid. Can you tell me one good reason for her to have done so, that is if what you are saying is in fact the case."
"I can only think of one possible reason and that is if she knew all along what her old man was doing, then she might be doing it out of some sort of guilt by association."
"So you think that she might have known for years that her dad has been forcing you to have sex with him."
"I don't know but I just can't think of anyone else that it could be."
"Well, the other week you were telling me that you have got her number. Why don't you try giving her a call and see what she has to say for herself. If it is her then I can sort of understand her helping you out but why the hell would she have got the solicitor to represent me as well, she has never even met me."

George was already making the call, both of them eager to know if it was her behind things and if so just why?

Tom waited impatiently for George to finish the call, which seemed to be going on for quite some time. He had deliberately gone through to the kitchen where he was unable to hear George's side of the conversation as he thought that it would give him more freedom to say what he wanted without Tom overhearing.

"You're alright to come back in now you idiot I have finished on the phone."

As Tom returned to the lounge he asked why George had called him an idiot.

"Well did you go through to the kitchen because you might have heard me saying that I love her and that I can't wait to get her back into bed or something. Remember what we agreed about there being no secrets. There was no need for you to have gone out of the room and I'll tell you exactly what the score is if you really are ready to have one hell of a shock."

"I take it from what you have just said that it is her then?"

George then told Tom what he had just heard from Samantha.

"It turns out that when the secret cameras were being installed in the family home that Clive had been at work throughout. Once the work had been completed the two guys that had installed it all ran her through how it worked so she would then be able to relay it to her father. Well to cut a long story short she retained the passwords and has been keeping a close eye on what her father has been getting up to for the last couple of years or so. She knew all along that her dad was blackmailing me into having sex with him and it turns out that she had watched what had taken place at Clive's place the other Sunday when the two of you had returned from the squash club. I had to laugh at the one thing that she said."

"What was that then George?"

"She said that she wished that my cock was as big when I was going with her as it is now."

"So that is why she has got involved, but how did she know that we were going to get pulled?"

"Because she heard him having a phone conversation with someone and knew that he had given this other guy a copy of the recording with instructions that if he were to disappear that it should be passed to the police."

"Does she know who the person was that was looking after the copy?"

"I did ask her but she wouldn't say. I think that by us not knowing then we can't get ourselves into even more trouble by going out to get him. It could be though that she simply doesn't know, I'm not sure either way."

"Well it's a good job that Clive hadn't got a clue about what she knew otherwise we wouldn't have been able to get him out of the house."

"And just look where that has got us. If we had just left things as they were then Clive would have still been alive and we wouldn't be having to face charges."

"No but we would have still been having to do everything that Clive told us to. Don't forget that if we hadn't done what we did then there was no way that Clive would have ever allowed you to have moved in with me."

"I am fully aware of that but which would you prefer, to have had a few nights with me sharing your bed and now facing years behind bars or to have been at Clive's beck and call?"

"The simple answer to that is if you are still waiting for me when I get released then the first of the two options without a shadow of doubt. If I have to spend ten years behind bars in order to spend the rest of my life with you then it will be a small price to pay."

"You mean that as well don't you Tom? You really do mean what you have just said."

"Yes George I do, the only question though is will you be there waiting when I do eventually get to walk out of where ever it is that they send me?"

"I can't answer that one Tom other than by saying that as things stand at the moment then I intend to be there when you walk out. The thing is I am not going to promise that I will be because neither of us can predict what will happen over such a long time apart."

"I hear what you are saying, and I would like to think that I will see you in exactly the same way as I do now. Anyway, I think that we have done about enough talking for the time being now how about the two of us popping along to the Indian and grabbing some food?"

"As long as you promise me that as soon as we have finished eating it we can head to bed. I for one hardly slept a wink last night and as soon as my head hits that pillow I'll be spark out."

"Not if I have anything to do with it if the offer is there."

"You Tom have got a one track mind, not that I am complaining. There is one thing though."

"I think I know what you are about to say. Are you thinking that I ought to contact Marcos and see where we stand as regards to still working for him?"

"Bloody hell, you have never told me that you are a mind reader."

"Well I was going to tell you about that while we ate our meal but now you have brought it up I rang him up as soon as I got out of the court."

"So go on then what is the score, have we still got a job or what?"

"Neither of us will be working until after the cases have been heard in court, and as for the house along the road it has been completely stripped. Plus, they have already opened up a different house about five minutes' walk away from here although he didn't tell me exactly where it is."

"So how the hell are we going to live and how are we going to carry on paying the rent for this place?"

"You worry too much, I told you that Marcos is a really decent guy and he realises that the only reason why I did what I did was to protect his goods. What he said to me over the phone was that we will both be on fifty percent of our wages until after the court stuff is all over. If you do not get a custodial then there will be a job waiting for you if you want to go back working for him."

"So even though we won't be doing anything he is still going to be giving you two grand a week and me five hundred?"

"As I said Marcos is a good boss to work for just as long as you don't cross him. If either of us had said too much to the police then he would have known about it in a shot and by now money would not be an issue for us."

"By that you mean that if we had told the police everything about the firm then Marcos would have had us killed by now?"

"That is about the sum of it."

It was now that they considered that it an ideal time to stop talking and having got his shoes on George was soon ready to accompany Tom to the Indian take-away.

It wasn't until they were tucking into their food that Tom thought that he would again try and find out what George was intending doing. So far he had told Tom that he was sticking around at the moment but Tom needed to know what George's long term plans were just to give himself some sort of peace of mind.

"So you have made it clear that you are staying here at the moment but can I ask for how long George? You said that at the moment you are intending to be there for me when I leave prison. But with the way that you said it I just couldn't help but read into your comment that there was more than just a little doubt that it would actually turn out to be the case."

"I told you things as truthfully as I am able to. I am only just eighteen and who knows what is going to happen in however many years you end up being sent down for. As I said as things are at the moment then yes, I am intending to wait for that day but if you are expecting me to promise you that I will be then you had better think again. I am not going to make you a promise that I am not sure that I will be able to keep. You should have realised now that I have got a very good appetite for sex, and the thought of me having to go without any for the next few years while I am in the prime of my life is beyond my thinking."

"I appreciate your honesty George. I guess that all I will have to do is make the most of having you around until I get in court and then once I have been sent away then all I will have to do is just hope and pray. I know that you going without sex will be a near impossibility for days let alone weeks and I wouldn't expect you

to abstain completely. All I would hope is that whenever you do
end up with someone that it is simply for sex and that your heart
still belongs to me."

"You never know what is round the corner though do you Tom,
let's face it did you think for one moment that the two of us
would fall in love overnight?"

"I hear what you are saying George and I guess that we will both
just have to wait and see what develops. At least with us both
being paid half pay between now and the court case then it will
allow me to put a fair bit of money away so you will be able to
keep this place on once I go away."

"Well if I go back working for Marcos after my case is over then
that shouldn't be an issue anyway because if I am getting a grand
a week then I will have plenty of cash to more than cover things.
You never know Tom I might even be able to afford to come and
visit you every now and again."

"I take it that you are joking when you said that. I hope that you
will be coming in to see me on a regular basis."

"To a large degree that depends on where you are sent to Tom. If
you end up the other end of the country then it will not be that
easy especially if I am working for Marcos full time. I don't think
he would like it if I were to say to him that I want a couple of
days off work every week so I can come to see you."

"You are right of course. It is just me worrying about how I will
survive in there. It will be hard enough anyway without
wondering what you are up to and if someone else is getting a
place in that heart of yours."

"All I will say to that Tom is that I promise you that if it looks as
though it is going to happen that I will tell you just as soon as I
realise it myself. Now how about the two of us going to bed
because every night that we have got together I intend making the
very most of."

Although neither of them had slept much while in the police cell
the previous night it was rapidly getting light outside before they
eventually settled down in order to get some well-deserved sleep.

They slept solidly until being disturbed by the intercom sounding
and it wasn't until Tom looked at the time that he realised that
he'd forgotten all about the solicitor coming. It was now eleven
o'clock and they were both still in bed. Tom dived out of bed
shaking George while doing so and informing him that the brief
was here and that they both needed to get up sharpish.. Tom went
to answer the call and told the solicitor that he would be just a
couple of minutes before he let him into the building, apologising
for not being ready to receive him.

In total the solicitor, Andrew Barber, was with them for well in
excess of two whole hours during which time he went into great
detail as to how he wanted them to play things when it came to
court. For George it was a case that with the evidence that they
had on him Andrew wanted them to approach things from the line
of George had already fallen for Tom by the time that he found
out, and that love had blinded him from rational thinking. As for
Tom though that was going to be handled from the viewpoint that
Tom had suffered for years with mental issues, and the offence
had only taken place after he had been pushed to the absolute
limit by his older brother, who had used and abused him for years.
It was well into the discussions that Andrew came out with a
comment that neither Tom nor George were happy hearing. He
informed them that for George to get the best result in court then
he thought it best that they did not continue to live together. In his
opinion if George could say in court that he had since split up
with Tom then it would go in his favour. Whereas if it became
known that they were still living under the same roof and sharing
the same bed then it would not help his case.

"Sorry Mr Barber but if it means that I get a heavier sentence then
so be it but there is no way that I am going to move out of here.
Tom and I will have limited time together as it is and I for one
intend to take advantage of every minute that we have got before
we are split up."

Tom looked across to where George was sat and although he was
happy to hear that George was so committed to him if it meant

that George would get a lighter sentence then it may well be something that they needed to seriously talk about.

"Hold on a minute George, from what Andrew has just said it will mean that you are much better off if the two of us split up. Now I know it is something that I would prefer never to happen but have you actually thought about what he has just said?"

"It doesn't need thinking about Tom, there is no way that I am going to leave you just so I get an easier time in court. Mr Barber, I am sorry but you will have to deal with things as they stand. I don't care if you tell them that I am still blinded by love or if I have just accepted the fact that I am living with a murderer, but we are going to stay together and that Sir is the end of that line of discussion."

"Can I just point out the fact that it may well make the difference between you getting off with a suspended sentence instead of having to serve at least a period of time in prison."

"I don't care if they do lock me up, with Tom being away I might as well be because with him not being at my side it will be like prison to me anyway."

Tom just sat there listening to what George was saying and it was then that he really understood that George had got exactly the same depth of feelings towards him as Tom had for George. He wanted to take him in his arms but with the brief still present and having realised that he wasn't as gay friendly as he might have been Tom thought better of it.

It was clear to both that the solicitor was not that pleased with hearing what George had said. However, he knew that he would have to go along with their decision, even if it meant things were going to be tougher in court for him to get the best result for George.

Andrew Barber had arrived at the flat just after eleven in the morning and it was approaching half one in the afternoon before he considered that they had covered everything that needed addressing at this stage. As he left his final comment was that he wanted them to reconsider their decision to stay together until the court case.

"Mr Barber, I don't know if you are married or not but if you are
and you love your wife would you leave her purely for your own
selfish reasons although not only would it break her heart if you
did so but it would also break your own?"
"I hear you George and to some degree I can understand what it is
that you are saying, all I ask is that it is something that the two of
you spend some time talking through. It is my professional
opinion that it will not do either of you any favours in court if you
continue the relationship is all I am saying."
With that being the final comment he went on his way, and just as
soon as Tom had closed the door he turned to George and pulled
him close to him.
"Thank you George." He said as he embraced him.
"What part are you actually thanking me for Tom? Telling him
that I wasn't about to go running back to my parent's house?"
"No, for making it perfectly clear to me that you love me just as
much as I do you. Can I just say though that it might be an idea
for us to do as the solicitor has said."
"What?" George almost shouted right into Tom's left ear. "Are
you saying that you think that I should leave you?"
"No what I was meaning is perhaps it is something that we should
talk about."
"You can forget that right away Tom, as I said to the brief I am
not going anywhere. Now if we are not likely to have any further
visitors today why don't we just go back to bed and pick up
where we left off last night?"
"I was going to suggest that we pop along the road as I am dying
to know if the house is just totally empty."
"I have a funny feeling that Marcos will want us to stay well clear
of all his houses for the time being, even the ones that are not
being used. You will need to contact him though in order to find
out how we are going to get paid each week."
"When I spoke to him on the phone yesterday afternoon that was
all agreed on, every Monday evening one of his guys will be
coming here with the cash for us. He even said that if we decided
to go away somewhere for a couple of weeks between now and

our day in court that if I let him know then he will pay us in advance so we are able to enjoy ourselves."

"I don't think that we would be able to go anywhere even if we wanted to, from what I understood of the bail conditions we wouldn't be allowed to go far."

Chapter 11

It was a total of five weeks before either of them appeared in Crown court and it was George who got his time in the dock first. Tom wanted to go with him in order to give him moral support but having had a very strong word from their solicitor he stayed at home with his phone constantly close by. Andrew Barber had told them that the case would probably be adjourned for the simple reason that before George could be found guilty they first had to establish Tom's guilt. The brief hadn't been wrong and the judge was not at all happy that George had been booked in to appear prior to Tom's case having been heard. George returned home to the flat where Tom was eagerly waiting.

"Well how did you get on then George, they obviously haven't locked you up."

"As Andrew said it has been adjourned until after yours and the judge was not at all happy. I'll tell you one thing when I go back in there I hope it isn't the same one because he seems like a right stroppy sod. The solicitor was saying that he was a relief judge that does the circuit just filling in where needed so hopefully neither of us will have him."

"Was he really that bad then?"

"Put it this way I think if it had been the trial then I am pretty sure that I wouldn't have been coming back here anytime soon."

"That's a point that we haven't even considered and I think it is something that we need to talk about, just in case."

"I think that I have just thought of exactly the same thing. Are you thinking about this place if we both do get sent down and what will happen with not just the flat but all our stuff?"

"That is exactly what has just dawned on me. Do you think that we could speak to Marcos and get him to cover it for a short period?"

"What makes you say a short period?"

"Because from what Mr Barber has said you will be very unlucky
to get sent down at all but if you do it won't be for very long.
What was it he said about six months maximum and that you'd
only have to spend half of that inside. That means that even if we
look at the worst case scenario you will only be in for about
twelve or thirteen weeks, and we have already got about ten
weeks rent money put to one side."
"You are forgetting that Andrew Barber predicted that short a
time before I refused to leave you. He has already made it quite
clear that I might get a heavier sentence because we are still
together."
"I guess that we could sit here talking about what might or might
not happen for ages but at the end of the day we won't know until
the time comes. Were you given a new date when you will have
to appear?"
"No, they can't do that until after your case has been concluded,
at least it means that we have definitely still got four weeks
together."
"Twenty six days and counting. I want us to make the very most
of every hour of them as well."
"In that case I was going to go and get out of this suit anyway and
from what you have just said I might as well not bother to put my
jeans and a t-shirt on for now."
With that they went through to the bedroom but despite their
intentions to stay in there for some time they were soon
interrupted by George's mobile ringing.
"I had better get it Tom just in case it is the solicitor needing to
talk to me about something."
Without bothering to get dressed George went through to the
lounge where he had left his phone and answered the call.
To his surprise it was Samantha, and she was asking if the two of
them were at home and if so would it be okay for her to come
round to see them. Although George asked why she wanted to
visit Sam just told him that all would be revealed when she gets
here. He reluctantly agreed and as soon as she was given the go
ahead George was told that she was only a mile or so away and

that she would be with them within ten minutes. Having ended the call George went through to the bedroom and gave Tom the news.

"Why is she coming?" Tom enquired, a puzzled expression on his face.

"I would like to know the answer to that question myself. I did ask her and basically all she said that we would find out when she got here. I have got a funny feeling that it has got something to do with the recordings that her dad had got of us though."

"You don't think that she is going to try and blackmail us into doing something for her do you?"

"I don't know but if you think about it she knows that for the last two years her dad had got me running round in circles for him. If she is going to try and use them then I have got no idea as to what she might want me or us to do."

They had only just finished getting dressed when the intercom sounded heralding the arrival of Samantha. George let her in and very soon they were all seated in the lounge.

"Firstly Samantha can I just thank you on behalf of George and myself for getting us a decent solicitor, we really didn't expect you to have got involved."

"Tom after what my father has done for the past couple of years I felt that I needed to, however it is turning out to be a lot more costly than I thought it would which is the main reason for me having come round."

"Well if you want us to come up with some money towards it Sam then that is going to be really difficult. At the moment we are trying to get enough saved up so we can keep this place on if George does have to spend a short period of time in prison. According to what Mr Barber has said there is a chance that he might have to spend up to three months inside."

"I thought that would be the case and that you wouldn't have any spare cash hanging about. I have been watching some of my dad's recordings and it was when I was watching the one of you Tom when you first went round to dad's house that it got me thinking of a way that you can contribute towards the costs."

Tom immediately thought back to what had taken place and it only took him a matter of seconds before he was sure that he knew exactly what she was referring to.

"If I knew who your dad used to deal with Samantha then I would be more than willing to start donating sperm if that is what you were meaning."

"Well it just so happens Tom that I have found all the details and have been in touch with them and they are very eager to receive donations as there is a real shortage. When I asked just how much they needed their reply was simply as much as I could get hold of. I was shocked to find out that my dad had told you the truth and that they pay five hundred pounds for every load though."

"Well, if it will help and if they want it I will donate mine like I used to as well. I don't know how much the solicitor is costing but I think that between the two of us as long as you can get hold of enough beakers then we should be able to fill quite a few every week."

"That George is very kind of you to offer, but I had already assumed that you would do it anyway. Now when I spoke to them earlier today they informed me that at the moment there is a real demand and that their stocks are virtually exhausted, so I guess that we had better get on and start filling their gap."

With that she reached into her shopping bag and one after another started producing beakers from it.

Both Tom and George sat there watching and counting as they continued to be produced.

"So we can see that you have brought eight, I guess the question is how quick do you want us to try and get them filled and how are we going to get them to you?"

"That Tom is really easy." She looked at her watch. "It is only just gone three now and from what I saw in that film of yours you are both more than capable of shooting your loads at least twice an hour. If you do both use a beaker each time then I would say that by six I should be on my way."

"Are you saying what I think you are Sam, are you trying to say that you want us to get filling them right here and now while you are here?"

"Yes George, that is exactly what I am saying, and I assume that neither of you have any objection."

"So you'll just sit out here while Tom and me get to work in the bedroom, is that what you are saying?"

"Well seeing as I have seen you both totally naked on film I thought that it would be far better if you started filling them just where you are. I am sorry I did bring with me some of my dad's films for you to watch but I see that you haven't got a telly so that idea is out."

"Just to clarify things, you are expecting us to strip off in front of you and to start filling those beakers while you watch?"

"Don't pretend to be getting all shy on me now Tom, as I say I have already seen you on film and I must admit that I am a little curious as to see if you are as good looking in the flesh as it were."

"I think that I speak for Tom as well as myself Sam, but I would not be happy doing it with you watching, no offence meant."

"I had this funny feeling that you might come out with something like that and I had to spend many hours watching various recordings before I had got what I needed. You see my father had foolishly left the new password on the kitchen worktop so I was able to gain access of the cameras in the house just along the road. Now I am not going to go into too much detail, but I believe that neither of you would want to face additional charges of supplying vast quantities of drugs to the local dealers would you?"

"Tom, you don't know Sam as well as I do but believe me she is just like her father was as regards to finding a way to get exactly what she wants. If she has got recordings of us doing transactions in the house then we can say goodbye to freedom for a hell of a long time if we don't do exactly what she says."

"So how can we be sure that you will not use the recordings even if we do what you are asking?"

"Well you trusted my old man and George will tell you that I am
more than able to keep secrets if I need to. As long as you both do
everything that I ask then you have my word that I will not hand
the recordings over to the police. If however you refuse then that
is exactly what will happen. Oh, and by the way Tom just in case
it might cross your mind to stop me there is a copy being held by
someone and if I disappear then you know what they will do with
it don't you?"
"You have watched us talking at the house on how we were going
to get your old man off the scene haven't you?"
"I have George and between you I have learnt how to cover my
own back just in case. Now are the two of you going to get those
clothes off because I really don't want to be here all night getting
these beakers filled."
George looked at Tom and Tom at George. They both knew that
Samantha had got them over a barrel and reluctantly they started
removing their own clothes, firstly the t-shirt and then the jeans.
"Boys you really disappoint me, looking at those boxer shorts it
doesn't look as if either of you are even slightly hard. I think that
you both need to come over here and stand in front of me."
Sheepishly the two of them moved closer to where Samantha was
sat and when they both went to stop when they were a couple of
feet away she beckoned them closer.
As soon as they were close enough she reached out and grabbed
both of their private parts, one in each hand.
"Now I know that I always used to be able to get yours hard in no
time George and from what I have heard Tom saying on the
recordings he has no problem getting hard when there is a girl on
it."
With the two of them just stood there submissively and in total
disbelief as to what was happening Samantha then pulled down
their boxers, firstly George's and then closely after Tom's were
pulled down to the floor.
"Well you have got me in quite a dilemma now boys because both
of these look really appetising but I have only got the one mouth.
Which of you wants my mouth round theirs first?"

Although since meeting George Tom had said that never again was he ever going to have sex with a female the way she was working her hand on it Tom's was getting increasingly stiff at an alarming speed. He looked down at George's and was relieved to see that he was in a similar state.

"Well seeing as neither of you are going to speak I guess I will just have to take it in turn."

 Firstly, she moved her head onto George's and then after a few seconds switched to Tom's. For the next couple of minutes she kept alternating a few seconds on the one and then moving onto the other.

It was after a few minutes had passed that the two guys were aware that Samantha was clearly beginning to enjoy herself and this was confirmed when they saw her starting to unbutton her blouse before slipping it from her shoulders then pulling her arms free of it.

Tom could not help but look down at her and had to admit to himself that she had got a really good upper body, and that the bra that she was wearing looked as if it was hiding something that he wouldn't mind having a proper look at. To his shock it was when Samantha had got her mouth on George's that he watched as George reached round her back and undid the bra before pulling it clear.

"What do you think then Tom. Now you can see why I was with her although I was gay. Not only is she good with her mouth Samantha has got a really nice body as well."

"I must admit from what I can see you are not wrong. Mind you she has got an advantage over us, our pants are down round our ankles."

"I have got a funny feeling that Samantha will soon be rectifying that if I know her."

"Well Tom I know that George really doesn't like doing a similar thing with his mouth as I am with mine, well not on a girl anyway, but from what I heard you saying to my dad it is something that you always used to like doing. While I carry on sucking on George's why don't you get my jeans down and get to work?"

Tom looked across to George and as soon as he caught his eye George nodded as if to say, 'Tom you had better do as she says otherwise we are going to be in trouble'.

"I'll tell you one thing George you have grown quite a bit since I last had this in my mouth, has it been put to use with a girl since we split up?"

"Not once, you know that I am totally gay Samantha so why would I have used it on a girl?"

By this time Tom had not only lowered both the jeans and panties but was also putting his hands to work, the left on her breasts and the right one between her legs, which she had opened wide in order to accommodate him.

"I think that things are going to take a whole lot longer than I had initially thought they would guys." Samantha exclaimed, clearly enjoying what Tom was doing.

"Why's that then Sam, I know for a fact that we can both shoot a good load each time and that we can get all eight of those beakers full within the two hours."

"Tom, can you remember what happened when you were over my dad's place and why the beakers were not being filled as fast as they could have been?"

"That was because there was only the one of us that was using the beakers when we shot our loads."

"Well done Tom, I think you had better go to the top of the class. Between the two of you I am now getting that horny that I think you are going to have to take it in turns using the beakers, because each time one of you are not going to need one."

Neither Tom nor George knew exactly what she was meaning, was she implying that she wanted them to take it in turns shagging her or was she meaning that she was intending keeping her mouth in action. It was George that thought it best to find out just what she had in mind.

"So are you saying that you want us to take it in turns shagging you Sam or are you wanting to taste what we have got to offer. If

I remember rightly you always used to love doing that as much as when I got it between your legs."

She pulled her mouth free and told George that he could shoot his load in her mouth just as soon as he was ready, as for Tom though he was going to have to shag her. She made it clear that with him having had so much experience in the past with girls that she thought that he would know how to please her. Adding that he had better.

Tom realised just what she meant by her comment and that he would have to ensure that it wasn't only him that reached a climax because if he didn't manage to get her to one then he just knew that she would be not happy in the least.

"Get a beaker then Tom because I want to watch you filling it while at the same time George can be doing the same with my mouth."

It was gone eleven that night before all eight beakers were being put back into the shopping bag, all of which had now got a good sample of both the guys sperm, four loads from each of them.

"Well guys that was quite enjoyable I must say, all I hope is that you enjoyed it as much as I did."

"Not meaning to sound horrible but I think that we would have enjoyed things better if it had been just the two of us Sam."

"Well George that is really sad to hear because I think that by the time you both get your days in court you will have had plenty of opportunity to change your mind. I will be back round here at five o'clock tomorrow with a fresh stock of beakers for you guys."

"You are joking I hope." George responded in a rather harsh tone.

"No George I am not. You will both be here, and you had better be ready to please me just like you used to bend over to please my father. Do I make myself clear?"

Both Tom and George didn't reply but just nodded in resignation. As soon as she was out the door it was George who was the first to speak.

"What a bitch, she has got us both by the bollocks and doesn't she just know it? Mind you I could tell that at the one point you were really beginning to enjoy yourself. And I could read your mind when she undid her blouse and that was why I took her bra off. I knew you would be dying to see what they were like."

"I am not going to lie to you George as we have agreed that there are going to be no secrets between us. Samantha has got one beautiful body and I must admit that it was one of the best shags that I have had. I don't think that she has had a fella since you were last there because I had no problem bringing her to a climax."

"Do you really think that she has only ever had mine before you got in there earlier?"

"Well, if she has had any other guy then he was not very big and didn't really know what he was doing. I reckon that she hasn't had sex since you and her had it what two years ago."

"No wonder she is coming back round again tomorrow, she has got one hell of some catching up to do if that is the case."

"Do you think that she is intending to come here every evening until we go to court George?"

"I'm not certain but while we are being honest with each other I thought that I would really hate seeing you shagging her but I didn't, with her giving me head and with watching you did you notice how much I put in the beaker?"

"No, but from the way you are speaking I guess it must have been a pretty good amount."

"Put it this way Tom if it had been in your mouth at the time I don't think that you would have managed to swallow it all, there was that much."

"So I guess that we both got off on it then because I know for a fact that she would have felt what I put inside her, I reckon that I must have shot a hell of a lot from how it felt."

"The only thing though Tom is that with us both having shot so many times I for one am knackered now and although I would love us to have a session I don't think that I could manage it."

"I am the same George and besides, I guess we had better save ourselves for tomorrow because if we can't produce for her then we might end up in the shit."

With that they decided to head for bed but that there was going to be no sex between them only hugs and kisses.

Just as she had said at dead on five o'clock the following evening the intercom sounded and George buzzed her in.

As she came through the flat door they both noticed that unlike the previous afternoon where she had brought with her just the one bag today she was carrying two. It was George who picked up on it first.

"Don't tell me that both of those bags are containing beakers because I don't think that we would be able to manage more than what we did last night Samantha."

"You're alright George I have only brought eight beakers with me again, I have however brought a few other things along with me that will put a smile on Tom's face even if it doesn't put one on yours."

"Let me guess, you've raided your old man's wardrobe and have brought some of his toys with you."

"I have and I made sure that I brought the big dildo with me because from what I saw on the film Tom really did enjoy having that up him. If I remember right he reckoned that when it was in him that he shot more than he had ever done in his life, that is right isn't it Tom?"

"I must admit that it did feel like it. I hope that you have brought enough lube with you as well because without it there is no way that I would be able to take it."

"The lube is in the bag as well Tom and I am dying to feel you inside me while George works that dildo up your arse. I'll let you know if I think that you shoot any more with it than you do without. Now why don't all three of us get started because I would prefer to be away from here by ten tonight. That is unless I am enjoying myself that much that I decide to stay."

"When you say stay, I take it that you mean till a bit later than ten, am I right?"

"We will just have to see how much we all are enjoying ourselves won't we. I would hate to go and leave you feeling cheated and still wanting more."

"Put it this way Sam by the time you left last night there was no way that either of us could have managed to have sex with it just being the two of us as much as we wanted to. We were both totally knackered."

"Well George in that case I hope that you have saved yourselves today until now is all I can say otherwise you might end up disappointing me."

"There is just one question that I have got for you Sam before we start, when we were talking last night Tom said that he thought that his was the first inside you since I was there two years ago, was he right?"

"Well Tom, you must know girls pretty well to have got that one right, was it that obvious and how could you tell?"

"Well, it was immediately clear that you were quite tight down below so I knew that there hadn't been too many there before me, and when you orgasmed I just got the feeling that it had been some time since you had experienced the same sensation."

"Your man has obviously used that cock of his on quite a few women in the past George, does that not bother you?"

"Not really because that was in the past, or at least it was until last night and I know that he enjoyed himself as much as you did, what you don't know though was that I got quite a kick out of seeing him at work in you."

"Well tonight shall we start by seeing if Tom gets the same sort of kick out of seeing you going there. Let's get rid of these clothes as we are wasting time."

With having said what she had Samantha wasted no time in getting undressed and was stood completely naked before either of the guys had even got their trousers fully off. By the time they were both naked George's member was still quite limp whereas Tom was sporting a very stiff cock, he'd been looking at Sam's breasts and liked what he saw.

"Well George by the look of things you have got some catching up to do. In fact, seeing as you are not ready to get that tool of yours into action yet you had better get one of my father's working instead."

With that Samantha pulled out the smaller of the two dildos that Tom had experienced on that Sunday when round at Clive's house.

"I'll lie on the floor and you can put this to use while Tom gets his to use in me."

With that Samantha virtually pulled Tom to the floor with her and as soon as he was on top she was willing him to get into action. With Tom having parted her legs he then entered her and it was now that he felt George's hand on his backside. He was aware that there was lube being applied and he secretly couldn't wait to feel the dildo entering him. Although he was well aware that it was when he got the larger one inside him that it really did bring him to places that he had never experienced either before or after.

"George do me a favour will you, once you have worked that one in me for a time can you get the other one into action because I think that Sam will really appreciate what happens when I have got that up me."

George didn't reply but instead started working the dildo firmly in and out of Tom's backside, he wanted to get it well prepared before introducing the bigger one.

"I'll tell you what, I think that I will be making a decent deposit myself in not too long, look at this."

George was now waving his member around for them both to see, He was well chuffed that it wasn't just pointing skyward but it was harder than it normally got.

"I take it that you are enjoying using that dildo on me then George?"

"Too right I am, and I can't wait to get the other one in there because that is something that I didn't get to see last time from this angle. Do you think that you could manage it now if I swap them over?"

"Give it a try, but take it really slow to start off with just in case I'm not quite ready for it."

With that George removed the smaller of the two dildos and having put a good amount of lube round the bigger one and also adding more to Tom's rear entrance he then started edging it in slowly. To his joy there was no comment from Tom telling him to stop and assumed that his partner must have been happy for him to continue feeding it in.

"Go on then George really give it to him because I can already tell that he is getting more excited than he has up till now, I think that his cock has almost doubled in size he is getting such a kick out of having that thing in him."

"Let's have a quick look at it then Tom and I'll soon tell Sam if she is right or not."

With that Tom pulled out of Sam briefly displaying an absolutely rigid member before driving it back into place.

"How much of it have you got in me George? it feels as though you have only got it just a little way in."

With that George now felt at ease to go harder with the dildo. Up until Tom's comment there had only been about a quarter of it inside the backside but with having heard Tom's comment George soon changed that. He kept moving it backwards and forwards, each time pushing it a little further inside Tom than the previous, until there was a good half of it entering him.

"Do you still want to feel more of it in you Tom or is that about as much as you are comfortable with?" George asked out of concern, as he didn't want to hurt Tom in any way.

"I'll let you know when to stop George, but you are alright to carry on as you were for the time being."

George continued to feed more and more of the huge dildo into Tom's backside and with every extra millimetre that Tom felt within him the more excited he got.

"Well Samantha I could just shoot my load in you but I don't think that you would get a really good judge of just how much I am about to shoot, wouldn't you prefer it in your mouth because then you will really know."

"I've got a better idea, when you are about to shoot tell us and George as soon as you hear Tom saying that he is coming I want you to lie on the floor next to me so I can watch him shoot all over your belly."

"I'll tell you what Sam, it is going to come out with such force that it will spray just about everywhere." Tom added aware that he would have difficulty in just keeping it to George's belly. When Tom felt that Samantha was orgasming it was enough for him and with the dildo now way inside him he informed them that he was just about to make a huge deposit. George for his part let go of the dildo leaving it still inside Tom's backside and hurriedly lay down by Samantha's side.

Tom pulled out and having rapidly moved across above George then started making his deposit. Jet after jet left him hitting George's stomach with such force that it then sprayed up hitting both George and Sam in the face as well as going just about everywhere else.

"Bloody hell Tom where the fuck is all that coming from, you have never shot that much when it has been just the two of us."

"That George is simply because I have never had that dildo inside me when it has just been us, that is why no other reason I can assure you."

Samantha was just in ore and as soon as she was sure that Tom had finished she then sat up and started rubbing George's belly, spreading Tom's spent juice evenly over it.

"And I thought that you liked the taste of my boyfriend's juices Sam, I would have thought that you would have used something other than your hand on it all."

Just as George had hoped Samantha rose to the bait and leaning right over him started licking the deposit up. For George this was one thing that he did enjoy taking place just about as much as anything and it was not long before he was again growing stiff, although he had used a beaker not long after introducing the larger of the two dildos into Tom's backside.

"Well Sam looking at George I think that when you have finished licking up all of mine that he will almost be ready to give you some more if you want it."

"As soon as he is stiff enough he had better give me it, but it won't be going in my mouth. George you are just about to go down memory lane, I want you to fuck me like you used to before you decided that men could give you more enjoyment. I'll warn you though that you had better put some effort into it because if I get to think that you are just going through the motions then that dildo is going up your arse and there will be no lube used. Do I make myself clear?"

George really wasn't looking forward to getting his tool anywhere near a female's vagina and even the thought of it was having a reaction on his dick. It had been getting quite hard but all of a sudden it was becoming softer by the second.

Tom spotted what was happening as he thought it might and soon introduced his hand onto the member in the hope that he could get George aroused again before Samantha realised what was happening. It was then that Tom had a thought.

Tom pushed George's legs apart and having dipped a couple of fingers of his left hand in the lube he introduced it to George's rear entry, his right hand still working on the now stiffening cock. As soon as Sam considered that she had cleaned up to a good enough level she then lay back on the carpet and having grabbed one of George's upper arms pulled him on top of her.

It was now that Tom had got a much better access to where he wanted to get to and having picked up the smaller of the two dildos introduced it to George's backside. His thinking was that they were both males and if it had given Tom so much excitement having one inside him then it should have the same impact on George, or at least he was hoping it would.

For George this was the first time he had ever had anything up his back passage other than Tom or Clive. With it being considerably larger it really was doing the trick and very soon he was aware that he too was as hard if not harder than he usually got, and fortunately the experience was such that he was able to enjoy what he himself was doing.

When Sam had first told George of what she wanted to take place he was sure that there would be no way that he could ever get her to a point of climax. With what Tom was doing with the dildo he soon became aware that he had achieved the unexpected and it was now that he considered that he had done enough to keep her quiet and he then had to force himself to reach climax as well. "George if I didn't know better I would think that you enjoyed that almost as much as I did, but I know that if it hadn't been for what Tom was doing behind your back that neither of us would have got anywhere. Thank you Tom."

As soon as George had withdrawn he excused himself and went through to the bathroom. Tom thought that he must have just needed to have a piss but the reason for George's rapid departure from the room was in order to get his head over the basin. Before he had started he had felt physically sick with what he was being asked to do but now that he had actually carried out Sam's demand he was emptying his stomach down the loo.

"You do know why your fella has gone to the bathroom don't you Tom?"

"At a guess I would say it is because he needed a piss."

"You really don't know him that well then do you? He will be in there throwing up you wait and see. As soon as he had shot his load I was watching his face and I could see the colour draining from it. When he gets back we'll ask him and I bet I am right." Sam stated confidently.

When George did return to the room some minutes later Sam wasted no time in establishing the fact that she had been right, pointing out that they needed to get to know each other one hell of a lot better before they start even thinking about getting engaged. It was a realisation that hit them both although they were not about to admit as much to their uninvited guest.

"Well Tom at least you are going out with a genuine gay guy, I feel sorry for George though because his boyfriend doesn't quite know which side of the fence he wants to be on. He says that he is now totally gay but from the way you shagged me then I doubt it very much if you are."

Tom was now thinking that Samantha was playing a little game and was trying to drive a wedge between the two of them for some reason. Could it be that she still had feelings towards George and this was her way of trying to get him back for herself or what. She was definitely up to something Tom was sure of it but as yet he wasn't totally clear as to what her motives were.

"So can I ask if that is it for today then Samantha?" Tom asked hoping that she would go and then he would be able to talk to George and perhaps then between the two of them they might just be able to work out what Sam was up to.

"I am finished for today but as for the two of you there are still seven beakers that need filling and the quicker they are all used then the quicker I can get on my way."

"Not being funny Samantha but with the amount that I shot earlier I am not too sure that I will be able to deliver enough to satisfy those that pay you."

"Well if you don't then we will just have to get that dildo back inside you, but we'll forget about the lube next time and see if that will have an impact."

Tom was rapidly getting fed up with this girl who had imposed herself into their life. As far as he was concerned George meant far too much to him to share him with Sam, or anyone else for that matter. He decided he would get those beakers used one way or another, and in the shortest time that he could manage. All he wanted was to get her out of the flat while he was still able to bite his tongue.

She sat there watching as Tom and George encouraged each other using a variety of methods to achieve the desired results and all seven of the beakers were put into use in record time, and it was about nine o'clock by the time they had the flat to themselves.

"What do you think she is up to George? You know her far better than I do but she is definitely up to something."

"I wish I knew, all I do know is that earlier I threw up more than I have done for years. If she ever expects me to repeat what I did this evening then I will just tell her to take the recordings to the police as twenty years behind bars would be better than having to shag her ever again."

"I did wonder if she has still got feelings for you and wants to split us up so she then has a clear run at you."

"Well if that is what she is thinking then she has got me all wrong, there is no way on this earth that I would ever willingly go with a girl ever again. I know that you can still be tempted in that direction but for me it turns my stomach just thinking about it." After some time talking they made their way through to the bedroom. Although they hadn't eaten since lunchtime neither of them were that bothered about food and just wanted to get in bed and go to sleep cuddled up together.

"By the way Sam didn't say anything about coming round again so do you think that she has had enough for the time being?"

"Sorry to disappoint you George but while you were throwing up in the bathroom she did make it perfectly clear to me that she would be round again the same time tomorrow with another eight beakers for us to use. She turned round and said that the solicitor is costing that much that even with her making four grand out of us every day it still isn't covering his bill."

"Well all I hope is that if she wants either of us to shag her that she will be happy with it being you every time from now on, because tonight was the very last time that she is ever going to know mine in her."

"The question that we really ought to be trying to come up with an answer to though George is how can we stop her?"

"From the way I see things there just isn't anyway that we can say no to her. It isn't just a case that she will tell the solicitor that his services are no longer required is it. With what she has got on us then if we do piss her off then I really do think that she would send copies of the recordings to the police. She had always got an evil side of her and by the look of things she has been perfecting her skills in that department."

"There must be something that we can do to put an end to this before it starts affecting our relationship, if it hasn't already."

"What makes you say that Tom?"

"Quite simple George, thanks to her you now know that I can still enjoy myself with a female despite what I had said to you about being totally gay now."

"Tom I know that you are only doing what you have to. Okay so you enjoy it but you are human after all and I don't hold it against you in any way."

"You may say that but I feel as though I have been lying to you all along. When I have to shag her I have got to admit that I do get enjoyment out of doing it. She has got one hell of a nice body and with her being quite tight down below I do find that it does really excite me more than I thought it would."

"So whose body do you prefer than Tom, hers or mine?"

"It's two totally different things George, just in case you hadn't noticed she is a female. It isn't like comparing one guys body to another is it?"

"No I know that Tom but being honest with me which would you prefer to have lay beside you every night in bed?"

"That George goes without saying. Yes, I enjoy shagging her but that I can assure you is all it is, just a shag. If you don't know by now that there is only the one person that I love then I must be doing something seriously wrong."

"Sorry Tom, that was a stupid thing for me to have come out with. I know you love me just as much as I love you."

"Can you see what is already beginning to happen George? She is already putting friction between the two of us and if we don't find a way of stopping her games then I am worried that it will end up getting too much for our relationship to be able to handle."

"Let's get to sleep and we can try and come up with some sort of idea tomorrow before she turns up again."

It took George no time at all in falling to sleep, for Tom however it was a very different matter. For more than four hours Tom just lay there trying to think of some way that they would be able to put an end to the nonsense that Samantha had brought to their front door. Yes, as far as he was concerned he had got no problem with both George and himself continuing to supply sperm in order to help cover the cost of the solicitor, but that was about all he was now prepared to continue doing. He went over and over things in his head, yes, he knew very well that Sam would have been able to get some real good footage of them dealing sizable quantities of drugs to various parties. He also knew that if the police did get their hands on the recording them both he and George could say goodbye to freedom for years to come. What he was unable to come up with however was a way to put an end to Samantha's little game. At long last Tom thought of a way that there might well be an avenue open to them but it would rely on George agreeing to what he had in mind. Although part of him wanted to talk to George about what he had thought of he decided not to wake him and instead he snuggled into his partner and allowed himself to doze off.

Chapter 12

It was just turned eleven in the morning when Tom was woken by
George who had now brought a coffee through for him.
"Morning sleeping beauty, did shagging my ex take that much out
of you that you needed so much sleep?"
"Morning George, the reason why I have slept till now was
because it must have been getting on for four this morning before
I eventually dozed off."
"How come you took that long getting to sleep?"
"I was lay here trying to come up with some way that we can stop
Samantha carrying on doing what she is."
"And did you manage to come up with anything because if you
did then I would really like to hear what you have thought up."
"I did have a thought but I don't know if you are going to go
along with it."
"I'm listening Tom."
Tom then went through with George what he had thought of
doing. It was to his relief that George not only told him that in his
opinion it might well work he went on to tell Tom that he would
do whatever was needed if it meant that they would then be able
to get back to how things were between them.
"I wasn't too sure that you would think that it was a good idea
and worth us trying."
"Not only do I think it is a good idea Tom I am definitely up for
giving it a try. When you get out of that bed and dressed let's
head straight into the city centre and buy what we need. That way
if we get back here early enough we might be able to have a bit of
fun with it being just the two of us before she arrives."
With the thought of possibly getting shot of Samantha Tom was
showered and fully dressed before his coffee had time to cool
down enough to be at a drinkable temperature.
"I take it there is a private shop in Coventry that sells what we are
after, is there Tom?"

"I have never stepped foot in the place but I know exactly where there is one and I would be amazed if they haven't got everything that we want."

"In that case shall I phone for a taxi, or are we going to walk into the centre?"

Having told George that there was a shortcut through a few alleys they were soon setting off.

On reaching the shop they were both relieved to see that it stocked everything that Tom had earlier mentioned and having spent in excess of a hundred and fifty pounds on the various objects they were soon heading back home.

"There was one other thing that I was going to ask you George, I know that you occasionally like to smoke a bit of weed, do you know if Samantha smokes the stuff as well?"

"She loves it more than I do. If you are thinking what I think you might be then that is a brilliant idea. Are you thinking that if we get her stoned then she will be more than willing to go ahead with things?"

"Well, it will make her more relaxed and that can only help, when we get close to home I'll pop round to one of Dave's runners and buy an eighth off him. I take it you have got some papers and backy or do we need to nip in the corner shop and buy that as well?"

"I can go one better than that Tom, you needn't go round to Dave's guy because I have still got about half an ounce in one of my bags that Clive got for me weeks ago, and it is some really nice stuff as well."

Although their initial idea was to get home early enough to have some fun between the two of them before their visitor was due to arrive they were that focussed on making sure that they both knew what was planned that sex took a back seat. If what they had got lined up worked then there would be plenty of time in the coming days for them to enjoy each other.

Just as she had the previous day Samantha arrived dead on time, and as soon as she was in the flat and while she was emptying her two bags George sparked up a rather well loaded spliff and was very soon passing it over to Samantha.

"Try some of this, it's a hell of a lot better than we always used to smoke round at your old man's place."

She took a small toke of the spliff and very soon was taking a second pull on it, this time drawing harder and taking it right down. Both George and Tom were watching and liking what they were seeing.

"So Samantha, can I ask you a question?"

"Go on then Tom."

"Have you ever had sex when you have been totally wrecked, because I'll tell you one thing for nothing you will get a real high from it?"

"I haven't but this stuff is that good I think that it will be something that I am going to experience today. George have you got any more of this because I don't think that the one joint will get me stoned?"

"Well it just so happens that I have already got another three spliffs rolled ready for you. You forget that I know that you love the stuff and that once you start smoking then there is hardly any stopping you."

With that they all relaxed a little, for Samantha the joints were rapidly beginning to take effect and for the two guys it appeared as though their plan might just be being made one hell of a lot easier thanks to the cannabis she was inhaling.

Tom watched and could not believe quite what he was seeing, normally if there was a joint ablaze then it would be passed round the room or at the very least offered to those present. For Sam she was just happy to sit there and smoke the whole spliff herself and then lighting another, not that he was too upset about what was happening.

It was only twenty minutes later by the time Samantha put the remains of the second spliff in the ashtray and turned her attention to the guys.

"Well Tom, you told me that sex when you are stoned is fab so why don't you prove it to me. I would ask George to but after him throwing up last night I don't think that he will be too keen to go there again. Are you ready to give me a real good fucking then Tom?"

"Well it just so happens that George and I have been talking about you during the day and he tells me that you like trying something new. Now according to what George has said he has never had you from behind and with him being the only one that you have been with other than me then I take it you have never had that pleasure?"

"I don't fancy you shagging me up the backside if that is what you are on about."

"Don't worry Samantha I think I know the difference between the two holes, but I think that it is something that you will enjoy, and while I am inside you you can be sucking on George at the same time. How does that sound?"

It was clear in an instant that with the cannabis Samantha was now just about as open to suggestions as she would ever be. Tom seized the moment and having got her to her feet he started undressing her while at the same time she fumbled at trying to undo his shirt buttons.

Shortly after Sam was stood up bent double with Tom behind her while George, with his trousers and pants round his ankles, was stood directly in front of her, Sam's mouth already in action as she started to feel Tom entering her.

With Sam's head being right down the two guys were able to mouth to each other how they were going to progress things.

"So Sam you know you brought over some toys for Tom's benefit yesterday, I see you only brought the one bag today. Was that because you thought that we should be the ones that would provide the toys today?" It was George that had asked the question.

Sam removed her mouth from round the member in order to respond to his question.

"Why have you got some toys here then?"

"We hadn't Sam but today we went out especially for you and got a couple of things that Tom with all his experience with girls just knows that you will get a kick out of trying. I take it you are still game for a laugh like you used to be"

George knew that with the way he had phrased the comment that she would see it as a challenge and as such would not back down from accepting it.

"You know me George better than anyone and if you remember when I have had a smoke I am always game for a laugh."

"In that case wait there and I'll be back in just a moment, Tom will carry on putting a smile on your face and I'll be back in just a jiffy then you can get your mouth back to work on mine."

With that George pulled himself clear of Sam's mouth and went through to the bedroom returning moments later carrying a large brown paper bag. Without allowing Sam to get a look at its contents he went behind her and to where Tom was still at work and having pulled the one item out prepared it ready for use.

"Sam, can you still touch your toes like you used to because if you do then I know that Tom can then get deeper into you, and I reckon that you will enjoy it a hell of a lot more than you are at the moment."

With that Samantha reached both arms down and was very soon proving that yes, she was still clearly able to touch her toes. As she did so Tom made certain that he made things more enjoyable for her, hoping that she would pass comment to the fact.

"So what do you think Samantha, are you liking that more now than when you were just bent over slightly? Tom asked.

"Fucking hell Tom that is great, the only thing though is that I don't know just how long I will be able to stay bent over like this as much as I am enjoying what you are doing."

"Let me help you with that Sam." George interrupted as he introduced a pair of wrist to ankle restraints and wasted no time in getting them locked into place on the right arm and leg. He then picked up the other half of the set and although he had to tease Sam into lowering her left arm back down he was soon fitting that one too.

Just as soon as the second of the two restraints were in place George tapped Tom on the leg and gave him the thumbs up.

"Right Sam, now if you remember from watching those tapes of your fathers that he got me to do things that I really didn't want to take place. Well I never got a chance to get my own back on him so I guess that I will have to make do with his daughter."
With that he withdrew his penis from her vagina and started inserting it into her back passage.
It wasn't until Tom was almost all of the way inside her that both him and George realised that Sam must be totally out of her head from the effects of the spliffs she had smoked. She hadn't put up much of a fight against the restraints having been put into place on her and now she was not objecting to what Tom was doing, although she had earlier voiced her objection to it taking place.
"I can't see what sort of face she is pulling, do me a favour George and have a look and tell me if you think that she is enjoying this as much as I am."
With that George went round the front of Sam and having got down on his knees to be on a level with her head he then answered Tom's question.
"I think you must be doing something wrong Tom because looking at her she is really enjoying having your dick in the wrong hole. In fact by the looks of things she is getting as much enjoyment out of having you up her bum as you do when I do the same to you."
"In that case George do you think that she would enjoy having the same size dildo up there as both her father and her insisted on me experiencing?"
With that George went back to the paper bag and having taken their main purchase out he then took it round to where Samantha would be able to have a good look at it.
"So what do you think then Sam, do you think that we could get this as far inside you as your father did to Tom?"
The effects of the cannabis immediately gave way to shear panic on seeing the size of dildo that George was waving under her nose. It didn't need to have a tape measure taken to it to confirm that it was even bigger than the one that had been used on Tom.
"You ain't getting that thing anywhere near me!" She exclaimed.

"Just in case you hadn't realised you are in no way in a position to stop us. Now shall I let Tom finish off and shoot his load up your arse before we see just how much of this you are able to take before you start screaming the place down?"

"You know what we forgot to buy though George don't you, we forgot to get any lube."

"I guess in that case we will just have to make do without any. I take it you have no objection have you Sam?"

George was beginning to enjoy getting one over on his ex-girlfriend. She had made the most of having them under her control and now the tide was rapidly beginning to turn.

Sam was now struggling, trying to free her wrists from the restraints.

"Just relax Sam. Firstly there is no way that you will ever get out of those things until we see fit to unlock them, and besides you wiggling like you are is spoiling my fun. Be a good girl and stay still at least until I have offloaded in you. Then at least you will have some sort of moisture there for when George starts getting the dildo in use."

Tom was now really working her backside with some vigour and knew that it would not be long before he would be making way for George to introduce the toy. He knew that if he were to let go of her hips that she would without doubt try and pull herself forward and free of him but there was no way that he was going to allow that to happen. From past occasions he was well aware that when a girl first experienced the warm sensation within her then it would be an almost certain thing that she would want to experience the very same thing again in the not too distant future. It was Tom's thinking that if the plan did fail then at least there might be an alternative avenue for George to go down that he would be more comfortable doing to her. Tom's thinking was that if George enjoyed shagging him up the arse so much then he could see no reason why George wouldn't get satisfaction out of doing the same thing to Sam.

"Come on Tom, I think that Sam is really looking forward to feeling what this is like all the way inside her." George laughed.

It was at this point that both George and Tom heard the crying and having bent right down again in order to look into her face George soon told Tom that she was crying her eyes out.

"What's the matter Sam, am I doing it wrong because if so I am sorry but for me it just feels fine. Or is it the thought of George getting our little toy to work that is concerning you?"

"Come on Sam, aren't you going to give Tom an answer?" George then placed the dildo on the carpet and on looking up at Tom with a huge smile.

"I've got a much better idea Tom, we'll save the dildo for when it is just the two of us. Now Sam, I know you are really into all of the social media sites and I think that you will really enjoy hearing of what I have just thought of doing. Tom you carry on enjoying yourself while I nip to the kitchen, I think you are going to enjoy this as well."

With that George disappeared into the kitchen only to return carrying a couple of carrots as well as a good sized parsnip. He placed them on the floor by Tom's feet and then went and picked up Tom's smart phone.

"Are you nearly there yet Tom?"

"I can be if you want me to George, why what have you got lined up?"

"Well as soon as you have had your fun then I will get to work filming Samantha while you get to work using the carrots and parsnip. I think that she will not want images of her going out on all the social media sites of her having vegetables entering her various holes. What do you think Sam, do you think that your followers would increase all of a sudden when word gets out that you can be seen with a carrot up your fanny while at the same time having a parsnip sticking out of your arse?"

It was only now that Tom realised just what it was that George had thought up and he couldn't help but burst out laughing at some volume.

"That is evil George, but I love it. Now Sam what George has just said is going to take place, and like yourself we will make sure that someone that we can trust totally will have a copy of the recording. If you ever even think of using the footage of us dealing drugs then think about everyone that you have ever known seeing you with carrots and parsnips where they should never go. Now do you get the message?"

"I won't use the footage that I have got of either of you, there is no need for you to carry out your threats, you have my word."

"Sorry Sam but we just can't take the risk of you not going back on what you have just said as soon as we have released you from the restraints, without having something recorded first. Now hurry up and get your part done Tom so we can get this filmed and then her out of this place once and for all."

With that Tom did as he was asked and was very soon making a deposit inside her anal passage. Once finished he then withdrew and having immediately pulled up his trousers and pants he then picked up the veg. With a carrot in his left hand and the parsnip in his right he then introduced them to Sam's anatomy while George filmed what was taking place.

"Make sure that there is a really good shot of her face as well George, so there is no mistaking who it was that had got these things sticking out of her."

With that George moved round getting every angle of Sam in the shot while making certain that at no time was there more than just part of Tom's hand visible to the possible future viewers. As soon as George considered that the task was complete he informed both Tom and Sam that he had done it.

"I think that before we unlock her George we really ought to have a look at what you have managed to capture just in case we need to take more footage."

With Sam still stood with both of her wrists still firmly fastened to her ankles Tom and George sat on the floor in front of her so all three of them were able to watch what George had filmed. The footage lasted for little more than a minute but it was that clear as to who the female was and what was happening that Sam's crying started all over again.

"So what do you think then Sam, do you think that all of your followers would enjoy watching that? I think if we ever put this out then you would become a worldwide sensation overnight." George laughed.

"Right then young lady, we are going to release those restraints now but before we do we will make things quite clear to you. Firstly, if you ever go to the police or anywhere else with the footage of George and me dealing drugs then this will go out on all the social media sites. In addition, you will carry on paying the solicitor to represent us until both of our cases have been heard, otherwise we will put some of this out on the media sites. Now George and I have talked at length and we do feel that it is only right that we do help to pay for our brief. As such you can bring ten beakers round here when we ask you for them, and then you can pick them up when we are ready. No longer will you be here to see us filling them and no longer will you be using either of us to fill you either. Now is that perfectly clear and have we got your agreement?"

Between the sobs she confirmed that Tom's request would be honoured by her. Adding that her old man had left that much cash as well as the house that she really did not need them to contribute towards the cost of the solicitor but it had just been a game that she had been playing with them.

On hearing what Sam had said it was George who decided that he needed to say something.

"In that case then Sam as you don't need the money from our sperm donations if you would be as good as to give us the contact details then we might very well deal with them direct. As you know very soon we might be rather pushed for money to keep this place on, and it might just be an avenue that we decide to go down."

"I have got their names and phone number on my phone and as soon as you let me out of these things I'll get them for you."

"Just before we do let you loose are you sure you don't want me to give you another fuck first." It was Tom asking her but from the tone of voice she knew that it was not a genuine offer, if it had been then she might just have taken him up on it.

As soon as the restraints were removed a rather stoned and embarrassed Samantha hurriedly got herself dressed and as soon as she had given the guys the contact details they required she was on her way out of the door, leaving the unused beakers on the lounge carpet.

"Well George I don't know if my original idea would have got the desired result but with what you came up with I think that we can safely say that our secrets are forever safe."

"What's more Tom is if I think that you are missing her ever then I can put the footage onto your laptop and then you will be able to watch it till your heart is content."

"My heart is content with having her out of our hair and you in my life George, but I wouldn't mind seeing it on a bigger screen than just your phone to see how well it has come out."

"Now are you just saying that because you want to see it out of curiosity or is it because you like seeing her naked and are already missing her?"

"You know the answer to that one, now come on I'll get my lap top started up and we can both watch it and then we can head to bed and have some fun."

"Is that with or without the aid of your new toy that we bought earlier?"

"Am I right in thinking that you had already thought of using the veg and that you allowed me to buy the dildo with your intentions all the time being that it would only ever be used on me?"

"The answer to that one Tom you will never really know the answer to, now will you."

For the next three weeks Tom and George spent the majority of their time locked away in the flat, only leaving it in order to get shopping in for George to reveal just how good a cook he was to his partner. To George's surprise on the odd occasion when he had suggested that they head out for an Indian it had been Tom who had voiced that he would prefer to eat whatever George was up for cooking them.

Andrew, the solicitor, had spoken to them via phone on a number of occasions and was continuing to voice he thought it best that the two of them would be far better off if they were to end their relationship. It was only five days before Tom was due to appear in crown court that he finally accepted the fact that there was no way that he was going to convince them enough for it to take place. Andrew did however achieve one thing, he actually got George to agree not to attend court for Tom's hearing, something that George was not at all happy about but had agreed to after Tom had begged him.

For the last seventy two hours before Tom was to leave for the court both were that concerned about what was to be their fate that sex took very much a back seat as all they were interested with was building as deep a bond between them as was possible. For Tom he was hoping that it would be sufficient to keep George loyal to him while Tom was locked up for however long the judge deemed fit.

It was 8:42am on the Wednesday morning when Tom left the flat, jumping in a taxi outside in which he was going to travel to the court. He had with him a kit bag stuffed full of clothes as the solicitor had advised. Both Tom and George were resigned to the fact that there was no way that Tom would be returning home anytime in the near future, the only thing that was remaining was to see just how long it was to be for.

George had established from the brief what time the court usually adjourn for lunch and when they ended the proceedings at the end of each day. Knowing that Tom was due to appear at 10:30am he thought it pointless ringing the brief at lunchtime, however at 4:32pm he was straight on his phone.

"Hello, is that Mr Barber?"

"It is, and I needn't ask who that is. Afternoon George, I dare say you are ringing for a progress report on how Tom is getting on?"

"You're right of course. I know that it is only the end of the first day but how are things looking?"

"As I had told you today was mainly going through formalities such as swearing in the jury and other formalities, the evidence will not really be heard until tomorrow morning and that will, or at least could take up both tomorrow and the whole of Friday. I did warn you that it could be next Wednesday or even Thursday before the jury are sent out in order to make their decision."

"I know that sir but how is Tom handling things?"

"Obviously, he is concerned as you would imagine would be the case, however he seems to be holding himself together quite well up till now. What I am able to inform you is that he will remain in custody until the case comes to a conclusion."

"You had already warned us that it would be the case which is why Tom brought his bag with him. I have got one question though that I would like you to answer, it isn't the same judge that was on duty the day that I appeared is it?"

"No George, at least that is one thing that Tom has in his favour, and I will just add that I have had dealings with the judge that is overseeing proceedings before and I can tell you that he will not allow the fact that Tom was, or is, in a gay relationship affect things in any way."

"I take it that he has already been made aware of the fact that Tom and I are still together then?"

"It hasn't been mentioned yet but it is bound to be brought to the court's attention before the trial is over. The prosecution will almost certainly bring the subject up in the hope that there are some on the jury that are anti."

"If Tom is going to be held over the weekend will there be any chance of me getting to visit him either Saturday or Sunday?"

"I'm sorry George but there is no way that I will be able to get that agreed. Anyway I dare say you have got loads more questions that you want to fire in my direction but I had only just walked out of the courtroom when you called, and I really do need to go and speak with the clerk of the court, so I am afraid I will have to end the call."

Having agreed that it would be okay for George to give him a ring the following lunchtime the call was concluded.

It was just turned ten that evening when George decided to turn in for the night and it wasn't until he had pulled the duvet over him that it dawned on him that he was going to be spending the first night in this bed without having Tom at his side. He lay there for what seemed like hours getting deeper and deeper into his thoughts. How long, and how many nights was this going to prove to be the case. How many nights was he going to have to spend separated from Tom.

Daylight was forcing its way through the curtains before George finally drifted off to sleep, and it was to his amazement that when he looked at the clock on waking that he saw it was now approaching midday.

Having got up George sat in the lounge looking at the clock every few minutes, eager for it to display the fact that it was 1pm as it was only then that he would be able to give the brief a call in order to get a progress report.

"Hello Mr Barber, it's George here. I was just ringing to find out how things are going."

"As I think I told you during your call yesterday we won't really know anything until the middle of next week. All I can inform you at the moment is that I will be fighting as hard as I am able to get Tom the shortest term inside as I am able. Having said that though I am not going to build your hopes up on false promises. Tom will, with all the evidence, be facing a custodial sentence and I can tell you that it will be for a number of years, just how many that turns out to be we will not know until next week. I am sorry as I know that is not what you wanted to hear but I am afraid it is how things stand. To save you from having to call me again I will give you a call when we finish tomorrow, although as I have already implied there will not be much more that I will have to tell you than you already know."

"I know you are probably thinking that I am being a real pain sir but I am worried about Tom which is why I keep calling."

"I appreciate that will be the case but as I have already said I will phone you tomorrow, but when I do don't expect to hear anything other than what I have already told you."

With that it was call over.

George sat in the armchair allowing his imagination to run wild until his thoughts were interrupted with his phone ringing.

Chapter 13

"Hello you, I thought I would give you a quick ring just to make sure you were okay."

"Bloody hell, you are the last person I expected to be hearing from after the other week."

"I have been speaking with Andrew Barber, and he was just saying that he thinks you are finding things really tough. Are you alright and are you eating?"

"Of course I am not alright Sam, and as for me eating I don't mind admitting that I haven't ate a thing since Tom walked out of here yesterday morning."

"In that case George expect your intercom to be buzzing in about half an hour. Oh, and it isn't optional but I am going to come over to make sure that you at least eat something."

"There is no need for you to do that Sam, besides, I am not at all hungry."

"As I said George it isn't optional. I will be there in a little while."

With that the phone went dead before Sam allowed George to give any further protest.

 George sat there in the armchair wondering why Sam was so keen to come and pay him a visit. He was concerned that she might be heading over in order to try and blackmail him into carrying out similar acts to those he had to perform on her previous visits.

George did not have to wait for long before the intercom sounded and he was hearing Sam's voice coming over the speaker. Reluctantly he allowed her into the building, and on seeing her coming up the staircase he was relieved to see that the only thing she was carrying was a carrier bag from the local takeaway. He was relieved because he had wondered if she was going to turn up with beakers that she would then expect him to be filling.

"You needn't have come over Sam", George proclaimed as she entered the flat."

"We both know that if I hadn't then you would have gone to bed tonight without eating anything, and you would probably have not eaten a thing again tomorrow either. At least with me being here tonight I can make certain that you get something in that stomach of yours. Now are you going to put this lot on plates or do you want me to?"

George took the bag from her and went through to the kitchen having established what was in it and what was for who.

Once plated he took both meals back through to the lounge where Sam immediately started filling her face, George on the other hand sat with plate on his lap motionless. Not only was he not hungry but he was also not in the least relaxed with having Sam there in the flat and without Andrew to support him.

"I haven't bought you that just for you to sit there looking at it, George I'll tell you now that I will not be leaving here until you have emptied that plate, so unless you intend eating it cold I suggest you start."

George knew Sam well enough to know that when she said that she wouldn't leave without him having eaten that was exactly what would transpire. Having accepted the situation George started slowly taking forkful after forkful into his mouth.

Between eating George decided that he had to ask a question.

"Sam so what have you really come here for?"

"You will probably not believe me when I tell you. The only reason is to make sure that you are looking after yourself. When I spoke to Andrew Barber on the phone earlier I got the impression that he was getting increasingly concerned about you. I am not stupid you know. I am well aware that for some unknown reason you and Tom have got a real thing between you, and I know that with you being here on your own you will be spending all your time worrying about him. Now I know what I did the other week was out of order and I am sorry for having put you through what I did. Having said that I must admit I did enjoy most of what took place."

"What, so are you trying to say that one of the main reasons for you coming over was so you could apologise?"

"No, as I have already told you, the main reason was because I wanted to check up on you, to make sure you were looking after yourself. Believe it or not George I do still care about you."

"Yes, so much so that the other week you forced me to do something that you knew very well would cause me to head to the bathroom and throw up."

"As I have already said I am sorry about that. I guess it started out with the intention of having a bit of a laugh at yours and Tom's expense, but then I got carried away and things got out of hand. There was one other thing that I was wanting to talk to you about."

"What's that?" George asked, fearful of what he was about to hear in reply.

"I was going to ask you how you were off for money. Don't get me wrong I am not trying to get any out of you. What I mean is have you now managed to get enough saved up to cover the rent on this place if you do end up being sent down for a time?"

"So far we have managed to get about fifteen week's worth of rent put to one side, which if everything goes well it might just about be enough. That is as long as the brief manages to get me the lower end of what he is predicting will be handed down to me. If I get sent down for any longer then I guess when I am released the first thing that I will be doing is looking for a roof over my head,"

"Have you got a date yet for when you have got to appear?"

"No Sam, they can't firm that up until after Tom's case is finished, and that could be a few more weeks before they have got round to telling him how long he has got to spend inside. According to the brief before the judge determines how long Tom has got to serve he will want something called a pre-sentencing report or something like that."

"Yes, Andrew told me the same. So it could be weeks before you end up in court then?"

"That's right. Just reading between the lines from what Andrew has said it could be as much as another two months before they get round to having me in the dock."

"Do you know if they will allow you to visit Tom before you get your day in court?"

"I haven't asked because I have got a funny feeling that I would not like hearing the answer that came my way. Come on Sam, I have known you for long enough to know when you are not telling me everything. What is the real reason for you being here?"

"Okay, I'll level with you. Yes I am concerned that you will not be bothering to take care of yourself, but there is something else that I want to talk to you about."

"I just knew you weren't telling me everything. What else is there?"

"I don't know if I told you but since my dad died I have been living back at his, the other day I started clearing some of his stuff out and came across a computer memory stick hidden away in one of his draws in the bedroom. Well me being the nosey bitch that I am I shoved it in the computer to see what was on it."

"Carry on, I'm listening." George said, his curiosity now raised.

"When I started opening up the various files I came across this one that I can't decide if I should hand over to the police or not."

"That sounds serious, what the hell is on it?"

"It relates to a bank account that I didn't even know he had, and in it there are thousands of pounds, and I mean thousands."

"So, it's probably a savings account that he has been paying into for years ready for when he retired."

"No it isn't,. there are detailed accounts of every payment made and what each one was linked to. I spent hours looking through it and the more I studied it the more I wasn't liking what I was finding out."

"Come on Sam, tell me what it's to do with then?"

"Each payment that he got was for either a young boy or girl that he, from what I can make out, sold to someone by the name of Charles down in London."

"And you didn't know anything about that line of work that he was into by the way you are talking."

"No, why did you?"

"Put it this way Sam, if your dad had got to know me a year or so earlier then you would probably have found my name in those files as well."

"Are you saying what I think you are. Are you trying to tell me that he would have sold you somehow?"

"Yes. The one evening I got a phone call from your old man asking for me to go round to his. Well I'll make it brief. There was a guy there from London who wanted to check me out and once he had seen me he decided that I was too old for what he had in mind. Your dad used to find young gullible boys and sell them on to be sex slaves down in London."

"You're having me on?"

"No I am not Sam. Can I ask what you have done with the memory stick?"

"I've got it hidden away back at home, why?"

"Because I have just had an idea."

"Go on then George, what are you thinking?"

"I am thinking that if the court found out what your dad was up to it might help Tom out, especially if we get the brief to put across to the court that Tom had discovered this and he was so incensed by it that it caused him to take the line of action he did. I reckon that if the judge and jury heard exactly what your old man had been up to then Tom might get a much lighter sentence."

"So what do you want me to do then George?"

"It is up to you, it is your dad after all, but I think that if the brief was to have a good look at it then he would be the best one to say if putting it before the judge would be a wise move or not. As I say though it has got to be your decision."

Instead of answering George Sam, having picked her bag up from off the floor, pulled out her mobile and started making a call. George sat opposite her hoping that she was calling the solicitor.

"Hello, is that Andrew Barber?"

George sat there listening to every word that Sam said into the telephone, trying at the same time to work out what was being said at the other end of the call. He had to wait for a good ten minutes for the call to be ended before he was made aware of the fullness of what had been discussed.

Sam informed him that she had arranged to meet up with Mr Barber in the courthouse foyer first thing in the morning, and that she would have the memory stick with her. The brief would then have a look at it before the day's proceedings started and depending on what he thought would then depend on what route of action he would take. She did tell George that Andrew did give her the impression that it could well have quite an influence on the case.

With Sam having to be up early in the morning and after being satisfied with the amount of food that George had eaten it was not long before she was heading home to Warwick. It had been agreed that she would give George a call as soon as she had finished with the solicitor in the morning.

It was not long after closing the door behind Samantha that George headed for the bed. Tonight though, and unlike the previous he did manage to get to sleep without much delay. For the first time since he and Tom were first arrested he was feeling more than just a little optimistic that things might turn out a lot better than they had all been predicting.

It was shortly after ten the next morning when George's phone started ringing and having looked at the caller display he answered it eager to hear what was going to be said.

"Hello Sam, what did the solicitor have to say?"

"I knew you would be sat there with phone in hand itching to hear from me, it hardly had chance to ring once before you answered it. In answer to your question I have just finished with the solicitor and he has gone off to try and arrange a meeting with both the judge and the prosecution team before they head into the courtroom. He will also be having a talk with Tom in order to bring him into the picture. Mr Barber wants me to head back home to try and find whatever paperwork I can about this bank account. He said that we will need to be able to prove that it was my dad's memory stick but as long as we can then it could work out to be good for both you and Tom. I hope you don't mind but I did mention to him that you already knew about what my dad was involved in, and he asked me to tell you that he'll probably be ringing you during their lunch break to have a talk about it. I hope you didn't mind me telling him."

"Sam, if it means that Tom gets a shorter sentence then I will happily come to the court and stand in the witness box and swear to the fact. I will have no problem telling them that I could have been one of those entries on that file. Sorry Sam, but your dad was a real bastard and I don't care who knows just what shit he was in to."

"If you had said that to me before I found out what I have we would have fallen out over it, but knowing what I do now then I have to agree with you. There was one thing that the solicitor said that you might be able to help with. He asked if there was any way we would be able to identify the boys behind the various entries. Have you ever met any of the lads who did end up going to London?"

"I have never met any of them but when you were round here yesterday am I right in thinking that you said that there were initials against each entry?"

"Yes, why?"

"In that case I will get dressed and down the library as fast as I can. I will look up in the local papers over the last few years of any reported missing child and hopefully we will be able to tie some of those entries up to missing kids."

"That sounds like hours and hours of searching and I don't know if you will have enough time."

"I think they have now got all the back copies on computer so I am hoping that I can just type in a search for missing children and then a list will appear. If that is the case then I will then just have to look up the relevant dates to get all the details. I think that even if I only manage to come up with one or two that seem to match up it will be a help."

"Are you going to the library in the city centre, because if so I will grab a bus and come over to give you a hand after I have had a look for bank statements back at home."

"Cheers Sam, yes I will be heading for the one in the centre but finding those bank details sounds as if it is more important. Why don't you give me a call once you know what you are doing, better still send me a text because if I am in the library they won't like it if my phone rings."

Having agreed to do as asked Sam ended the call allowing her to get on her way back home, for George it allowed him to get dressed and on his way out heading for the library.

By the time that Sam joined George in the library he had already got five names of boys, all under the age of fifteen, that had allegedly run away from home in the nearby area. To George's delight Sam had thought to bring a list of all the initials with her. It took less than a couple of minutes before three of the names that George had come up with appeared to tie in with entries on Sam's fathers records.

"By the way San, I forgot to ask if you managed to find anything in the house relating to the bank account."

"Initially I couldn't find anything, but when I had another look at the files on his computer I struck lucky. The stupid sod had set it up with internet banking and because he always used the same passwords and security questions for everything it took me no time to find everything. Out of all the various payments that he received they only ever came from one of three different accounts. I bet if the police trace them back to who sent the money through it might even end up reuniting some of the kids back up with their families."

"Wouldn't that be nice, as long as they are still alive and haven't been messed up to such a degree that it creates even more of a problem for them."

They carried on with their research until George's phone started
ringing.

"It's the brief, I had better run outside to take the call." George
told Sam.

Within a matter of seconds George was talking to the solicitor,
Sam right at his side. He informed Andrew that not only had Sam
come up trumps with regard to the bank account details but
between them they had now found the names of five kids that had
disappeared, and not only did the initials tie up with the entries
but the dates of the payments also were about right. It was only
after telling the solicitor everything that they had uncovered that
George asked how things were going and what the outcome of the
meeting he had this morning was.

He remained silent while listening to what Andrew had to say,
much to the annoyance of Sam who was eager to be brought up to
date on the developments. What George was hearing brought a
smile to his face, the first time there had been one there for
weeks. Having seen how George was reacting to what he was
being told over the phone it only added to the impatience that
Sam was feeling, and no sooner had George removed the phone
from his ear she did not hesitate to ask what the state of play was.

"Well Sam, from what the brief has just said with a bit of luck
Tom might be spending a lot less time away than we thought, and
Andrew implied that when it is my turn in court I might not even
be sent down. He is going to give me another call as soon as they
finish for the day and said that he might even end up coming over
to see me this evening to talk everything through."

"That's great news. Do you think it would be a good idea if I
were to come back with you? That way he will be able to see
everything that I have found at the same time and we can spend
some time with the three of us tying things together."

"I guess it won't do any harm, as long as you don't try force
feeding me again like you did last night." George couldn't believe
that he had just made a joke out of the situation.

"By the way you are talking I have got a funny feeling that you
will be eating without me having to stand over you."

The two of them carried on looking stuff up on the library's database until 4pm at which time they headed back to the flat, stopping off at McDonalds on their way.

By seven that evening there were three of them in the flat going over everything that had been unearthed during the day.

"Right George, can I ask you a question, did Tom ever give you any reason to think that his brother was tied in with what Sam's father was involved in?"

"No, he did say that they had met a few times round at the house but from what I can remember that is all. Why do you ask?"

"I was thinking that if we could tie Gavin and Clive together then we could use that to assist with the case. As things stand Clive's name is a dirty word as far as the judge is concerned, and if we are able to tar Tom's brother Gavin in on the same business then I think that Tom having killed him will be seen as doing humanity a huge favour."

"With them both being dead then how the hell can we prove that?"

"Easier than you think George, they are not here to dispute anything we tell the court."

"Am I understanding you, are you trying to say that if I were to stand up in court and tell them that I had not only told Tom about Clive trying to get me sold off down to London. But in addition, that I knew Tom's own brother was in on it all as well then the court would just accept it as being fact."

"If that was your understanding of what was taking place then I feel sure that if you brought it to the courts attention it certainly would not do any harm."

"Mr Barber just let me know when you want me to turn up at the court and I will be there. Tom's brother was a drug addict and we all know that they will do just about anything in order to fund their addiction. By the time I have finished those in court will want to knight Tom for services to the country rather than send him to prison for murder."

"When you get up in the witness box don't get carried away, if you know what I mean."

"Mr Barber I know exactly what you are saying. Trust me, I will
spend every hour I have between now and then rehearsing what I
will be saying, and I will run it past you beforehand."
Throughout majority of the conversation Sam had just been sat
there listening to the brief and George talking until she suddenly
realised that she had got something to add to the conversation.
"George, while you two have been talking I have been looking
round the room. See that picture of Tom with another guy over on
that cabinet, has Tom ever mentioned who the other guy is
because I have seen him before."
"Yes, that's a photo of Tom and his brother from when they were
on holiday about ten years ago. Where do you know him from?"
"Mr Barber, how would you like to be able to present video
evidence to support what George is going to tell the court?"
"Sorry Sam but I am not following you,"
"I think I have mentioned to you that my dad had got cameras
rigged up in the house and that I have access to all the files. Well
the other day when I was going through some of them I am
certain that Tom's brother was on some of the footage. If I can
find it again then that will prove without doubt that the two of
them were more than just passing friends."
"Sam, if you can come up with footage showing them together
then I think that will assist me no end when defending both Tom
and George."
"Sam, I know that the cameras that were installed in the house
that Tom worked in have got sound recording as well, have those
at your dads got the same?"
"Yes, that's how I got to find out exactly how he was
blackmailing both you and Tom. I know what you are thinking
and no I haven't listened to what Gavin and Clive were talking
about, if that was going to be your next question."
"With a bit of luck Sam when you do find it again and listen to
what they are saying it might reveal some very interesting stuff."
"George, I wouldn't build your hopes up too much. It could be
that Gavin had been there purely to do a few odd jobs around the
place or even a bit of gardening."

"I hear what you are saying Mr Barber, but from what Tom has
told me about his brother I can't see him travelling all the way
over to Warwick without there being serious money involved."
Having agreed that all three of them would simply have to wait to
see what Sam can come up with both Mr Barber and Sam were
soon leaving George and Tom's flat.
It was not even 10pm when George went to the bedroom, having
eaten a couple of rounds of cheese on toast, and in no time he was
dead to the world,
He woke up by the sound of his phone ringing and with there
being no sign of daylight he glanced at the bedside clock before
answering the call. It wasn't even four in the morning and George
immediately thought that it could only spell bad news,
"Hello." He grumbled, still half asleep.
"Morning George, I know that I will have woken you but I
thought you would want to hear what I have got to tell you."
  It was on hearing what Sam had said that George rapidly gained
a lot more alertness and was soon asking what she had to say for
herself. He lay there listening to every word that was coming over
the call. Sam revealed that she had found a total of six occasions
on tape where Gavin had visited her father, but it wasn't until she
said that although the first three she had listened to hadn't brought
up anything of any use it was on the next recording that things
changed in quite a big way.
George listened as Sam elaborated further.
"You were right when you said last night that Gavin wouldn't
have bothered coming all the way over to Warwick if there hadn't
been serious money involved, he got paid two grand for a job that
my old man got him to carry out."
"Tell me more Sam."
"Although if you were to listen in on their conversation without
knowing all the rest of the stuff it wouldn't make much sense,
however when added to everything else that we have uncovered it
is really clear that my dad paid him for grabbing a boy as he left
school. Have you got those names and dates handy because if so

can you see if there was someone with the first name starting with a M, and if so what date was it?”

George climbed out of bed and went through to the bedroom where he had left all the paperwork after the solicitor had finished looking through it the previous evening.

“There are two with the initial M, the one is a Martin and that was just over two years ago, the other was a Michael, he went missing 16th April last year. Do either of those tie in with what you have got your end?”

“It must have been Michael that they were talking about. Hold on while I grab those records of payments into the account and see if they match up as well.”

After a pause of little over a minute Sam informed George that everything tallied. Gavin had grabbed the boy from outside the school gates on the Tuesday afternoon, which was the 16th April, he had met up with Sam’s dad the next day and received two grand in cash, then on the Thursday of the same week there had been a payment made into the account for ten thousand. As an after thought she added that there were initials against the payment of MC.

“That would be the one then Sam because the surname of the lad who went missing was Chapman. So that proves Gavin helped to grab kids for Clive. Now in my reckoning if the courts were told about this and that our solicitor told them that Tom had just found out what had been going on then it wouldn’t be at all surprising if Tom hadn’t acted in the way he had. With what Gavin had been up to, if it ever became public knowledge then that would have caused Tom huge problems. I know they will say that you can never justify killing anyone, but if there were ever an instance where you could then this must be pretty damn close to being it.”

“What do you think we ought to do with all this information, are we better off handing it all over to the police without delay, or should we give it all to Mr Barber and let him deal with it?”

“Seeing as we spent over two hours last night with the brief going through things I think he would be the best avenue. With all his legal knowhow he will know exactly what is the best avenue to go down.”

“I guess you are right George, do you think that it would be best if we both were waiting outside the court building first thing in the morning so we can grab hold of him when he arrives?”

“If you try and get to me by about eight then I will give him a quick call. If he does want us to meet him at the courthouse then it will only take us about ten minutes in a taxi from here before we reach the place. That is if you are not too knackered, because to have found everything out that you have you couldn’t have been to bed.”

“You’re right, as soon as I got in I started going through all the footage, doing different searches. I will be okay though, after we have seen Mr Barber I will have plenty of time to catch up on sleep. Getting all this lot to him has got to take priority. George, if we manage to get Tom out of having to serve any time in prison do you think he will do something for me as a thank you? Before you bite my head off I said that as a joke, I was only kidding.”

“I was going to say that if it does turn out to be the case then I will get the dildo working at the same time so you get the best that Tom can give you.”

“Anyway George I am going to try and catch two or three hours kip but I’ll make certain that I am over your place before eight. I guess you will go and catch another hour or two sleep as well.” Having ended the call George went back to bed with the intention of having another couple of hours sleep, however after an hour of just tossing and turning he gave up. By seven he had showered, shaved, had breakfast and was on his third cup of coffee of the day. There was just the one thing that repeatedly went round and round in his head, the one question, was Tom going to end up in prison and if so for how long?

Sam arrived fifteen minutes early and by eight they were both on their way out through the front door. George had given Mr Barber a call and he soon requested that they meet up with him as soon as they were able to get a taxi to the court buildings.

Once they had met up with the brief and after having furnished him with everything they had managed to find out Andrew Barber told them to get on their way as he needed to arrange meetings with both the judge as well as the prosecution team. His thoughts, or at least what he was hoping to achieve, was that after bringing this new information to their attention would be that the case against his client would be dropped. His personal feelings were that Tom had done society a huge favour in killing his brother as without him the world would be a better place.

After having had a brief chat with Sam George informed the brief that if he did want either of them for any reason then they would both be available at short notice as Sam would be spending the day at his flat, and that ten minutes warning would be enough time for them to get to the courthouse. With that they left Andrew, both hoping that he was as successful as they were all hoping he would be.

Once back at the flat the two of them tried to relax, both checking the time on a regular basis. It was not until after the court would have finished for the day that George's phone started ringing.

"Hello Mr Barber, we have been sat here all day waiting for your call, how did things go?"

"If you are asking if they have decided not to pursue the case against Tom then I am afraid I have got to say that despite my best efforts I was unable to achieve that argument."

"So does that mean that Tom is still facing years behind bars?" George asked, immediately thinking the worst.

"I believe that yes, he will have to spend some time in a prison, however from what the judge said when sentencing he will be as lenient as the guidelines will allow him."

"So what does that mean then sir?"

"It means that the judge will use whatever argument he can in order to justify the shortest possible custodial term as he can. Plus the prosecution team have agreed not to challenge any sentence that is handed down."

"As I have already asked sir, what exactly does that mean?"

"I have got a feeling that Tom could end up with as few as three or four years, and that only half of that he will have to serve in prison with the remainder being on licence."

"So am I understanding you right, are you saying that he could be out in as little as eighteen months, and that in the worst case it will be just the two years?"

"With the way things appear, and in addition to what has been said then yes I believe that will be the case. Having said that I am not guaranteeing it."

"Can I ask you in that case what you think I will get sentenced to when it comes round to my turn in the dock?"

"To a large degree that will depend on if you are allocated the same judge as is overseeing Tom's trial. If we are lucky and it is the same judge then we should be alright."

"Sorry for being persistent but what do you mean by alright, are you saying that I might not even have to spend any time banged up?"

"I am not going to answer that at this stage, as I am afraid it will all depend on the judge on the day. You have my assurance however that I will be speaking to the judge and requesting that he tries to be sitting when it does come round to your day in court."

"Okay, I understand that. With it being Friday tomorrow do you think that the jury will be sent out to make their decision, or is there still loads of stuff to be heard before that happens?"

"It will be Monday afternoon at the very earliest before that takes place however there is one other piece of news that I have got to tell you, sorry two pieces."

"What are they sir?"

"Firstly, that all the information that Sam and you passed to me has now been handed over to the police. The other bit of news that I have, which I know will make you happy, is that the judge has agreed to allow you to have one two hour visit with Tom over the weekend, I did however have to commit you to a day and time."

"So when can I see him, and where?"

"I have been informed that due to the overcrowding situation in all the closest locations, that Tom will be spending the weekend in the cells at Coventry police station. I have committed you to visit him Saturday morning at eleven o'clock. I hope that fits in with anything that you might have planned."

"Mr Barber even if I had got other stuff arranged I would have cancelled it. Ten Saturday morning is fine with me and thank you very much for having achieved getting it authorised. Thank you."

It was on this high note that the phone conversation was drawn to a conclusion and a very anxious Sam could now be brought up to date with all of the developments.

"Well that really is good news isn't it George?"

"It sounds as though it is going to be, but Mr Barber did say that nothing is for certain and I guess we will just have to wait until Tom is sentenced before we can relax fully. It all seems to be looking too good, and I can't help feeling that something is going to go wrong and that tom will end up having to spend a hell of a lot longer than two years locked away."

"Don't be so negative George, if Mr Barber has said that it will probably be no more than two years then he isn't likely to have said it without being confident of it being the case."

"I know what you are saying but I just can't help thinking that something will go wrong."

"Let's wait and see. At least you can go to visit your man on Saturday, which is one thing that the solicitor had said would not be allowed. Now are you going to be okay here on your own, because if so I'm going to head back to Warwick, and when I get there I will be heading straight for my bed."

"Sam, you get on your way, and thanks very much for everything that you have done. If it does turn out as good as the brief reckons then both Tom and I owe you in a really big way."

"After everything that my dad has put you through over the last couple of years George you owe me nothing, and again I am sorry for having put you and Tom through all that rubbish the other week, I was bang out of order. All I hope is that once all this lot has been drawn to an end is that the three of us might be able to become good friends. The two of us have always got on well and I think Tom is an alright guy as well."

"Yes, I guess you can take it in turn coming to visit us both in nick, Tom the one week and me the other."

"It might not even come to that, you heard what Mr Barber reckons, anyway I'm going to get on my way."

Without any further conversation Sam left the flat and headed for the bus station in order to make her way back home. For George though all that he was left doing was sitting in the same armchair as he had been all day and dwelling on every negative thing he could bring to mind.

It was 2:10pm the following day when George next heard from anyone and was still sat in the same chair having fallen asleep in it late into the previous night.

"Hello". He muttered on answering the phone call.

"Is that you George, it's Mr Barber here, are you free to talk?"

"I didn't expect to be hearing from you until the court finished for the day, is there something wrong?" George was immediately in full panic mode.

"On the contrary young man. Now you know that I said that the judge had agreed for you to visit Tom on Saturday, I'm afraid that you will not now be able to."

George dived in before allowing the solicitor to say any more.

"Come on sir, what's gone wrong for the visit to have been cancelled?"

"Nothing has gone wrong at all George, and if you will allow me to finish I will tell you exactly what is happening. Now the reason why you will not be able to visit Tom in the police station is due to the fact that he will not be there. I hope you have got food in the house because you will be getting a visitor in approximately an hour and I know that when he gets there he will almost certainly be wanting something nice to eat as the food he has been getting delivered to his cell would not have been filling nor would it have been of any quality."

"Does that mean what I think it does, are you saying that Tom is on his way home?"

"He will be just as soon as all the relevant paperwork here is completed. If I can put you in the picture as to the state of play. Tom is being allowed home for the weekend but will have to return here first thing Monday morning for judgement to be passed. The judge has instructed the jury to take the weekend to come to their decision, however he did stress to them that he wanted them to consider everything they had heard, and that they were to try to put themselves in Tom's position and for them to ask themselves what they would have done if it had been them. Basically the judge was trying to influence them into returning a not guilty to murder but rather to find him guilty of one of the lesser charges that are on offer."

"So what exactly does that mean then Sir?"

"It means George, that if they come back having found Tom not guilty of pre-meditated murder that the judge will then have greater flexibility when it comes to sentencing. Which is exactly what I was referring to last evening when I informed you that it might be as little as eighteen months."

"Can I ask you a question please Mr Barber, with the way things have turned out would it now be okay if I came with Tom on Monday?"

"With the way things have turned out George I can't see that there will be any harm done if you were to accompany him. He will need to bring his kit bag with him again though. Do not expect him to be returning home with you by the end of the day."

"I understand that and was expecting it to be the case. It will be really good to have him here with me over the weekend though."

"George, I need to get on because I have to be present when all the paperwork is gone through and the quicker we can get that dealt with then the sooner Tom will get home."

"Would it be an idea for me to get a taxi over to pick him up?"

"No need for you to do that as I will bring him to you just as soon as we have finished this end. As I have said expect him in about an hour."

As soon as the call was finished George went straight through to the kitchen in order to check out what food there was, his aim was to cook Tom something special. It was while looking through the cupboards that he decided on taking a completely different route.

"Hello, Wang Lee Restaurant."

"Hello, is it possible to book a table for two for this evening please, somewhere round eight o'clock if you can?"

As soon as he heard the key going in the downstairs door lock George went and opened the front door to their flat in order to greet his partner.

"I bet you didn't expect to be seeing me here?"

"I didn't until Mr Barber phoned and told me. Shall I get the kettle on to make you a drink before anything?"

"No George, the first thing I want is a hug and kiss from you if there is one on offer."

With no more being said they spent the next five minutes in each other's arms.

"Now you can get the kettle on if you are still offering as I am gagging for a decent hot drink."

"The solicitor said that you would be as hungry as hell with what they have been serving up in the police station for you to eat. Was he right?"

"I think I could eat a horse as it happens but I don't want you spending loads of time tucked away in the kitchen because I want what time we have to spend it wisely."

"As it happens I was hoping that you would come out with something along those lines. It's nearly four now so we have got about three hours before we need to get showered and changed."

"What are you talking about George?"

"We have got to be showered and changed by 7:40 this evening."

"Sorry, I'm not following. Why have we got to bother getting showered and dressed, I know I haven't been able to even have a proper wash since Tuesday morning but I didn't think that I smelt that bad."

"You silly arse. The reason why we have got to be ready for 7:40 is because that is when the taxi will be picking us up. If you

remember where we went for my birthday then that should tell
you everything.”
“Are you saying that we have got a table booked at Wang Lee for
tonight?”
“We have, a table for two at eight. I did say back then that I
wanted us to only go there when we had got something very
special to celebrate, and from my side of things you being here till
Monday morning is very much something worth celebrating. I
hope you feel the same Tom.”
“Well with everything that is going on if we had gone along with
what we had agreed, that the next time we were going to go there
would be for our engagement then we would have had a long wait
George.”
“From what Mr Barber said on the phone earlier it might not be
that long. From what he said to me it implied that you might not
get sent down at all.”
“I wouldn’t hold your breath on that one because I am not
building my hopes up.”
“From what you just said I get the impression that you have
already accepted that you are going to be locked away for
sometime. What makes you think Mr Barber has got it wrong?”
“I think that with me having pleaded guilty to killing Gavin there
is no way that I am going to walk out of the courtroom on
Monday.”
“I guess all we can do is wait and hope. I really do hope that Mr
Barber is right and that you are wrong, I really do.”
“If I get five years or less I will consider myself very lucky, but
even if I do get away with five I will still have to spend two and a
half years away. My biggest concern is that while I am banged up
you will find someone else.”
“Tom, can you do me a favour please, can we not talk about stuff
like that for the weekend, if these are going to be our last days
together for years then let us make the most of them.”
“I will try but I can’t promise that I will not slip up and bring the
subject up from time to time. No matter what I do it is right at the
front of my thinking.”

"I know it must be worrying you as it's hard enough for me to deal with. At least tonight will you try to enjoy us being together?"

"I'll do my best George. So changing the subject from what Mr Barber has told me it sounds as though your ex-girlfriend has really helped with things."

"She has been a real diamond actually, oh and by the way she apologised for what she had put us through the other week. From what she said I got the impression that if you hadn't given her such a good shag the first night then she wouldn't have bothered coming back."

"So that is something else that is all my fault then."

"I said it as a joke Tom."

"I know you did but you must admit that everything in our lives that is bad all stems from me. Me losing my job is my fault, you losing your job, my fault. Me facing a prison sentence, my fault. You ending up in court, my fault. And most importantly, if you find someone else to replace me while I am in nick will be my fault. Over the last few nights I have spent hours thinking things through and have decided that it would be totally wrong of me to expect you to hang on for me."

"Tom, we had this conversation the other night, and we agreed that I will try and stay loyal. Again I promise you that if you do end up inside and I find someone else then I will let you know. I emphasise the 'if' because that is not what I am aiming to do. Tom I love you and even if you get sent down for ten years in five years' time I expect to be there when you walk out through those prison gates. Now we have got a couple of hours before we need to start getting ourselves ready to go out, and I know how I would like to spend that time. Why don't we go through to the bedroom for a bit."

"I was hoping you would say something along those lines because although it is something that I really do want to happen there was no way that I was going to broach the subject."

They made their way through to the bedroom where conversation was non-existent other than the occasional 'I love you' being

voiced. Needless to say that they had only just readied themselves
when the taxi arrived, and in no time they were being shown to
their table in the restaurant.

"So what will it be then Tom, are we having the same as last
time?"

"Yes, but unfortunately I haven't got a ring with me tonight."

"From what Mr Barber implied earlier it won't be too long before
that does happen. Just think Tom, if things do go as well as they
could for you on Monday then it could turn out that we are back
in here a lot sooner than either of us had thought."

"As I said back at the flat I can't see that happening somehow
George. There is something else that I have just thought of, do
you think it was a wise decision for us to come here this
evening?"

"What makes you ask that Tom, I thought that you being here was
something well worth celebrating."

"For the simple reason George that we are supposed to be
watching every penny so we then have enough to cover the rent
while we are out of circulation."

"Firstly, I don't think it will be for as long as we had envisaged,
and secondly Sam has very kindly said that she will cover any
shortfall. So Tom, no matter what happens we will still have the
flat for when all this is over."

"Oh yes, and what will Sam want in return is the only question
that springs into my mind?"

"I honestly believed her when she said that there would be no
catch, and she felt it was the right thing for her to do, especially
with the fact that if it hadn't been for our actions she would not be
sitting on the small fortune that she is now."

"The way you are singing her praises are you sure you are not
thinking of turning straight and planning on getting back with her
just as soon as I am banged up."

Tom had said it in jest and with a smile on his face otherwise
George would have reacted to his last comment by standing up
and walking out of the place. Instead in response to Tom's

comment he stood up and having moved round the table to where Tom was seated delivered a kiss on his partners lips.

"I hope you know that me going back with Sam is the last thing on my mind. All I hope is that very soon we will be in here again, each of us having something in our pockets ready to put on the other's finger."

"Can we get on with ordering the food because having had very little sleep over the last few nights I am looking forward to our bed."

"What for though, is that to make up for lost sleep, or lost fun?"

"Both as it happens, but you will have to forgive me if I am not to my usual standard in the sex department."

"When we get back we'll head straight to bed and get straight off to sleep. As long as I have got your arms around me other stuff can wait. We have got all weekend to do other stuff, and I am itching to see if you can handle that new dildo that we bought."

"If I had realised at the time that you were intending using it on me then there is no way that I would have suggested ever getting one quite as big as that thing is."

"Just think though Tom, if you do get sent down then if I have got you used to taking that thing then you will be okay when you go and get showered in prison. You'll even be safe to bend over to pick up the bar of soap."

"Very funny George, but the only thing that I ever want up there is what you have got hidden away in those trousers of yours. That is unless you are the one who is handling the dildo."

With having gained the waiters attention the food was ordered.

Once they had eaten as much as they were going to Tom wasted no time in asking for the bill.

"There is nothing to pay sir, the owner has told me that he will cover the expense, and in addition that he wishes you good fortune for the week ahead. We all hope that it will not be long before we have occasion to be serving you again."

As the waiter started to walk away it was Tom who called him back.

"Are you sure you have got thee right table, as I can't understand why we do not have to pay."

"You are a valued customer and Mr Lee has been following developments as regards to the case. I know that he had his sister in the court today so she could report back on any progress."

"In that case can you say thank you to Mr Lee for me, but we really did not expect a free night."

"We are all hoping Sir that we will be able to celebrate with you one evening during the coming week. Mr Lee has mentioned that if he thought it would be beneficial then he would have offered to stand up in court to give a character reference."

"Can you please pass on our thanks to Mr Lee, also if you could tell him that he isn't the only one who is hoping that we return here very soon."

"As George has just said will you please pass on our thanks to Mr Lee."

With that and knowing there was a taxi rank only a few metres along the road they left in order to get home.

Chapter 14

The weekend flew by for both of them and it was soon time to once again pack Tom's bags ready to head off to court. It was now Monday morning.

"How come you are getting all dressed up George?"

"That Tom, is because I am coming with you. I didn't tell you but when I spoke to Mr Barber on Friday I asked him if it would be okay for me to come there with you this morning and he said that it was fine. So I won't be waiting for a phone call to find out how you got on because I will know just as soon as anyone."

"George, what I said when I arrived home on Friday I meant you know. I don't expect you to wait around for years until I get released. You are young and have got your whole life ahead of you, go out, have fun, and find yourself another guy that you can make as happy as you have made me over the short time that we have been together."

"Thanks for the offer, but no thanks. I love you Tom and I will stick around waiting for you. No matter what happens I intend visiting you every week while you are inside and then be there to meet you when you walk out of prison. That is if you do even get sent down."

"George, I love you as well, which is why I have said what I have. Please, if I am sent down for any real period will you promise me now that you will put what we have had behind you and start anew."

"It isn't going to happen so forget it. As I have already said, if I do meet anyone else then you will be the first person who knows about it, but I honestly think that even if I went looking I wouldn't be able to find anyone that comes anywhere near you."

"I guess we could carry on going round and round in circles, shall
we just agree that if someone does come into your life then I will
not hold it against you in any way."
"I hear what you are saying, now the taxi should be here in five
minutes so how about a kiss and cuddle before it arrives."
They were still in each other's embrace when a car horn sounded
outside, signalling the cab's arrival.

To George's amazement the public gallery in courtroom three
was absolutely packed, so much so that the usher ended up having
to turn people away. George sat there and watched as one by one
different officials made their way in. Time dragged by as he
listened to the various formalities being gone through and it
wasn't until he heard the judge asking the spokesperson of the
jury if they had come to a decision that he focussed fully on what
was being said.
It was to George's great delight when he heard the spokesperson
return a not guilty response to the question of did they find the
defendant guilty of murder. It was however not so good when he
heard them answer guilty to that of manslaughter. It was now that
George regretted having not asked Mr Barber more details on the
various outcomes. He sat there listening as the judge began to
speak once more.
Having thanked the jury for their time and dedication the judge
then went on to address the courtroom.
"If the case that we had been hearing was that of either the victim
or that of his accomplish then I would have had no reservation in
applying the most severe of sentences that I was able, this
however is very much different. In all my years of being a judge I
have not once heard a case as this. I have listened to both the
arguments brought by both the prosecution team and those of the
defence. In addition I have listened to the testimonies of those
who have given evidence. More often than not I would have
delayed passing sentence until such time as I have been furnished
with certain reports, however that is not the case. I am governed
by strict parameters that I have to apply, and thus it is with regret

that I sentence the defendant to a minimum period of three and a half years, being the shortest I am allowed against the offence. Half the term to be spent in custody, with the remainder on licence. The court is adjourned."
George sat there, the tears flowing. The thought of Tom being locked away for over twenty months was one that he didn't know if he could handle, yet at the same time he knew it was one that he had got to find a way of accepting. He promised to himself there and then that if at all possible there would not be a week go by that he didn't visit Tom in prison, and that he would be waiting, counting down every single day before once again they be re-united.
It wasn't before the public gallery was all but empty that George was approached by Mr Barber.
"Well George on the whole I think it a good result."
"So what was that you were saying to me on Friday about Tom possibly not having to serve any time locked up?"
 "I appreciate it is not the outcome that you were hoping to hear, however as soon as the jury found Tom guilty of manslaughter then the judge's hands were tied. You must understand that the judge has very strict guidelines that no matter what his personal views he has to adhere to. If it had been a different judge then Tom could have been facing as much as a twelve year spell."
"I hear what you are saying Mr Barber but is there no way that we can appeal against the sentence?"
"I am sorry but it would be a futile exercise. Tom himself pleaded guilty to manslaughter so there is not a lot that we have to argue. The only way that we could possibly get the length of custodial reduced is by involving psychologists and psychiatrists, having said that I would not recommend it an avenue that we go down."
"Surely if it means that Tom might end up spending less time inside then it has got to be worth trying."
"George, there is a very strong possibility that if we do take that path then it may well result in a greater period of time apart from each other. If we get psychiatric reports stating that Tom was not of a sound mind when he committed the offence then it is not

beyond the realms of possibility that he ends up having to spend a much lengthier period within an institute for the mentally unstable."

"I hear what you are saying, but it doesn't seem fair."

"I appreciate that it is not the outcome we were hoping for however if you think about it, when Tom committed the act he did not know at the time that his brother had been involved in child abduction. If the judge knew this to be the case then I feel sure a further two years, if not more would have been ahead of Tom. No George, I would strongly recommend that we accept things as they are as to pursue things may well turn out counterproductive."

Having listened to all that Mr Barber had said it was with reluctance that George accepted that he had no option than to carry on with things as they stand. It was now that he asked the brief one more question.

"With Tom being sent down for three and a half years then what am I to expect when it is my turn in the dock?"

"I have already discovered that the same judge that was residing over Tom's case will be doing so over yours, which in itself is very good news. Now you have heard as we all have that the judge would have given Tom less than he did if able. Relating to your case then I really am feeling positive. The facts are, you were not an accessory to the murder in any way, nor were you involved in a relationship with Tom at the time of the offence having been committed. The only one possible avenue the prosecution have is to say that when you were made aware of the crime having been committed that you then did not report it to the authorities, As far as the court will know you may well have only discovered the facts a day or two prior to the arrests having been carried out, during which we will say that you were wrestling with the options open to you. We can say that on the morning of the arrest that you had already decided that later that day you would be going to the police station to report all."

"I had known from the second night after we had met though."

"You know that, I know that, but the court were not there to listen in on the pillow talk were they."

It was a statement rather than a question that Mr Barber had voiced and George knew that he was not expected to give any answer.

Once the conversation regarding to Tom's sentence had been exhausted there was one more thing that George needed to ask, no two.

"Mr Barber, when am I likely to hear of my court date, and I will be able to visit Tom between now and then won't I?"

"With regard to your court date, I would imagine that within a matter of a few days we will hear when that has been set for. With respect to if you will be allowed to visit Tom then I feel that the relevant authorities will not permit that to take place. With the two cases being tightly connected I believe that it will not be possible."

"So Tom will be stuck inside prison without being able to receive any visitors, is that what you are saying?"

"No George, what I have just said is that they will not authorise you to visit him. If you would like me to I am prepared to pop in and see him, as long as my work load permits. In addition I believe that Sam has got to know Tom quite well and I can not see any reason why the powers that be would not allow her to visit Tom on a regular basis."

"Once my day in court is all over, and as long as I don't get sent down as well, would I then be allowed to visit him?"

"I cannot see any reason for them then not to allow it to happen, in addition if they were to try and prevent your visits then I would fight to get that decision overturned. Yes George, I believe that once your case has been heard there will be nothing to stop you from visiting Tom in whichever prison he is being held. Now Tom will be being held in a cell downstairs until a vehicle arrives in which to transport him to prison. I would like to get to have a few words with him before he heads off, so if you will excuse me I had better get on my way."

"Okay Mr Barber, will you give him my love please and tell him that I will be visiting him just as soon as I am allowed,"
"I will pass on your comments George, and I will be in touch just as soon as I hear anything relating to your day in court."
With the brief now leaving him George decided that he might as well get on his way. The thought of him living alone in the flat, Tom's flat, for months was one that he did not feel comfortable with.
Having left the court he made his way on foot home. Throughout the twenty minute or so walk all he could think about was would Tom be able to handle life on the inside, and the other thing was would he himself be able to handle it if he were to be given a term in nick.

George had to wait an agonising forty-two days before it was his turn to stand in the dock. Forty-two days and nights during which there was not one hour pass by without him wondering how his partner was coping. Sam had been in to visit Tom on three occasions and after each had reported back to George that Tom appeared to be handling prison okay.
Unlike with Tom's appearance George's case took just two and a half days before the jury were sent out to make their decision. Mr Barber informed George that the jury might take as long as a day before notifying the clerk of the court that they had come to a verdict on which they were all agreed, and that with it now being 2:30pm it may well be the following morning before George would hear the outcome. The brief also warned George that unlike with Tom where the judge did not want sentencing reports before passing sentence that it may well not be the case now. To both George's and Mr Barber's surprise they were being instructed to re-enter courtroom four within an hour. This to Mr Barber's opinion could be either a very good thing or might turn out to be the opposite.
Once all had taken their place it was only twenty five minutes before George knew his future. The judge had sentence him to a

term of eighteen months, suspended for a similar period of time.
George was to remain a free man,
 "Right George, at a guess the first thing you will want to know is
when can you pay Tom a visit? During recess this morning I did
have an opportunity to speak with the judge and he assured me
that as long as you were not incarcerated then he would make it
perfectly clear to the relevant powers that he could see no reason
for your visits not to be allowed to proceed. Now there will be the
usual checks carried out but I cannot see anything preventing you
from having your for visit within a week."
"Thank you Mr Barber, that was going to be my first question.
There is one other question that I have for you though. Tom and I
made you aware of what work we used to be involved with. Can I
ask what the situation would be if I was found to be once again
involved in that line of work. Would I automatically then have to
serve the two years that I have just been handed as well as any
other that it is deemed I deserve."
"That is a good question and my advice would be for you not to
return to those sorts of activities. Consider yourself fortunate to
have got the result you have today and if I were you I would not
do anything that might give cause for you to end up in a prison.
Do I make myself clear?"
"Perfectly. I only asked because the flat we have is not cheap to
run and I will need to have decent earnings in order to keep it
going."
"I understand that, but there is help out there which should allow
you to manage until such times that you secure a permanent job."
"Will I be able to get any assistance with transport costs to and
from Exeter prison as from what Sam has told me it costs getting
on for a hundred pounds a time?"
"There are provisions in place as well as a number of charities
that can assist you on that.

For the following eighteen months there was not one week where
George did not visit Tom in prison at least the once, and on
several occasions he had done so twice. He'd now got a full time

job working as a parts man in one of the local car main
dealerships, with the boss ensuring that his hours were tailored to
fit in with his requirements. In addition he was still making
regular donations of his sperm meaning that there was no need for
him to have to beg for handouts from any direction. During his
visits he had broached the question as to what Tom was intending
doing work wise when he was to get released, however Tom was
not ready to think about that at this point in time, he would wait
until that day came and decide then.
Sam had stayed in touch and on a number of occasions she had
accompanied George on his trips to prison, although it meant that
on those times the conversations between George ad Tom were
restricted.
Tom's release date was for Wednesday 18th June, and George had
got everything planned for what he considered as being a very big
day. He met his partner at the prison gates at just turned ten in the
morning and it took five hours before they were walking in
through the front door of the flat. It wasn't until they had been at
home for a couple of hours, time that had been spent catching up
for lost time before George made an announcement.
"Tom, I hope you are okay with it, but I have booked us a table at
the Chinese restaurant this evening to celebrate your release."
"If you had waited for a week it would have given me an
opportunity to get to a jewellers in order to buy something."
Little did Tom know but George had already got an engagement
ring ready to present Tom with over their meal. In addition there
was going to be a photographer present. This was one occasion
where George really did want the events to be filmed